Anne McCaffrey, a [illegible] ...per, is [illegible] ...and best... [illegible] fant... writers. She is the author of the hugely successful *Dragonriders of Pern* series and makes her home in a castle in Ireland.

Elizabeth Ann Scarborough is the author of *Channeling Cleopatra* and the Nebular Award-winning *The Healer's War*, as well as more than twenty science fiction and fantasy novels. She lives in the Puget Sound area of Washington State.

Anne McCaffrey's books can be read individually or as series. However, for greatest enjoyment the following sequences are recommended:

The Dragon Books

DRAGONFLIGHT

DRAGONQUEST

DRAGONSONG

DRAGONSINGER: HARPER OF PERN

THE WHITE DRAGON

DRAGONDRUMS

MORETA: DRAGONLADY OF PERN

NERILKA'S STORY & THE COELURA

DRAGONSDAWN

THE RENEGADES OF PERN

ALL THE WEYRS OF PERN

THE CHRONICLES OF PERN: FIRST FALL

THE DOLPHINS OF PERN

RED STAR RISING: THE SECOND CHRONICLES OF PERN

(published in US as DRAGONSEYE)

THE MASTERHARPER OF PERN

THE SKIES OF PERN

and with Todd McCaffrey:

DRAGON'S KIN

By Todd McCaffrey:

DRAGONSBLOOD*

Crystal Singer Books

THE CRYSTAL SINGER

KILLASHANDRA

Tower and the Hive Sequence

THE ROWAN

DAMIA

DAMIA'S CHILDREN

LYON'S PRIDE

THE TOWER AND THE HIVE

Catteni Sequence

FREEDOM'S LANDING

FREEDOM'S CHOICE

FREEDOM'S CHALLENGE

FREEDOM'S RANSOM

The Acorna Series

ACORNA (with Margaret Ball)

ACORNA'S QUEST (with Margaret Ball)

ACORNA'S PEOPLE (with Elizabeth Ann Scarborough)

ACORNA'S WORLD (with Elizabeth Ann Scarborough)

ACORNA'S SEARCH (with Elizabeth Ann Scarborough)

ACORNA'S REBELS (with Elizabeth Ann Scarborough)

ACORNA'S TRIUMPH (with Elizabeth Ann Scarborough)

Individual Titles

RESTOREE

DECISION AT DOONA

THE SHIP WHO SANG

GET OFF THE UNICORN

THE GIRL WHO HEARD DRAGONS

BLACK HORSES FOR THE KING

NIMISHA'S SHIP

A GIFT OF DRAGONS

Written in collaboration with Elizabeth Ann Scarborough

POWERS THAT BE

POWER LINES

POWER PLAY

* to be published

ACORNA'S TRIUMPH

Anne McCaffrey

and

Elizabeth Ann Scarborough

CORGI BOOKS

ACORNA'S TRIUMPH
A CORGI BOOK: 0 552 15275 7

First publication in Great Britain

PRINTING HISTORY
Corgi edition published 2004

1 3 5 7 9 10 8 6 4 2

Set in 11/12.5pt Palatino by
Falcon Oast Graphic Art Ltd.

Corgi Books are published by Transworld Publishers,
61–63 Uxbridge Road, London W5 5SA,
a division of The Random House Group Ltd,
in Australia by Random House Australia (Pty) Ltd,
20 Alfred Street, Milsons Point, Sydney, NSW 2061, Australia,
in New Zealand by Random House New Zealand Ltd,
18 Poland Road, Glenfield, Auckland 10, New Zealand
and in South Africa by Random House (Pty) Ltd,
Endulini, 5a Jubilee Road, Parktown 2193, South Africa.

Printed and bound in Great Britain by
Cox & Wyman Ltd, Reading, Berkshire.

Papers used by Transworld Publishers are natural, recyclable products made from wood grown in sustainable forests. The manufacturing processes conform to the environmental regulations of the country of origin.

In fond memory of Connie Johnson:
math teacher, bibliophile, adventuress, and friend

ACKNOWLEDGMENTS

Our thanks go to Rick Reaser, science and salvage consultant and Ambassador to the Sulfur Beings, for his continuing advice and support. Also we wish to thank our editors Denise Little at Tekno Books and Diana Gill at HarperCollins for their suggestions and help, with special thanks to Denise for being the Keeper of Acorna's Database of names and Linyaari words. Thanks are also due to Margaret Ball, cowriter with Anne McCaffrey on the first two Acorna books, for inventing the Linyaari language, among other things. And we would most particularly like to thank Martin H. Greenberg, without whose trust and support this project would have been impossible to continue.

Acorna's Triumph

One

Acorna moaned. She struggled desperately to regain control of herself. As always, she was powerless. She could only watch as the room changed and the time portraits swirled around her like dervishes.

The white lights symbolizing Linyaari blurred, blinked out, returned. Vhiliinyar's panoramas changed from lush to blighted, then became fertile again in a dizzying kaleidoscope of shape, color, time, and place. The images shifted to the deafening *boom-boom boom-boom boom-boom* of a drumbeat.

It doesn't really move that fast, she thought in an oddly detached way. *And where are those drums coming from?*

Then she knew that the drumlike booming was the frenzied pounding of her own heart. Her blood seemed to be trying to leap out of her skin with each beat of her pulse. She struggled upright and reached for the door but something felt odd. She looked back to see herself still lying on the floor of the ancient time laboratory. *How strange,* she thought. Her hands twitched as she tried once more to rise. She had to get to the door.

Aari would be coming through it soon. Coming with her. And the danger. She could not remember what the danger was, but she knew it was something horrible and unexpected, even though she realized that she had been through this same sequence countless times during many other sleep cycles. She knew what the danger was. She just didn't remember it.

Didn't *want* to remember it.

But she had to. If only she could open the door quickly enough, get herself through it, get *him* inside, and close it fast enough and hard enough, the terrible thing wouldn't happen.

The room stopped spinning, and time stood still. She rose.

Where is the door? she thought. Then she thought, *What door?* She could see grass and rivers, craters and furrows, mountains and trees, but no door. *But there has to be a door . . .*

And then she walked through the wall, coming into the room. She wore a shipsuit and helmet and she was covered in something green and slimy. Right behind her came Aari.

That was it. That was when she had to shut the door. *But there* was *no door,* she thought. She struggled to reach out again, but then realized she was still lying on the floor.

Klik-klak, klik-klak. The sound entered the room with her ship-suited self and Aari. It was like the beating of her heart, but a different tone. Its volume increased, and the regular beat quickened and loosened into an overwhelming cacophony of *klikity-klak-klikity-klak-klak*ings.

She reached for Aari. He didn't seem to see her. He turned and raised his arms.

Behind him, Khleevi swarmed into the room, their mandibles and pincers *klak*ing, their antennae rubbing, their immense jaws devouring the floors and walls. Once more, the insect race was bent on destroying Vhiliinyar and the Linyaari who had returned to populate it.

Acorna felt rather than saw something looming over her. Just as she was sure her death was certain, she was grabbed and shaken.

'Khornya, Khornya, wake up! What's the matter?'

Acorna opened her eyes and looked up into the concerned face of her young friend Maati. They were both inside the time lab within the great ruined office building that was among the remains of the lost ancient city of Kubiilikaan. This city was the original home of the shape-shifting people who were the forebearers of Acorna and Maati's race, the Linyaari, along with the unicorn-like Ancestors. Long buried and forgotten, the city was the only part of the Linyaari home planet that had escaped the depredations of the Khleevi invasion safe within its sophisticated shields beneath the surface of Vhiliinyar.

The walls of the time lab were not spinning now, but as usual the static maps of the planet were dotted with small points of white light that indicated the places where Linyaari personnel were located. Many teams were back on the planet's surface, mapping, surveying, and otherwise planning each phase of the planet's renewal by regional applications of the terraforming process.

'Khornya, are you all right? You look funny,' Maati said.

'I had a bad dream. That's all,' Acorna assured her. Dream fragments filled her head. She looked around for the phantom door that had haunted her dream, but of course it wasn't there. The room was vast and spartan and very clinical-looking. Only Acorna's bedroll and the pool of water in the center from which a beam of energy rose to pierce the ceiling and each story above it saved the chamber from the sterile ambience of a typical research facility.

'What kind of dream?' Maati asked.

'I can't even remember what it was about now. Something about the Khleevi.'

'No wonder you were crying out and trying to run in your sleep,' Maati said. She laid her horn gently against Acorna's head to soothe her friend and heal her of the residual effects of the dream.

'Thanks,' Acorna said. 'But I'm fine now, really.'

'You shouldn't be spending all your time down here alone,' Maati scolded. 'You can't *pull* Aari out of that machine, you know.'

'I know,' Acorna admitted. 'It's not that I

expect that, it's just that now that I know that Aari is with one of the Ancestral Friends, and they're using the device to cross time and even send messages back, I want to figure out how they're doing it. And I *might* find Aari in the process,' she finished hopefully. 'You never know.'

Maati sighed. 'I miss him, too, Khornya. I barely got to know my older brother before he disappeared on us. But staying down here all the time is just plain unhealthy. That's probably why you're having all these bad dreams. Really, you should come up to the surface just for a little while,' Maati coaxed. 'You haven't been up in ages and ages, and you won't believe the progress we've made with the terraforming.'

'Of course I would,' Acorna said, but her attention was elsewhere. She rose to inspect a hole in the wall behind one of the great maps showing the time and place of each person on the planet's surface. For a moment the hole gave her an odd turn, reminding her of something terrible in her dream. But that was silly. It was just a dream. And she had put the hole there herself – though with much trepidation.

She'd wanted to see the workings of the map or whatever it was that was driving the time machine. 'I can see everything that's going on up there on the maps,' she told Maati. Returning her attention to the pictures on the surface of the wall, she gestured to the appropriate image as she spoke. 'The watersheds are all exactly where they ought to be now, the streams are flowing, the rivers and their currents are behaving properly, the tides are turning the seas at the correct times, the waterfalls are falling, and even the rain is coming at the correct appointed intervals. All that water must be making everything quite green.'

'Yes, but you don't care about that at all,' Maati said. 'You can't fool me. You only know about the waters because they're needed for the time travel. But honestly, Khornya, you've done so much to make Vhiliinyar live again. It isn't just the planning and the exploration. You made it happen. It was all because of you that we got the catseye chrysoberyls.'

'I wasn't exactly alone on that journey. Anyway, it's only because of Captain Becker's negotiating such a good price with Uncle Hafiz that we ended up out of debt and with credits to spare to fund the rebirth of this planet.' Captain Becker was her good friend, Jonas P. Becker, pilot of the *Condor*, flag and only ship of Becker Interplanetary Salvage and Recycling Enterprises, Ltd.

Becker, a canny businessman himself, was undaunted by the bargaining skills of Acorna's adoptive uncle, Hafiz Harakamian, the semi-retired former head of the also interplanetary enterprises of House Harakamian. Unlike Becker's business, Hafiz's boasted many ships, flitters, and other vehicles, a portion of one moon, and all of another.

'It was pure good luck that we found the catseyes just when we needed to refine our terraforming process, so that we could restore sections of the planet instead of doing everything at once.' Acorna was fully awake now and ready to return to her investigations. Maati and the others who had already voiced similar concerns about her only fussed because they cared, Acorna knew, but it was distracting. If she was going to justify spending all her time in the time lab, she had to make it pay off by conducting real research.

With a pointed glance at Maati, she pulled down her goggles, turned on a special saw, and with a whirring of the blade enlarged the hole she'd made so it was big enough to stick her head through.

Maati made a face. 'It's nice to know that you've been listening to what we tell you when we come to visit you. But you can't fool me. It's not like you've seen anything up there for yourself. And this is a feast day. The best grasses of the season are all ready to harvest. Please come up and graze with us. Everyone will be there.'

'Not everyone,' Acorna said.

'Not Aari, I know,' Maati agreed reluctantly. 'I'm sorry. I know how hard it's been on you. I know that you feel like you've missed contact with him while others have received telepathic inquiries from him.'

Acorna frowned and withdrew her head from the hole in the panel. 'You didn't tell me that when I talked to you from Makahomia. You said "indications." You didn't say "telepathic inquiries."'

'Okay, I didn't. But it was no big deal. Aari's communications were very sporadic and scattered, and no one was really sure what they meant until they talked to each other and to you,' Maati protested. 'This has been frustrating for Mother and Father and me, too. At least you were doing something useful on Makahomia. That's why we decided to join you. And Aari's okay. You found that out yourself when you heard that message from him that the priest gave you down on Makahomia. You know very well that if . . . no . . . *when* he comes back it will be at some wildly romantic moment, when you need rescuing or help fighting some horrible enemy, and the rest of our people are being too analytical and fair-minded to be of any help at all.'

'You have a very big imagination, Maati,' Acorna said, dusting off her hands. 'We've finished off the Khleevi. I can't think of any other horrible enemies standing in line to be vanquished at the moment. And I think my own fair mind has just about analyzed this contraption. I'm beginning to understand how it works.'

'Really?' Maati was actually very interested in the time machine, so Acorna's ploy was successful. Maati crowded closer to see what Acorna was doing.

'Yes, and the better I understand it, the more it explains a few things to me. Like the thought messages from Aari. I have entered all of the instances reported to me. I found that, far from being random, they fit a definite pattern – the same pattern that the time/space mechanism follows. Only at certain intervals are there connecting ladders between the time and place Aari occupies and our own time and space. Though he has made a couple of jumps.'

'How do you know that?'

'I'll show you,' Acorna said, and passed her hand across a section where the column of liquid light rose from floor to ceiling. At once a familiar shape appeared in that unfamiliar place. It was a double helix, a shape typical of the cellular blueprints comprising most lifeforms.

'What is that?' Maati asked.

'Time,' Acorna said. 'And space also. Or a road map through both of them. Where the helix twists we intersect, but otherwise we travel separately. I've labeled the intersections between Aari and us in this interaction. There, and there, and there. See how they form a pattern?'

'Yeah,' Maati said. 'How did you find all that out?'

'Mostly by accident,' Acorna admitted. 'But after a couple of those accidents, things began to make more sense to me. And if the pattern holds, we're about due for another contact with Aari. So I've got too much work to do down here to spare the time to go to the surface.'

She waved her hand again, and the column shimmied and turned back into its amorphous self.

She crossed to the map of Vhiliinyar, which dominated the wall with the hole in it. While Acorna concentrated on her excavation work on the wall, Maati noticed that some white dots flickered near the underground lake, a couple of blocks downhill from their position. When white dots appeared on one of these maps, they indicated the presence of Linyaari in that location.

Acorna noticed the dots, too. There was a breathless catch in her voice as she inquired, 'Did anyone come with you when you came through the tunnels?'

Maati shook her head. 'No.'

To reach the underground city from the surface, people had to enter through the labyrinth of caves occupied in ancient times by the Ancestors and their attendants. The caves led up into the building through an opening a few feet from the door of the room she and Acorna were in.

Because of many previous accidents caused by malfunctions of the time device that had resulted in the disappearances of various beings, Aari among them, access to the area was carefully controlled, if not completely restricted. There shouldn't have been any Linyaari there to make those white dots on the map.

'We'd better see who it is,' Maati said, but

Acorna had already passed her and run out the door.

With Maati at her heels, Acorna took off, running so fast that she all but teleported herself to the shores of the lake.

Acorna had had a premonition the moment she saw the white dots. Maybe, after all this time, Aari had returned. There was an Aari feeling to those dots, and she just suddenly *knew* that he had returned. And then she saw him, standing with another Linyaari beside the underground lake. It was unmistakably Aari, though he looked more erect and confident, and his horn was beautiful and gleaming, unbent, no longer stunted, just as it had been in her dream back on Makahomia.

She was down the hill in an instant. Then her arms were around his neck, her head resting in the hollow of his shoulder, just as she'd wanted to be since the day he'd gone missing. Except that *his* arms did not embrace her back, though one hand did tap against her shoulder in a sort of awkward pat.

Behind her, Maati cried, 'Aari? Is it really you? Your horn is fixed! When did that happen? Where've you been? What—'

Aari held up his hand to stop Maati's stream of questions. 'Greetings,' he said. 'Yes, it is I. At least, I am Aari, and this is Laarye, and we have just arrived. If Grimalkin's calculations are correct, you would be' – he juggled Acorna aside slightly to hold his wrist to one ear – 'oh, yes, our beloved little sister Maati, unknown thus far to Laarye. And this affectionate lady' – he patted Acorna's shoulder again – 'is my own lifemate, Khornya.'

A sour taste rose in the back of Acorna's throat. Though Aari was here, something was terribly wrong. This wasn't the Aari that she knew and loved!

'I have received much data concerning you both,' Aari said. 'It is a pleasure to . . . er . . . renew . . . our acquaintance, I'm sure.'

(Acorna?) Maati thought, (What is going on here?)

(I don't know. Maybe he's been recaptured by the Khleevi, and this time instead of torturing him physically, they brainwashed him,) she told Maati telepathically.

(I assure you that is not true, Khornya,) Aari told her. (Grimalkin helped me navigate time so that both Laarye and I avoided the Khleevi altogether. Once I found Laarye, he and I jumped here. I confess it's extremely disorienting. I have in my recorder notes from myself about my capture on the other timeline, the torture, the death of my brother, and the realization that our homeworld had been destroyed. I have recorded meeting Captain Becker and Riidkiiyi, also meeting you and my sister, and also my healing. I have many other events recorded, but the one that truly causes me pain – is it true that in this timeline, Grandam Naadiina has died?)

(Yes, that's true,) Acorna said. (She died saving

her people. I'm glad you've taken good notes of your life in our timeline. I take it since you identified me as your lifemate, you also recall our joining?)

(I have it recorded as a most profoundly enjoyable experience,) Aari replied with a lusty gleam in his eye that reminded her of Thariinye. (I hope that soon we will have occasion to refresh my memory in this timeline to add verisimilitude to the recorded memory.)

Maati, who had been talking earnestly with Laarye, telling him about her childhood after their parents' disappearance and her role in their recovery, felt emanations coming from Acorna such as she had never felt when her friend was among only other Linyaari. Dangerous emanations. Highly combustible.

She didn't even have to eavesdrop on their thought-talk to hear it. Aari was putting up no shields, as if he was carrying on a casual conversation among a group of friends, as she had been told her people often had before the Khleevi came. Khornya was broadcasting on all frequencies, loud and clear enough for anybody to read.

Acorna recoiled from Aari's light embrace as if she were a Khleevi and he was coated with the Khleevi-killing plant slime that had helped them destroy their enemy. 'Perhaps you should have chosen that time to return,' Acorna suggested in an overly calm voice. Maati noticed that Acorna was now speaking aloud and guarding her thoughts. It seemed that this Aari was a stranger to her.

'Oh, I couldn't have done that,' Aari said. 'This is really the first opportunity to cross over to this side without contaminating any major part of what's gone on already: the only change, as Grimalkin explained this thoroughly to me – I wish he were here to explain it to you, but he had pressing business elsewhere – the only change is that I don't actually remember anything from the time Laarye and I left home together until now. It's an awfully big chunk of time, but Grimalkin thought it would be best if in this timeline, the capture by the Khleevi never happened. So he rescued both Laarye and me – or rather, he assisted me as I rescued both of us.'

'How thoughtful of him,' Acorna said. 'It's a pity he couldn't have spared the planet the whole Khleevi catastrophe and let us all just skip that part. It would have saved a fortune in terra-forming expenses.'

Aari had been chattering happily up to this point, but now he stopped and regarded Acorna more thoughtfully, 'You're upset,' he said with some surprise. 'Why are you upset, Khornya? According to my records, you love me. I would think you'd be happy I'd found a way to return to my people with my brother alive and without having had to endure that endless torture.'

'And all it cost you was the couple of *ghaanyi* of memories of our life together,' she said. 'I can easily see why it was worth the trade to you.'

Acorna was struggling to be reasonable and keep the hurt out of her voice, but it wasn't working. Then she amazed Maati by employing one of Captain Becker's favorite curse phrases. Acorna *never* cursed. 'Frack it all, Aari! I have searched through time on this world. I have caused the Ancestors to put a stop to the wholesale terraforming to return Vhiliinyar to its original state in case you returned to an unstable world. I have traveled to Makahomia, where all of us could have been killed by people who worshiped you and your friend Grimalkin as some sorts of deities. I got the message you left for me. But then . . . you . . . sounded like you. And now you've returned a stranger.'

He held up his wrist and listened to it again, then said, 'Oh, yes. That. Well, I left the message for you on Makahomia, but that was *before* the crucial jump. I appreciate all of your trouble, Khornya, but really, I was fine. Grimalkin and I just had to wait for the proper moment, as I believe I said in my note.'

Aari clearly didn't understand why she was so upset – maybe because Acorna didn't understand it herself. She knew that if someone had offered her the chance to make Aari's torture vanish, and his brother Laarye live, all at the cost of Aari's memories of their love, she would have willingly agreed. Grabbed at the chance, even. But . . . she hadn't been consulted. And those memories had been a central part of her life, too. Now, looking into Aari's beautiful but emotionally distant eyes, those precious memories felt as if they were part of some sort of dream, or maybe of a vid she'd seen. Or as if their shared experiences and emotions – some of the most beautiful in her life – hadn't really happened.

She felt discarded.

She knew that feeling was not exactly logical and reasonable. She should be happy that Aari was whole again. She should be ecstatic that he was no longer tormented by memories of what the Khleevi had done to him. She should be thrilled that he had even managed to save the life of his brother – Laarye's death had haunted him and left him wracked with guilt. But the way he had done it made her feel as if she was irrelevant in his life. And what was worse was that it felt as if, somewhere in his voyages in time, the Aari she knew and loved had melted away to be replaced with this . . . this . . . infuriating stranger. Even worse yet, her own Aari had cooperated in the destruction of the person he had been. He'd allowed their love to fade from his mind and heart.

She was a stranger to him. And *this* Aari was very much a stranger to her.

Maati was apparently taking all this much better than Acorna was. But Aari was only Maati's older brother, not her lifemate. And now Maati had her other brother back, and could get to know him. Maati had been born after Aari and Laarye were stranded on Vhiliinyar, where

Laarye had starved to death while he lay injured in a cave and Aari had been captured and tortured by the Khleevi. The only family Maati had known as she grew up was Grandam Naadiina, who had died heroically during the Khleevi attack on narhii-Vhiliinyar. After Aari was rescued, he and Maati had helped to save their parents, and now they had their *other* brother back. Maati's family was finally complete, so of course she was rejoicing. Maati loved Aari, of course, but she naturally did not know him as Acorna did – or had.

But for Acorna, this new twist on her relationship with Aari was just one thing too much. She had in fact moved mountains and oceans and the rivers of time to find him. Now that he was back, he'd forgotten all that they had shared. Aari looked at her like she was someone he'd met at a party once, not the love of his life. For Acorna, it was past bearing.

Acorna excused herself with a mumbled apology and returned the way she had come. Aari didn't even call after her – he started talking with Maati as if nothing out of the ordinary had just happened. Acorna kept on walking as she passed the room containing the time machine; for the first time in months she felt no urge to go inside it. Instead, she followed the hallway to the trapdoor leading to the cave connecting the abandoned underground city of Kubiilikhan with the surface.

She needed someone to talk to, preferably

someone who could not read minds, since hers wasn't fit to share with company at the moment. She wished Nadhari Kando was here. Acorna needed to talk to someone who could understand what she was feeling. Nadhari had seen and done so much that nothing surprised her or shocked her anymore. Nor was she one to *tsk-tsk* over the expression of negative emotions. When Nadhari felt negative emotions, whoever was causing her pain usually got to share that pain, and often got flattened in the process.

But Nadhari was back on Makahomia right now, too far away and much too busy to serve as Acorna's confidante. Acorna thought she would be able to confide in her aunt Neeva, but Neeva and her spaceship, the *Balakiire,* were on the Moon of Opportunity, known as MOO to its tenants and all those who loved it. Neeva was consulting with Linyaari scientists regarding the terraforming process. She, too, was busy with important work. Acorna would have to find someone else to talk to. But she couldn't think of anyone who would believe her, much less understand.

As she emerged from the cave into the open meadow made deliciously fragrant by sunshine and recent rain, courtesy of Dr. Hoa's weather wizardry, the *Condor*'s shuttle settled onto the surface.

Acorna smiled broadly. That expression might be interpreted as an aggressive act by the Linyaari people, but Acorna knew that Captain

Jonas P. Becker would see her human-style grin and correctly deduce that she was overjoyed to see him arrive. Becker and Mac – the android who affected an artificial horn attachment while on Vhiliinyar to spare Linyaari sensibilities about outsiders landing on their planet – and RK, the *Condor*'s feline first mate, all disembarked. Acorna had never been so happy to see a group of beings since the day her human foster fathers had pulled her out of her castaway life-support escape pod.

Acorna ran to meet her friends. Becker took one look at her face, and said, 'Acorna! Princess! What's the matter? You look like you've lost your best friend.' That was all it took. Acorna fell into his arms and, in a big rush, poured out what had happened and how she felt about it all. At the end of her story, Becker let her weep on his shoulder while Mac patted her head awkwardly and RK twined around her ankles mewing anxiously, just as if he didn't know how to thought-speak, though Acorna knew all too well that he did.

'Captain, I know it's silly,' she said, drying her eyes and wiping her nose inelegantly on her sleeve since she lacked a handkerchief. 'All I've done since he went missing is try to get him back. Now he's back, but—'

'Silly? Naah, it's not silly. Sounds to me like Aari is suffering from a bad case of mistaken identity – he doesn't know who the heck he is. You know, maybe Karina Harakamian can sort him out. She's the kind of person who is always trying to help the kind of people who are trying to find themselves.'

'Maybe. I suppose he'll have to figure that out on his own, though,' Acorna said, thinking that the problem from her point of view was more that Aari didn't know who *she* was. 'He doesn't seem to need any help from me. Maati, at least, seems to be just fine with him.'

'I wouldn't be too sure of that,' Becker said. 'He just got here. These things take time. You're not the only one who will have to adjust to the new Aari.'

'There may be more to adjust to than Aari's changed personality,' she said. 'Aari's experience with the time device and Grimalkin brings up many new questions about the time shift equipment's capabilities.'

'There's more to adjust to than just that. I came to bring you some good news. Rafik is coming to MOO.'

'When?'

Becker gave one of his usual 'precise' replies. 'Pretty shortly. If you hop aboard and we take off now, we can probably get back there by the time he arrives. That is, if you want to see him, of course.'

He was teasing. Acorna wasn't in the mood to laugh at his little sally, but she smiled politely, and said, 'I certainly do.'

'That's great. It will do you good to see one of your foster dads again.'

Acorna felt the gloom that had settled onto her lighten just a bit. 'It will indeed. I would love to see Rafik. The break will give me time to think about my situation. In the long term, I believe what I really need to do is to continue to educate myself about how the time device works. Perhaps the new – perhaps Aari can help me with some of the insights he has gained into its process while time-traveling with his friend. I can't help but believe there must be a way to regain my Aari without losing Laarye or making Aari undergo Khleevi torture again.'

'I'll say this, Princess, if anybody can do it, you can.' He shifted his weight from one foot to the other for a moment, then said, 'If you want to wait out here, I'll just go in and say hi to Aari – even if he probably doesn't remember me.'

Acorna waited with less patience than she usually exhibited, but occupied herself with admiring the changes wrought on Vhiliinyar's surface. She'd been so busy in the underground city that she'd not taken the time to appreciate all the changes on the planet's surface. A majestic mountain range rose where once hills of rubble stood. Wildflowers sprinkled the meadows and grew in such profusion at the base of the distant foothills that the brilliant blossoms shone like stars against a background of a thousand shades of blue. Streams and rivers ribboned through the periwinkle meadows and a wide lavender lake that in time would become an inland sea spread between her and the mountains. She grazed thoughtfully on the delicious grasses provided.

But in a shorter time than she expected, Becker and Mac reemerged, trailed by Aari, Laarye, and Maati.

Becker looked very uncomfortable. 'Hey, Princess. What a treat! Maati and her brothers want to ride back to MOO with us to see their parents. Won't that be exciting?'

'Oh,' she said. She wished she could change her mind about going, but the plea in Becker's eyes for her to accompany them was too strong for her to resist. She had hoped to have time to talk with Becker in the familiar surroundings of the *Condor*. She truly did not want to be closed up in the tight confines of the *Condor* with the new, remote Aari.

However, she reminded herself that Rafik was coming to MOO. Her aunt Neeva was already on MOO, along with her uncle Hafiz and his wife. She could look forward to seeing them. She would find the time and space and people on MOO to confide in. But still her spirits sank as the new Aari beamed brightly down at her. It was going to feel like a long, long space voyage.

Her silence was not too noticeable, since Aari chatted in Linyaari to Becker about the things his recorded memory told him about the *Condor*, and Becker asked Aari about his adventures with Grimalkin. Becker also filled Aari in on the trip he, Mac, Nadhari, Acorna, and particularly RK had taken that landed them accidentally in Makahomia.

RK, who had always been very fond of Aari, held back from the new, improved version of his friend. When Aari reached out to stroke the cat, RK sniffed at his fingers, hissed, and batted them away. Then the cat jumped onto Laarye's knee to sniff him instead.

Maati was talking to Laarye about the rescue of her parents that she and Thariinye had staged.

Laarye kept nodding as if that was familiar to him, and Maati said, 'You know all about it?'

'Yes, Aari filled me in. His account varies in some small details from your own story but is essentially the same.'

'How is it different?'

'Aari told how he saved everyone and how he and Captain Becker cleverly devised a way to destroy the exoskeleton of the Khleevi using a plant toxin. This enabled him to save you and Khornya and Thariinye. Then he also located your parents.'

Maati frowned. 'Yeah, that's different,' she said in a non-committal voice.

Docking with the *Condor* saved Maati from making further explanations.

Once aboard the ship, as if by mutual consent, the Linyaari spread out. At Becker's suggestion, Laarye and Aari took Maati's LAANYE, the Linyaari language decoding device, and retired to the 'library.' This was a cabin that had once been stuffed with hard-copy books Becker had salvaged from dumps and landfills on various worlds. Mac had installed a vid screen and also patches to the main computer for those wishing to play vids, of which the library also boasted a considerable number. This current version of Aari had not been exposed to Standard Galactic, the human tongue through most of known space, though he knew that he was supposed to know it. This was, in fact, recorded in his memory storage unit. But Grimalkin had not recorded any clues to the language itself in the memory unit, and so Aari would have to relearn it. Since Standard was the language of MOO and much of the multiverse, Maati suggested to Laarye that he, too, needed to become fluent in it.

Acorna left them to it and sought out a place where she could be alone on the ship. She thought that Maati would go to the library with her brothers to coach them and point out the really *good* books and vids, but instead the young Linyaari girl sought Acorna out where she was tending the hydroponics bed.

'Can I help?' Maati asked.

'I thought you'd want to help your brothers,' Acorna said, wondering how weeds managed to creep into even the most controlled environments.

'I thought you wouldn't want to spend a minute away from Aari,' Maati retorted, more sharply than she had ever spoken to Acorna before. 'But I don't feel that way. I thought they needed to process all that learning stuff on their own.'

Acorna said nothing in reply, but kept weeding.

Finally, Maati could stand it no longer, and said, 'You know about ghosts?'

'Yes, I've heard of them,' Acorna said. 'I am surprised that you have.'

'Those stories are weird, but I like them – especially the ones where the atmosphere is sort of scary but the ghosts are nice. Ever since I read the first one, I've liked the idea that something of the spirit of someone who dies can stay with people they care about. But now I'm not so sure. Talking to Laarye is a lot like talking to a ghost. Talking to Aari – well, I keep thinking of him as Aari Whole-Horn, because he doesn't seem like the same person as *our* Aari. He's more like a visually enhanced holo or something. Do you know what I mean?'

Acorna nodded. She straightened slowly up from the garden, offering a handful of grass to Maati, who was still standing. 'Yes, I know exactly what you mean. It's as if he is a shell that looks like Aari, walks and talks a bit like him, but that's where the similarity ends. And yet, he is a person, just as much as *our* Aari, and probably just as lovable if we give him a chance. Maybe when your brothers meet your parents again, and we see them in the context of the family members they already knew, they will begin to seem more real.'

'Oh, sure,' Maati said. 'Of course they will. But it's funny, Khornya. I always thought my parents were dead, but when they came back I never felt about them the way I do about Laarye and Aari Whole-Horn.'

'You need to stop calling him that or he'll read

you and be offended,' Acorna cautioned. 'He may be stranger than we wish he was, but he still reads thought-talk.'

'Maybe we should wear horn-hats until we get used to the boys,' Maati suggested with a giggle, referring to the sometimes rather comical creations intended not only to costume and ornament a Linyaari horn for a dance or other festive occasion, but to shield some of the wearer's more spontaneous thoughts as well.

'I'll bet Eedi saved some of them from that party when I first arrived or narhii-Vhiliinyar,' Acorna said mischievously. 'We should borrow some from her. I want the one with the pink pompom on the end.'

'No fair,' Maati said, giggling. 'I wanted that one!' And off they went, talking of commonplaces and silly apparel and other nonstressful things until the voyage was nearly over.

When they finally docked on MOO, Becker looked out the viewport, and said, 'Damn. They forgot the brass band. Everybody else seems to be here though.'

Though he was exaggerating slightly, Maati's (and Aari's and Laarye's) parents Miiri and Kaarlye, and the Harakamians and their entourage of servants and security personnel awaited their arrival in the lavishly appointed terminal. Rafik Nadezda's vessel had set down just before the *Condor* did. He, too, was waiting at the terminal to greet them.

On Acorna's last arrival on MOO, not more

than two months ago, the terminal had consisted of a com shed in a temporary building. The new building was spacious and full of glass and plant life, artwork, and deep, comfortable seating. The Makahomian catseye chrysoberyls had enriched both the Linyaari and Hafiz immeasurably, and the improvements on both MOO and Vhiliinyar were the result of that influx of wealth.

Miiri and Kaarlye rushed forward to greet their children, and Acorna stepped aside, only to be swept up in a big hug by Rafik. One of her triad of foster fathers, the three asteroid miners who had rescued her infant self from her escape pod, Rafik was now the active head of House Harakamian enterprises. Rafik's uncle Hafiz had named him as heir in preference to his own son. These days Hafiz claimed to be retired, and loudly extolled his nephew's business sense and stewardship. MOO and the rehabilitation of the Linyaari worlds were Hafiz's idea of a retirement sideline.

Acorna returned Rafik's hug enthusiastically.

Finally, Rafik held Acorna at arm's length and looked her over with a paternal eye. 'I didn't think it was possible but, yes, you're even prettier than you were the last time I saw you. How *are* you, Acorna?'

Rafik was a little gray at the temples, but it suited him, and his dark eyes, thickly fringed with curling lashes, were as shrewd and merry as ever. Though his waistline remained trim, Acorna noticed a family resemblance between

Rafik and Hafiz that had not been as obvious to her previously.

'Just fine, now that you're here,' she said, linking arms with him. 'It is so good to see you again! You must tell me what brings you here. And I want to hear all about Calum and Gill and the Kendoro sisters. And Pal, too, of course.'

'There is much to tell. You're going to have a half brother or sister pretty soon, for one thing,' he said. 'Mercy is pregnant.'

'Wonderful! Calum must be over the moon. He loves children so. He will love having a baby of his own to coo over.'

'He's happy as a hungry Linyaari in the height of grazing season. Gill and Judit have been spending most of their time at Maganos Moonbase. I don't get up there very often, but I hear from them by com unit quite a bit. We all miss you, of course.'

'I miss you all, too.'

'But we've been worried about you. Aari, your lifemate, we heard that he disappeared?'

She took a deep breath and nodded.

'Well, yes, he did. It's been a long, hard time for me. But I have news, as well. Aari seems to be back, sort of. That's him there with his family. I'm keeping a little distance from him right now.' She nodded to where Aari, with great poise, was telling his parents how he and Grimalkin had located Laarye in time to prevent him from starving to death and brought him back through time to restore him to the family.

'He just got back, and you're already estranged?' Rafik asked, shocked. 'I thought you would shake the universe apart looking for him. What happened?'

But before she could tell him, they met Hafiz and Karina Harakamian. Hafiz wore his usual rich robes embroidered with gold and glimmering with jewels, while Karina, also as usual, was floating in an oceanic drift of lavender, lilac, violet, and purple draperies, the colors subtly blending with each other in a beautiful whole, the layers difficult to sort out. What was not subtle was the jewelry she currently sported. Gone were her amethysts and tanzanites, and in their place was a collar of perfectly matched orchid-hued golf-ball-size catseye chrysoberyls.

Becker did a double take that Acorna could sense even though her back was to him. 'Wow! You are wearing enough power there to terraform a galaxy, lady.'

'I *know*,' Karina said, stroking her necklace in a pleased fashion. 'Lovely, isn't it? It was difficult to choose the right ones from all of those you brought home, but when I saw these in my colors, I just knew I had to have them. Especially after what you told us about the reverence in which these sacred stones are held, and how only the most devout priests and priestesses wear them. Haffy was a bit stuffy about it at first, but I pointed out to him that as the panspiritual leader of our little colony, I have a certain image to maintain. That means such powerful talismans as these should at least be represented by a few little samples in my personal collection. So he had that adorable Rocky Reamer design this necklace for me and gave it to me as a gift for our two year, four months, three weeks, two days, five hours, and six minutes anniversary. Unfortunately, Rocky hasn't yet finished the matching earrings, bracelet, and ring, but the necklace makes quite a statement on its own, don't you think?'

'Statement! It's an entire library, and then some,' Becker said.

Karina looked crestfallen and frowned slightly. 'You don't think it's a bit plain on its own like this?'

Acorna felt that she could sincerely say, 'You would be the hit of any Linyaari ball with that, Karina. It really is stunning.'

'I know they only wore one gem at a time on Makahomia, but their culture was rather primitive, from what you say. And they didn't have the means to set gems properly, as Rocky does,' Karina said. 'And then, too, they were not – from what you say of the high priest – truly evolved and enlightened beings. I doubt many of them could have maintained their sanity, much less control, in the presence of such powerful talismans as these. I myself must struggle as I wear it to remain in charge of the stones, to channel their emanations, and it is only because of my years of dedicated study and selfless discipline that I am able to succeed.'

'Yeah, well,' Becker said, stifling a smile, turning away, and looking desperately for an excuse to end the conversation.

Rafik took his aunt's hand and kissed it, saying, 'And the power becomes you mightily, treasure of my adopted father.'

Acorna wanted to giggle. Rafik's manners were now – or perhaps it was here – *so* different than they had been aboard the asteroid mining ship where he, Calum, and Gill had raised her from babyhood. He couldn't have picked a better time to show up. Having him here steadied her and lessened the emotional vertigo she experienced from dealing with the new Aari.

She was also very tired from keeping her thoughts shielded from everyone. She should be – was – glad to see her lifemate alive and well again. And not everyone had the chance to undo such a horrible chapter in life as Aari's torture by the Khleevi. She felt, if not guilty, as least as if her fellow Linyaari would not easily forgive her selfish unhappiness in the face of Aari's unexpected return.

Hafiz beamed at her and sandwiched her hands between his own. 'You have much cause to celebrate today, granddaughter of my heart. Rafik is here and also your own lost husband.'

'Lifemate, dearest,' Karina whispered out of the side of her mouth, which she hid with the edge of a heavily beringed hand. 'The Linyaari have lifemates, not formal marriages.'

He waved her objection away. 'It is all the

same. Better in fact, since Linyaari remain faithful throughout their lives to one beloved spouse.'

Becker cleared his throat. 'Uh, Hafiz, could I speak with you privately for a minute?'

'What is it, you wily camel trader, you?' asked Hafiz, waving his plump forefinger under Becker's nose in a jovial fashion. Hafiz referred to the deal Becker had made on behalf of the Linyaari for the catseyes. The old man had paid almost current market price for the precious and highly useful gems before realizing that the Linyaari and Becker were carting home enough to drive the price down significantly should they all become available at once. Furthermore, since the Linyaari had been heavily into debt to Hafiz for his help in fighting off the Khleevi and rebuilding their devastated worlds, very little money had changed hands.

Still, Hafiz consoled himself with the thought that, though the Linyaari debt was wiped out and they had sufficient future credits granted for the remaining processes that would be required to revive both planets, Hafiz himself was able to make a handsome profit by selling some of the unusually large and fine catseyes he acquired at well above the usual rate. He was also making deals to sell others in the future. And under his capable and profitable guidance, the market would not be flooded, because the bulk of the stones were safely stored in one of the Harakamian warehouses on MOO, ready to be released at the whim and will of one Hafiz

Harakamian. When the time – and the price – was appropriate, of course.

Becker suspected Rafik might have come not only to see Acorna, but also to take possession of more of the stones to market on Kezdet.

Karina linked arms with her husband, not wanting to be left out of possibly profitable discussions, for despite her well-cultivated ethereal airs, she was as canny in her way as Hafiz.

This left Acorna more or less alone with Rafik, if she didn't count Aari's family and the security personnel.

Acorna realized what Becker was doing and was grateful for the opportunity to confide in Rafik. She pulled her adopted father aside and quietly explained about Aari and Laarye and the time machine, along with the little she had learned about Grimalkin, Aari's companion on his voyages through time.

As they conferred, they walked out of the terminal toward the guest quarters where Hafiz usually lodged his most important visitors. To get there, one walked through Hafiz's ornamental gardens. The moment they stepped into the bubble, the exotic fragrances assailing their nostrils told Acorna, even before she saw the brilliant blossoms, that the garden had been revived. The flowers were bigger and brighter than ever, and more fragrant. Here and there along the path elaborate fountains radiated fine sprays of moisture to cool the faces and throats of passersby.

Only a short time ago the surface of MOO had

been barren, the irrigation systems ripped up to provide conduits for the waters of Vhiliinyar. To free up the supplies needed to revive the battered planet, Karina and Hafiz had instituted water rationing on MOO, and had themselves submitted with a fortitude that amazed everyone who only knew them as luxury-loving potentates of their own private moon. During the hard times, Hafiz had softened the austerity of the ruined gardens to some degree with extravagant holograms that he created for that purpose, but they naturally did not emit the same perfumes or cooling spray that the real gardens did.

Acorna and Rafik slowed as they strolled, both to secure the necessary privacy and to enjoy the beautiful surroundings. 'You've heard my problems,' Acorna said when she had finished relating them to her adopted father. 'Now tell me to what we owe the honor of your visit? Is it the catseyes?'

'Partly, yes. And partly for other family reasons. I am so relieved that you came when you did, and with a development dramatic enough to distract Hafiz from his current campaign to find me a wife. Now that I am his heir, he says, it is time I married and provided him with little heirs and heiresses. He dismisses my argument that you are an appropriate heir for us both. He tells me that you, my dear, have other falafel to fry. I'm just glad I'm not Neo-Hadithian after all, or he'd probably try to get me to marry four women at once to improve my chances of fathering his "grandchildren." I can't understand him, Acorna. He is twice my age and had only one son – whom he couldn't stand. Now, all of a sudden, he's acting like a mother with a virgin daughter. And it's *my* life he's arranging for me.'

'Acorna laughed, 'Don't you want to find a wife, Rafik?'

'Yes,' he said. '*I* do. I don't want Hafiz to find one for me. And I don't want to find just any nice girl with a nice family that has a nice fortune that goes with her. I don't want to be an intergalactic playboy like Hafiz was in his younger days. I want to find *my own* wife, someone as special to me as Judit and Mercy are to Gill and Calum.'

'Well,' Acorna said ruefully. 'If you find her, take my advice and don't let her get involved with time travelers.'

'Poor Acorna.' Rafik put his arm around her slim shoulders and gave her a hug. 'It's going to be all right, you know,' he told her. 'You and Aari fell in love with each other once, and you will do it again. However much he has changed because of experiences he's had or hasn't had, he's the same person inside and will be drawn back to you. And once the strangeness goes away, you'll get to fall for him all over again.'

'Do you think so?' she asked, hoping against all logic that, because of the closeness of their relationship, somehow Rafik knew things about her she herself didn't know.

'I do,' he said.

Two

Dinner was a lavish affair. Hafiz's kitchens prepared a very good simulation of a fatted calf for the return of the prodigal heir. The Linyaari, of course, followed their own dietary agenda and dined on the beautifully arranged buds and grasses in the floral centerpieces while the other diners enjoyed gourmet delicacies from more substantial dishes.

The *Balakiire* landed while the feast was in progress, but Neeva, Khaari, and Melireenya were all too space-weary from their journey to join in the feast. They'd come through a meteor shower on the way back, and had had a very tense time of it.

(We just wanted to stop and say hello,) Neeva told Acorna through mind-speech as Melireenya and Khaari, slightly behind her, yawned and gave perfunctory waves of their hands to her and the other diners. (We'll graze later. I see you have someone more interesting to talk to than your old mother-sister anyway. It is well that you are together with Aari once more, Khornya. I am pleased for you.)

Clearly Neeva's tiredness kept her from picking up on Acorna's inner conflict.

Nevertheless, Acorna did her best to seem pleased, too. Under her family's watchful eye, she tried to be more welcoming to Aari.

'Can you tell us something of your experiences before you met up with Laarye again?' she asked. 'I have been studying the time device, and I think I've begun to understand how it works. But I admit I am still curious about why you and Grimalkin traveled to Makahomia.'

'Yes, Aari, I should very much like to hear that for myself,' Hafiz said. 'I trust you had some other plan in mind than that generations later your contributions to the history of that planet would eventually cost me my security chief.' He inclined his head toward a tall uniformed man scrutinizing the area from the perimeter of the bubble. 'The new fellow, Smythe-Wesson here, is a former Red Bracelet himself. While I find that somewhat reassuring, he does not inspire the same sort of confidence I had in Commander Kando.' Hafiz sighed a deep, put-upon sigh.

Thrilled as he was about the catseyes and the immense profits they would bring him, Hafiz had yet to forgive Acorna and her friends for allowing Nadhari Kando to remain on Makahomia.

Aari cheerily waved a dahlia through the air as he flung his hands wide, and said, 'Oh, that!

Well, Grimalkin, as you seem to have gathered, Khornya, is a feline shape-shifter. He is an empath and therefore much less egotistical than others among the Friends, but he shares Riid-Kiiyi's belief that those who are not cats are less fortunate than he. He was very happy to help me with my mission to rescue Laarye, but said we had to wait for exactly the right time and place to intersect with our home dimension so that I would be there to save my brother without falling prey to the Khleevi again. Even though he time-travels a lot, Grimalkin does not like to *waste* time, so he insisted we begin positioning ourselves by journeying to Makahomia, where he knew from the journals Nadhari will someday write that we were needed. It was also an excellent opportunity to re-fashion some of the inhabitants there in his own image. I don't actually remember any of it, mind you, but I have it all here in the recording he helped me make so I would remember myself from the other timeline.'

'That sounds *confusing*,' Maati said.

Aari shrugged. 'Perhaps it was, but he understood it. He is far older and wiser and much more brilliant than I, of course, but I trust his interpretations.'

Acorna felt peeved all over again. If Grimalkin was so much older, wiser, and brilliant than Aari – and presumably, herself – why couldn't he have returned Aari to her with his memory intact? Aari spoke of Grimalkin so enthusiastically that she thought that maybe he regretted returning to her. Perhaps her lover would rather be with his new friend.

Though Acorna carefully shielded these thoughts, Maati laid a hand on hers consolingly.

Hafiz had also grown bored with Aari's explanation of Grimalkin's explanation of time and space. Karina yawned and stretched, burped, and covered her mouth delicately with two fingers.

Hafiz then tapped his wineglass with a jeweled dagger. 'And now, honored guests, a special surprise. I have engaged something special for your enjoyment tonight. It is not a hologrammatic entertainment. Tonight you will see actual human performers of great skill and talent, and not incidentally, beauty, imported at enormous expense from the Akemilisan harems. Prepare yourselves to appreciate the astounding aerial acrobatics of Aziza and the Ornaments of Akemi!

'And now, in the time-honored custom of my people I say' – and he clapped twice, sharply – 'bring on the dancing girls!'

In a rainbow cyclone of veils and gauzy gaudy gold-encrusted split skirts and puffy pants, their bosoms and hips adorned by silk clothing heavily encrusted with jangling gold coins and jewels, the dancers whirled from the taller bits of shrubbery onto the patio where the diners sat digesting the superb meal.

Their feet were bare, except for tasteful toe

rings and little chains of coins worn as anklets, as were their midriffs.

'Nice,' Becker whispered to Hafiz. 'Are they just visiting or did you persuade them to be your in-house troupe?'

'They were on their way to another engagement when their ship developed trouble,' Hafiz whispered back. His right eye acquired a twinkle as the left one winked shut, as if he was enjoying a joke that was still a mystery to everyone else. 'One of our – associates – evacuated them to her vessel, then persuaded them to come here. Lovely, eh?'

Becker didn't respond because his jaw had dropped too far to make speech possible.

The ladies appeared boneless. Not for them the skeletal look popular in some of the human ports. Their smooth, rounded flesh undulated effortlessly in time to a drumbeat that varied so that it made Acorna think at some times of a stalking tiger, at others of a cornered gazelle. Their eyes were lined with a black substance that made them look huge, while veils first concealed the lower part of their faces, then were whipped away just as, with an explosion of frothing cloth, the women turned to show the serpentine movements of their backs and shoulders.

She heard Hafiz say to Becker, 'The Three Prophets teach that a woman should be modest. See how modest they are, with their veils concealing their identities? And, yet, how lovely. And I do think that to be a good wife, a woman should be well versed in the womanly arts.'

'You're not thinking of taking another wife, Hafiz?'

Karina's complacent smile faltered a bit, and she speared her husband with a rapier glance. He licked his lips and drummed his fingers on the sash around his paunch in time to the music. 'No, no,' he said with just a touch of regret. 'Such barbaric customs are practiced only by blasphemers of the true path, such as the Neo-Hadithians. My interest in these ladies is for the sake of my heir. It is time Rafik began to think of finding a wife. A man's life should not be all business and good works. He should have a family as well. I once believed that it was important to have sons, until I had one, and he was worthless. On the other hand, I adopted my beautiful granddaughter, who is a jewel beyond price, so I am thinking Rafik must father many children of both sexes, so that he has many heirs to choose from and I have many grandchildren to comfort me in my advancing years.'

'*I'll* comfort you, my dynamo of the desert,' Karina whispered.

'And I you, O pearl of pulchritude, and our grandchildren shall comfort us both.'

The drum tempo changed again, and the troupe split off to leave a single dancer, her gossamer veils folded over her body like the wings of a sleeping butterfly. She emerged slowly, stretched backward, elongating her torso and extending her head back toward her ankles. Just as they thought she was going to do a back-bend, she simply rolled her torso backward and then up again. Then she raised her arms above her head, facing them, her head moving back and forth like a snake's. Her feet rose above the ground and she rolled forward. It was not a tumble, simply a leisurely roll. She repeated these maneuvers in time with the music, her weightless body making lazy, graceful figure-eight arcs through the air.

As the music picked up, her movements, while grounded, and those in the air grew faster and more acrobatic; and then suddenly the rest of the troupe joined her, all spinning madly, the large faceted jewels in the middles of their coin belts flashing as if lit from within with each turn. And then, like the fluff of seedpods twirling in a high wind, each dancer in turn swept her hand before her belt and spun up into the air, the soles of her feet nearly a meter off the ground.

Karina clapped her hands delightedly.

'Oh, Haffy, this is a truly inspiring performance! Even I, who have studied the sacred erotic dances of ancient Babylon and Nineveh with high priestesses channeled from those cultures, have never seen such steps.'

'Truly they make an artistic tool of the simple antigravity belts they wear beneath their coins,' Hafiz agreed.

The girls spun downward again and, with their feet firmly planted on the ground, swept their veils before them and split off into the shrubbery to leave the stage to another soloist.

Becker was immediately enthralled by the new dancer. She was swathed in veils and skirts that whirled and shifted with her movements rising and falling, appearing and disappearing. The spacer was reminded of one of the clear-faceted kaleidoscopes you could buy at nanobug markets. The kind that took their colors from whatever was around them. If you looked through one of them at a sunlit coastal morning, sky blue, sea green, sun yellow, and spun it around and around, he thought maybe you could come close to the effect the dancer created. But, of course, it wouldn't be nearly as tantalizing as the flashes of pale skin and bright gold-green eyes glimpsed among the veils and her long, butter yellow hair. Her head was crowned with a circlet of coins that held a green veil whose tail covered her lower face, but there was something familiar about her.

As the tempo picked up, she suddenly approached and cast one of the veils around him. Then, fixing him in a green gaze made more exotic than it might have been by the kohl surrounding her eyes, she waggled her eyebrows up and down at him. Lifting one hip, then the other, she slowly worked her way into a shimmy, the coins at her hips flipping and clanking. She crooked her finger, beckoning, and he stood up and shook his lower half, too, though it didn't have the same effect.

Laughing, she pushed him back down and deposited her harem-pants-clad behind on his lap. 'Better stick to salvage, Becker,' she said in unexotic Basic.

'Andina! When did you get here?'

'I would have come to meet you, but I didn't want to spoil the surprise,' she told him.

'I didn't know you performed. I thought you were in the cleaning business.'

'I am. But these girls got stranded on a backwater asteroid populated by uncouth space bums not unlike you. I gave them a lift, and they gave me lessons for part of their fare. I persuaded them to let me bring them here instead of to the gig they were headed for when their ship began acting up. I figured Hafiz would pay them enough that they could reimburse me for the trip and fix their ship as well.'

'And if they couldn't fix it, you knew they could always sell it to me for salvage,' Becker said.

They said a lot of other things, as well, things that Acorna was too polite to listen to.

It appeared that Andina had started a trend when she got Becker up to dance with her, and some of the other dancers began to do likewise. Each dancer swooped, using her veils like wings, to the table, picked up a wineglass, set it on her head, lowered herself to the floor, did a lot of astounding muscular contractions with her abdomen and a few flips, rose again, wineglass still balanced, whirled into the air with it still on her forehead, then, without spilling a drop, whirled back to the table, gave each glass to its owner, and made a gesture that they were to down the contents, then whipped a silken veil around the party in question and dragged him (and sometimes her) out onto the dance floor. They repeated this until each diner had a turn, each glass of wine had been aerated, and most of the diners were on their feet and laughing.

As the gentleman at the head of the table, Hafiz would have been chosen first, except that when a lissome, sloe-eyed beauty undulated toward him, Karina sprang into action, placing herself between the dancer and her husband and waving her lavender draperies in a comparatively graceless and unprofessional but nonetheless effective fashion. The dancer applauded Karina with the ululating cry called a *zaghareet*, bowed to them both, and did her trick with both of their wineglasses. Hafiz and Karina were by then so absorbed in each other that they barely noticed. Still, they dutifully quaffed their wine when the dancer returned it to them, then they left the party with their arms as far around each others' convex waists as their ample bodies would allow.

The youngest member of the troupe was the daughter of one of the dancers. Like the other dancers, she seemed fascinated if somewhat confused by the Linyaari, who ate the centerpieces and drank only water. The other dancers avoided eye contact with the Linyaari diners, but finally the young girl's curiosity overcame her reserve, and she chose Maati to dance with her. Maati jumped in enthusiastically and imitated the girl's movements. Both of them giggled at the Linyaari girl's awkwardness. The dancer giggled even more when she realized Maati was female. 'What is your name?' the girl asked as she whipped a veil off some part of her costume and handed it to Maati, showing her how to tie it around her haunches.

Maati told her, and added, 'It means harmony, like in music.'

'Ah, my name is Layla. It means evening, in case one is living someplace where that makes any difference,' Layla replied. She then did an aerial flip, after which she extracted a belt from beneath the coins at her waist and handed it to Maati.

Layla made a little circle in the air with her upraised index finger.

Maati nodded excitedly and clasped the belt in place just below her waist. She spun as the little dancer directed, making one or two complete revolutions before she got dizzy and stumbled upward, putting one foot out to catch herself and meeting only air. She was almost a full meter off the ground! Her new friend steadied her and pulled her back down. Maati returned the antigrav belt, but she seemed sorry to have to do so.

Then she saw Laarye laughing at her and Layla, so they pulled him up to join them. He shifted from one foot to the other, watching them with a studious expression, then burst into a sort of prance as he circled them, holding one end of the veil until they were both entangled in it.

Rafik, whose wineglass was upside down beside his plate, was pulled from Acorna's side when the lead dancer, clad in crimson-and-teal paisley velvet pants and a great deal of clanking gold, did handsprings up to him and captured him with a red veil.

(Culturally fascinating, don't you think?) Aari asked, using thought-talk. (I wonder if those concealing cloths they wear over their faces and wave around themselves serve a function similar to horn-hats. Do you know?)

(I don't think the purpose is the same,) Acorna replied politely, if a little stiffly. (I believe they are part of a tableau recreating a historical mating ritual.)

'So are horn-hats,' Aari said, as if reminding her. 'It seems to me, and of course, in this time-line this is the first encounter I have had with human culture, that the cloths they wave—'

'Veils,' Acorna supplied.

'*Vaals*,' he repeated obligingly, if inaccurately. 'I think they are intended to increase the magnetic field around the dancer's body, thereby attracting more potential mates, whereas the *vaals* covering the mouths of the dancers serve to intensify the psychic vibrations emanating from their ocular organs. Of course, I could not actually make out what the message was supposed to be, but I feel sure it had something to do with mating.'

'Actually,' Acorna said, 'from what I have read of the culture Uncle Hafiz comes from, the dance was originally performed by females encouraging other females when they are in labor with their young. The female about to give birth is supposed to emulate the abdominal movements of the dancers in order to hasten her baby's entrance into the world. Practicing the dance from the time they are young girls strengthens the muscles required to give birth as well.'

'Ahhh,' Aari said. 'I felt sure there was some deeper meaning. Do the acrobatic feats and the airborne activities also play a role in human childbirth?'

'Not that I'm aware of,' Acorna said, suppressing a smile in spite of herself. This was starting to sound like Aari after all, with his rather whimsical interpretations of other cultures. 'I believe the only function of those movements is to enhance the performance of the entertainers.'

She found her feet tapping and her hands patting her thighs as she listened to the music. Watching Laarye and the girls cavort, with Maati following Laarye's prance and the dancing girl joining in as if it was a new step, Acorna jumped to her feet, grabbed Aari's hand, and pulled him into the dance, too. The dancers shimmied and undulated for a moment or two while looking askance at the high-stepping Linyaari, then shrugged and fell in behind, so that Laarye was leading a line of dancers that soon took in the entire audience.

For the first time since Aari's arrival, Acorna's tension vanished, a thing of the past as if each dance step kicked it farther away. Aari capered and kicked behind her, and she sensed his own relief. He truly had not meant to hurt her – he didn't even know her. Perhaps Rafik was right – they needed to get to know each other all over again, then everything would be fine.

Finally, the giddiness of Acorna's relief turned to weariness. She said good night to Rafik and her friends and sought her usual sleeping mat in Hafiz's guest quarters.

Tired as she was, she hoped she'd sleep well. The sleep Maati had interrupted had been unsatisfactory, plagued as it was by dreams that in some way involved the Khleevi, from what she could recall. She did not wish to return to that kind of sleep again, but she told herself the bad dreams only came when she fell asleep in the time lab.

Hard as she tried to reassure herself, she could not find a comfortable position on the mat. Other thoughts, disturbing in a much pleasanter way, kept intruding, adding to her restlessness.

Aari's presence stirred her on a number of levels, including the most basic physical ones. She had become *used* to responding to him, and now, even though her mind was telling her it wasn't a good idea, her body still wanted to. She wondered again if there was a way the time device could be used to integrate her original Aari with the current one – so that memories of her and his other friends were not merely hearsay to him, but experiences he had been a part of, that had moved and changed him emotionally.

She had to admit, though, that the new Aari sure could dance.

But something else bothered her too much to allow her to sleep. While dancing with the entertainers, she had caught random snatches of thought from those around her.

'After . . . find out where . . . back to ship . . .'

Those thoughts, especially in a group of space travelers such as those at the dinner, could have been perfectly innocent. But she was almost certain she'd picked up the words from the dancers. And she felt that there was something secretive behind them, just as there was something profoundly unfriendly lurking behind the women's professional smiles.

Perhaps it was nothing. Maybe it was simply that the dancers had led rather difficult lives and feared to trust the people they met on their travels. The young girl Layla had seemed to like Maati. Those feelings had been genuine, Acorna was sure. Layla had gone out of her way to be amiable to the young Linyaari girl. Of course, Maati was easy to like.

It was certainly true, in Acorna's experience, that many humans found the Linyaari comforting to be around and enjoyed their company.

But the soothing Linyaari aura had not seemed to affect these dancers in the same way it did ordinary humans.

Acorna tossed and turned restlessly for perhaps two hours of Standard time. Maati was not sleeping on the pallet beside her as she usually did when they both visited MOO. Perhaps she, too, had been troubled by the thoughts of the newcomers.

Acorna finally decided that, between her thoughts and the energetic dancing, she was too stimulated to sleep. She got up from her pallet and quickly dressed. She would go for a walk in an attempt to calm herself into sleep mode.

Night and day were engineered events on MOO, so there were activities available for people whose bodies were on other schedules than the one programmed into the enormous envirobubbles housing each major area of MOO's multitude of domestic quarters. She might go to the lab, see if Aari's parents were working there, and get their impressions of their newly returned sons. Or perhaps she'd look for Maati. The girl was fond of hanging out in the com shed and talking to others who were the human equivalent of her age. She had made friends with many of the Moonbase students and the denizens of the *Haven* when they were in port.

Acorna walked out of the guest quarters and stepped onto the pedestrian thoroughfare connecting the various envirobubbles with each other. The terminal and docking bays were in one direction, the laboratories in the opposite one. She closed her eyes and conducted a mental search for her friends. She didn't call to them. She simply tried to locate them by tracking their auras. Her mental powers had grown tremendously since she first rejoined her people. The earliest glimmer of psychic ability she had demonstrated, the power simply to look at an asteroid through a com screen or view port and discern its mineral content, had matured into a sort of mental sonar that allowed her, when she concentrated, to discern many details about her environment and to locate specific features contained within it.

Never before had she attempted to use that sense in this particular way, but now, in her indecision, she searched for people as naturally as she would grasses or metals or other aspects of her surroundings.

Maati was headed away from the terminal. Becker and Andina were spending the night on the *Heloise*, Andina's ship. RK slept in the command seat of the *Condor* while Mac was recharging his energy source nearby. The laboratories were empty. Kaarlye and Miiri conversed earnestly with Laarye in the guest quarters. Rather to Acorna's surprise, Aari and Rafik were deep in conversation as they strolled toward the laboratories.

And the discontented, disquieting babble of dancer thoughts pattered across her mind like hail from the direction of the warehouses. *What were they doing there?* she wondered. She headed toward the dancers.

As she passed through the outer gardens near the darkened laboratories, she saw Aari and Rafik. They were walking together and talking earnestly among the ivory flowers and twisting vines lining the paved path that meandered through the gardens. As she passed she saw Aari glance in her direction.

But the dancers' voices, amplified by her telepathy, and the jumble of their thoughts occupied most of her concentration. Their thoughts assumed a melody and a beat that was much like the music they danced to. 'Open, open, open sesame,' one woman was thinking as she used a sonic saw on an intricate lock. 'Off, off, you never saw us, we were not here,' another one instructed the laser beams that usually guarded the warehouses as she disabled them. 'In with you and grab the rocks. Now run, run, run!'

And in counterpoint were the thoughts of two others.

'This seems all wrong.'

'You bet it does. We haven't been paid yet, and we have no transport off this rock.'

'Rocks, rocks, grab the rocks and run, run, run!'.

'How would this one look in my belly button?'

'Stop clowning, Layla, and run!'

'Run where?'

'To the spaceships, of course. Andina is a generous girl. She won't mind if we take her vessel for a little spin.'

'You planned that all along, didn't you, Aziza?'

'Of course I did, little chickpea. Now take your rocks and run.'

'What about the camera security?'

'Your mama and Naima are giving the guards a private show. Now *hurry*.'

Acorna had never before attempted to send an all-points bulletin to every Linyaari within her range, but now she did so. (Everybody, come quickly! The dancers are thieves, robbing Hafiz of the catseye stones. Hurry!)

The evening's entertainment had been tiring for most of them, and although she received responses from Maati, Laarye, Aari, and their parents, other Linyaari awakened sluggishly and asked her to clarify her message.

(No time. Just come. Now. *Quickly!*) she called. All the while she called she was running for the warehouses in hopes of intercepting the duplicitous dancers.

(We're right behind you, Khornya.) Aari's thought reached her as she practically skidded to a halt on the path, where she was immediately threatened with a stampede of black-clad dancers bearing large and apparently heavy valises. As she gained on them, the first one laughed and spun around, spinning herself aloft and high over Acorna's head. Acorna jumped for the next one and caught a handful of the dancer's full black pants. But the antigrav belts the dancers wore were quite powerful. Instead of Acorna dragging the dancer down, the woman dragged Acorna up with her.

Acorna reached up, twisting the black pants out of the way until the skin of her hand met flesh and bone.

The woman kicked, 'Let go! You're heavy! I can't very well carry you and the loot, too.'

'That – is – my – point – exactly,' Acorna said through gritted teeth, while the woman's companions zoomed between the path and the shadowy dome of the bubble. Aari and Rafik pelted down the path that lay before them, with the raven-robed dancers soaring over them like Halloween witches. Rafik, seeing what Acorna was doing, made a leap and brought down the lead dancer as he snared her at the knee. But she kicked him in the face and got away. Aari leaped higher than Acorna had ever seen anyone, Linyaari or human, leap before, and when his prey ducked, he twisted in midair to redirect his grab. Unfortunately, Aari seemed to be trying to grab her using only the last joint of his fingertips instead of his entire hands or forearms. His fingertips, of course, slipped off her. Before he could tighten his grip, she drew her knees up to her chest and somersaulted over their heads. He landed lightly on his toes, giving his hands an odd, comical look of pure disgust before bounding after the others.

The dancers gave their pursuers a wide berth

after that, making horizontal zigzags away from them to elude their grasping hands.

Rafik grabbed another one, though. He used a hand-over-hand technique to pull his quarry down. When his hand met her waist, he gave a tug and her antigrav belt dangled from his hand. Then she fell and he with her, both of them coming down hard on the path, knocking the wind from Rafik and also driving the dancer's knee into his solar plexus. She grabbed for her belt but couldn't free it. But before Acorna or Aari could rush to Rafik's aid, two of the other dancers did back flips in the air, still clutching their valises, but with their free hands grabbed their fellow thief and pulled her up with them.

The distraction as she worried about Rafik caused Acorna to lose her grasp on the dancer to whom she was clinging. With a slight kick, the thief slipped from her grip, and Acorna tumbled back to the ground. Picking herself up, she ran to Rafik. But before she could get there, Aari touched him with his horn to heal any injury done to him by the fall and the woman's knee.

'Ouch!' Rafik said, rising and rubbing his backside. 'I think your horn's on the blink, Aari. My butt still hurts.'

Aari's fingers went to his horn. 'Oh, no. Something must have happened during the time/space transfer. Grimalkin warned me that something like that might happen.'

Rafik waved Acorna way when she would

have healed the hurt, and said, 'It doesn't hurt *that* bad, honey.'

By the time he stood up, all of the thieves were far out of reach, spinning, flipping, somersaulting, and otherwise propelling themselves toward the terminal.

'I *like* those belts,' Rafik said. 'I want one.'

'You *have* one,' Acorna reminded him. 'Maybe if you put it on, it will deprive them of the advantage.'

Rafik held it out to her. 'I haven't been able to turn hand-springs in years.'

Acorna quickly slipped it on.

'Wait!' Aari said. 'You can't do that. They might hurt you. Hand it to me. I will capture them.'

Acorna spun herself into the air. 'Sorry,' and waved goodbye to him as she launched herself forward with a series of midair flips. This was fun! Since she was much taller than the dancers, each revolution of her long body covered more airspace than that of each dancer. She almost caught up with them, though thus far she actually had no idea what she was going to do with them once she had them.

However, just as she was gaining, they came to the door leading to the passage between bubbles. They had enough of a lead that they were able to spin themselves down, iris open the door, flee through it, and close it again before she reached them. She copied the motion they each executed before landing, passing her hand over the large jewel in the center of the belt. It spun her gently downward until her feet touched the path.

She pressed the panel to open the door but it remained tightly closed. Somehow the fugitives had jammed it. She sent out a mental call to her fellow Linyaari. A few more seemed to be awake now. (Somebody stop them! And someone please come and release this door. Where are the security guards?)

Nobody seemed to know the answer to that, but after what seemed an interminable time, during which Aari and Rafik also reached the door, Melireenya called out to them in mind-speech.

(We heard you, Khornya, loud and clear. Neeva has gone to find the guards and to try to intercept the thieves. Khaari is waking Hafiz and Karina. Ah, now I see how they jammed this portal closed. One of them twisted her serpent armband through the layers. Got it.)

The door irised open a bit jerkily, and Acorna, followed closely by Aari and Rafik, were through it and on the other side so quickly that Melireenya had to take a speedy backward hop to avoid being bowled over.

Acorna launched herself again into the air, though it seemed a bit futile at this point. She didn't like how dark the gardens and pathways remained, nor how few people were about despite the alarm she had raised through her fellow Linyaari.

Usually the recreation areas were well lit and

populated throughout most of the night, but she saw very few people up and about now, and no security guards. Hafiz was going to have enough kittens to staff a Makahomian temple. Furthermore, she knew that she and Becker were going to hear a great deal more from Hafiz about why they had allowed Nadhari Kando to remain behind when she still had a contract as *his* chief security guard. Such laxness never would have been tolerated under Nadhari's administration. Never mind that it had been Hafiz's laxness, not theirs, that had put the dancers on this planet.

The other connecting doors had not been closed, much less jammed, which told Acorna that the dancers were no longer concerned about pursuit.

As she finally gained the terminal, eerily silent and empty of travelers or personnel, she saw the *Heloise*, the *Condor*, and the *Balakiire* in their bays beyond the terminal's transparent outer walls.

She also saw the gantry attach itself to the *Heloise*'s hatch, which opened to permit a file of black-clad figures bearing valises to disappear through it.

Becker and Andina were still sleeping in the *Heloise*. She tried sending to Becker but only got a grumbling response. She could imagine him huffing through his mustache in irritation at being disturbed. (Captain, wake up. The *Heloise* is being boarded by thieves – the dancers have stolen the catseye chrysoberyls and are hijacking Andina's ship – with you in it.) She didn't leave her warning to telepathy alone but, as she transmitted silently to her friend, sought out the terminal communications station and grabbed a microphone. But, when she reached her goal, she looked back at the *Heloise* to see that the gantry was gone and exhaust was coming from the ship's jets. Then, gently and without interference, the *Heloise* lifted off as gracefully as her hijackers had danced.

THREE

'Heads will roll when Hafiz finds out what happened,' Rafik said. He lounged in a chair on the main deck of the *Condor*, watching Acorna adjust their current course in pursuit of the *Heloise*.

Acorna agreed. 'But the real excitement will be when Captain Becker learns he has been cat-napped – excuse me, kidnapped.' She gave RK a warning look. The cat had given her a mental nudge that made her say 'catnapped,' she was sure. The *Condor*'s feline first mate thought-talked in perfectly good Basic, as well as in Makahomian and Linyaari when he wanted to, but generally he seemed to find it entertaining to pretend that he conversed only in his native meows.

Rafik paid little attention. He was busy pursuing his own line of thought. 'I don't understand how this could have happened. Why did so few people respond to your alarm, Acorna? Why *didn't* the security team do its job? And even more puzzling is how those women knew about the stones and where they would be concealed. MOO *is* quite a ways from the beaten path, since this part of the universe is still largely a mystery to people in our galaxy. Their encounter with Andina Dmitri was certainly not random chance. Do you think she could be in on it?'

Acorna thought of the few times she had been around Andina when the owner of the Domestic Goddess Intergalactic Cleaning Corporation visited Becker. 'I've never caught any suspicious thoughts or felt uncomfortable or wary around her,' Acorna said. 'And she's quite well known in her field. If the dancers did have their own ship and it malfunctioned, as they claim, who would have known Andina was on her way to MOO?'

'And how did they manage to take over the ship and escape so quickly?' Rafik asked. 'It doesn't make any sense.'

The *Condor* had been following the trail of the *Heloise* for several hours. But, just as Rafik had predicted, when Hafiz's face appeared on the screen of the com unit it looked a bit disturbed. Still, in Acorna's opinion, Hafiz looked much calmer than Rafik had expected him to. In spite of the enormity of his loss, the old bandit appeared more bemused than angry. 'I don't suppose my new security chief is aboard your vessel and you have neglected to mention that to me?' Hafiz inquired.

'No, Uncle,' Rafik said.

'He does not seem to be among his fellows either – all of whom are recovering from foul headaches and the same deep sleep that captured so many of us. I am surprised, heir of my house, that you escaped the drugging of the drinks.'

'Aha, Uncle, the truth is I only escaped the drugging of the drinks because I didn't care for the drink in question.'

'You question the quality of my cellars?'

'No, I question the effects of their contents on my head and stomach – even when untreated with sleeping drugs. I can understand why you retired when still a young and vibrant man, O Uncle, for being the head of your household is adding years to my body while taking years from my life.'

'You have become as delicate as a flower petal, O my heir, for your body to reject the most delicious of nectars. This is a strange malady indeed for an asteroid miner who used to eat dehydrated rations for every meal.'

'They were not all dehydrated, my Uncle. Some were ration bars. And when Acorna came among us, she made us many excellent salads. Perhaps the drink that now suits the station to which you have elevated me is too rich for my lowborn digestion.' He shrugged. 'At least it has proved fortunate in this case.'

'Not so fortunate – at least until the thieves are apprehended, our sacred and valuable gems are regained, and our friends are safe once more,' Hafiz said.

Acorna noted wryly how Hafiz had ordered his priorities.

'Of course,' Rafik agreed. 'I hear and obey, O Uncle, obviously.'

'Yes,' Hafiz said. 'Very well, my boy. May the winds of good fortune be with you in your endeavors.'

'Thank you, Uncle,' Rafik said with a straight face, though Acorna could hear him thinking how odd the blessing of his uncle sounded in space, where there was no wind.

The ship's feline first mate rubbed against her shins and looked up into her face, then gave a mournful 'Meow.'

Acorna knelt to stroke RK's plushy brindled back. 'I miss our captain, too. But you will have to make do with the rest of us for the time being. Just believe, RK, that we will get him back as soon as we can.'

For his part, Captain Becker was not only fit to be tied, he *was* tied. It made him sad to think that an evening that had begun so promisingly had gone so sharply downhill. And so suddenly.

After quite a lot of Hafiz's best hooch and Andina's fetching hoochie-kooch, Becker had been feeling quite amorous. So he quickly agreed when Andina suggested, soon after she landed in his lap, that they return to her ship, where they could be assured of privacy. Though Hafiz's guest quarters were luxurious and imaginative, not to say downright exciting in some areas, the walls in his assigned cubicle were not thick. In some cases, they were little more than a holographic veil drawn between one space and another. And both Becker and Andina knew all about the hidden surveillance cameras and bugs Hafiz had secretly installed throughout. These were mainly to allow him to spy on business associates, in order to get the best of them. But that didn't mean the cameras weren't used at other times by other people for other purposes. Andina's crew had been given leave to go dirtside to enjoy the delights of MOO, so she and Becker knew they would have the ship to themselves.

Andina's quarters on the *Heloise* were far from Spartan and not nearly as haphazard as Becker's on the *Condor*. Everything was clean, of course, as befitted the ship of a professional cleaning expert. But the ambience Becker remembered had definitely changed. Usually Andina's cabin was as cozy and homey as if it was made of logs and set beside a roaring trout stream of the sort Becker read about in his old hard-copy books. It seemed his lady's reading had lately taken a different turn. The homemade quilt he remembered decorating her double-wide bunk had been replaced by a hot-pink-and-gold paisley silk coverlet, swathed with gold-shot veils of turquoise, purple, and saffron hanging from eye hooks above the bunk. Soft, sensual music similar to that the dancers had used began playing as she led him into her chamber. A tray of real wax candles glowed beside the bed, their flickering glow the only light in the room, except for a holo window with a faux outside view, in which a holo crescent moon beamed in upon them. They had just slipped into something more comfortable, and were about to get *really* comfortable, when the mood was spoiled by the beep of Andina's cabin's com unit.

'Yes?' she answered, 'what is it?'

'Captain Dmitri, this is Commander Smythe-Wesson, chief of security here on the Moon of Opportunity. I have an urgent security matter I must discuss with you. Permission to come aboard, please.'

'I am engaged in an urgent matter myself at present, Commander,' Andina said, as Becker nuzzled her neck. They were glad the com unit screen was not presently turned on. 'Can this not wait until morning?'

'No, ma'am. I would not have disturbed you if it could. It is a very grave matter, Captain, but I am not at liberty to discuss it via electronic means. Permission to board, please.'

'Oh, very well, then,' she said, sliding out of bed. She opened a wall locker and pulled out a shipsuit. Becker reluctantly resumed his own garments as he watched her creamy body disappear into a rip-proof, waterproof, fireproof, well-ventilated synthetic fabric casing. *Those old-time pashas and sheiks were lucky they lived back before com units were invented,* he thought sourly. *Otherwise, they'd never have made it through even one night without interruption, much less a thousand and one nights.*

'Maybe I should head on back to the *Condor*,' he suggested to Andina.

She looked troubled. 'Maybe. But I'd like it better if you'd stick around. I have no idea what all this is about. And with the crew ashore . . .'

'Oh, sure,' he said. Naturally she would feel better with him around to protect her. She was able to defend herself in the boardroom when bidding for jobs and navigating through space, but she was no Nadhari Kando. Which, much as he missed the formidable Nadhari sometimes, was kind of a relief. Andina was strong enough to have built an empire from excellent cleaning chemistry and superior elbow grease and was a very good shot with a wide variety of firearms, but when it came to hand-to-hand, she was a lover, not a fighter.

As it turned out, that was unfortunate. Smythe-Wesson had already entered the hatch when Becker received the mental alarm from Acorna. As soon as the security chief appeared, Becker said, 'I know you said your business with Andina was urgent, Commander, but I've just been notified that the belly dancers have raided Hafiz's store of catseye chrysoberyls, which has got to be more urgent. I'll be glad to go with you and help you catch them.'

'Will you?' Smythe-Wesson said, with a supercilious sneer that expressed doubt, at the very least. Right about then, Becker, who had been distracted what with one thing and another, noticed that Smythe-Wesson's sidearm was no longer in its holster. It was, in fact, pointing at Andina and Becker. 'I have a better idea. Why don't we just wait for them to come to us?'

Whereupon he forced the two of them back to Andina's cabin and made Andina bind Becker's hands and feet with tape, checking the bonds himself to make sure they were tight enough. Then, pushing Andina in front of him, the security chief shut the hatch door between him and Becker.

Becker concentrated very hard, trying to send a telepathic message to Acorna, as he had been able to do on Makahomia. But he got no answer, no sign that she read him. He figured she was in the middle of pursuing the dancers and her concentration was so focused on that she apparently didn't pick up his transmission.

Smythe-Wesson forced Andina to the bridge, to begin the liftoff sequence. Becker couldn't see them of course, but Andina cleverly opened the intercom from her end so he could hear her muttering through her preflight check. He imagined her hands moving deftly over the controls, her brow slightly furrowed with concentration. Which wouldn't do her or their captor a lot of good with no crew, he thought smugly. This ship was no *Condor*, which could be flown by one person. But just then he heard other footsteps enter the ship, other voices, high, female ones, laughing and talking as they hurried past the cabin to strap down for liftoff.

He fumed a little, frustrated by his helplessness, then began thinking about how to do something about it. He'd actually been in tighter spots trying to repair the *Condor* in space back in the days when he stored and shifted cargo alone. Back then every iota of space was consumed by cargo, and he'd had little maneuvering room.

He might have his hands and feet bound, but he had a lot of room to compensate for those little inconveniences.

Furthermore, he wasn't taped *to* anything. He scooted himself to the wall, inched up it, and punched the panel to open the first storage locker. The costume Andina had worn earlier that night hung incongruously above her bulky antigrav boots. Neither was terribly useful for his purposes. The next panel revealed more helpful contents. Here was a stash of Andina's personal cleaning supplies, low-tech antiques that were practically collectors' items these days, but still effective. They included a scraper and a pair of scissors. Tape was very hard to pull loose, but it was easier to cut than rope. Becker cut his hands loose within seconds, and in a few more seconds his feet were free.

Unfortunately, by that time the *Heloise* was rising above the thin native atmosphere of MOO. The increased gravity resulting from the acceleration of the launch pressed him to the floor. He lay well away from the metal lockers, allowing himself to sink into the soft Fellkastani carpet with which Andina had thoughtfully covered her deck. He wondered if his current position would leave her a Becker-shaped impression in the rug forever after. He hoped she wouldn't be using the carpet as a souvenir to help her remember the late Jonas Becker.

So far, everyone concerned in this catseye caper seemed merely larcenous rather than murderous, but the cash value of the stones in the galactic marketplace was enough to unbalance even the sanest criminal mind.

Certainly Hafiz's criminal mind was going to be considerably unbalanced by the theft. But that was just tough. A deal was a deal. Hafiz had already accepted the catseyes as full payment and then some for the Linyaari debt. It wasn't Becker's fault that the wily Hafiz couldn't hang on to the stones. The deal Becker had made for them with the old man would stand. Legally. That wouldn't matter to the Linyaari, however. They would feel morally obligated to Hafiz again if he didn't have the stones to offset the further expenses in reviving the Linyaari planets.

Now that his bonds were removed, Becker wondered what to do next. Maybe he could lure the dancers into Andina's seraglio with the power of his animal magnetism (well, RK liked him) and passionate promises? Yep, *that* was a likely plan. Meanwhile, maybe Andina could overpower Smythe-Wesson and fly *Heloise* back home. Yeah, right. The dancers, of course, would be so exhausted from their exertions with Becker that they would offer little resistance. As a plan, he liked it. It was a pretty safe bet that Andina *wouldn't* like it, but a person had to be prepared to make some sacrifices in the interests of freedom and criminal justice. Then, too, there was the other problem, which was that it wouldn't actually work. Still, it was more attractive than the alternative, which was that old standby of crawling through the ventilation ducts.

Becker let go of his little fantasy. Seducing all the dancing girls would be nice, but it was a long shot. *Really, really* long. The ventilation ducts were probably much more realistic. He sighed and, feeling distinctly grumpy, looked around for something to stand on so he could reach the overhead grating and locate the opening to the duct.

Andina's quarters were not as full of furnishings as they were of draperies. The only chair was bolted to the deck. The bed squished under his weight, and even when he bounced up on the mattress, he couldn't touch the ceiling.

But the bouncing made him think of the dancers, and he returned to the first storage locker and Andina's costume. Sure enough, under the coins and fringes, there was the antigrav belt. He feared it wouldn't fit him, but the girls wore the adjustable belt low around their hips, so by holding his breath and grunting a lot, he dragged the buckle across his gut until it closed.

He bounced into the air and nothing happened. It took him several tries before he remembered the little twirl the girls did, and the way they passed their hands over the jewel now twinkling just above his fly.

It appeared he was about to lose his dignity yet one more time, all in the name of expediency. So, placing the tip of his index finger on the crown of his head, while raising the pinkie of the same hand, he pirouetted, strumming across the jewel until he rose and bumped his head on the ceiling. Ouch. Obviously these things were made for playing the Palace, where the rafters were loftier.

After a little poking, prodding, and raiding Andina's cleaning tools again, he pulled the ventilator cover loose, only to find that the duct was much too small for him to crawl into, anti-grav belt or not.

Disgusted, he passed his hand over the belt and sank to the floor again, where he sat cross-legged, pondering his predicament.

He finally decided that the best way to get out of the room was to create a disturbance, use the belt to hover above the hatch, and fall upon whoever came to check on him. Then he could escape through the still-open hatch and pick them off one at a time.

Before he could decide whether fire, flood, or blood would best serve his needs, the decision was taken out of his hands.

'Fire!' yelled Smythe-Wesson. 'Fire in the head!' Then came the pattering of female feet and a lot of exclaiming and the sound of a very calm female voice giving orders on how best to quell the reported blaze.

Meanwhile, the door opened in front of him, and Andina came in, and said, 'Oh, Jonas, you're loose and safe! I might have known! Come on, there's a fire aboard. Help us put it out.'

Though the blaze had already consumed every flammable thing in the head and flames crawled across every other surface in the room, the dancers worked well as a team and had it pretty well quelled by the time Becker and Andina arrived. Fire extinguishers smothered the wild tongues of flame, and it looked as if the emergency was over, until the youngest dancer, the one who had befriended Maati, turned suddenly, and the hem of her long skirt brushed a smoldering ember. Flames flared up the costume and caught on to her hair faster than anyone could move. Becker lunged forward. Catching the flaming girl, he smothered as much of the fire as he could against his flameproof shipsuit, then rolled over and over with her, putting out the flames in their path and the ones devouring the girl's clothing and hair at the same time.

The women wielding the fire extinguishers turned the nozzles on the girl and Becker, while others of the women ripped off the girl's clothing. Becker's fireproof shipsuit had taken no harm, though Andina brushed his face with her hand and bits of char fell off. 'You're going to look funny with no brows or lashes for a while,' she said. 'And I'll clip off the rest of your beard and mustache – you won't want to shave with that burn on your face. But I think you'll do. My hero.'

A woman Becker presumed was her mother cradled the girl in her arms and rocked her, speaking rapidly in a language Becker didn't understand.

'Take her to my cabin,' Andina said, 'and keep her warm and elevate her feet. She's probably shocky right now. We also should get some fluids in her.'

Becker lifted the girl from the woman's arms and carried her to his erstwhile prison. He was very careful how he laid her down on the bed, but bits of her skin came away on his hands and suit anyway.

Her mother was at her side immediately and the other women clustered close, but when they tried to cover the girl's red and blistering body, she moaned and thrashed, which made her whimper piteously. Andina turned up the thermostat.

'We must give her something for the pain,' said the lead dancer, apparently also the leader of the other women.

'I have a mild analgesic in my first-aid kit,' Andina said. 'I understand with bad burns that there is little pain at the beginning.'

'What we need to do,' Becker said grimly, 'is turn this bird around and go back to MOO so the Linyaari can take care of her. They could heal her like *that*.' He snapped his fingers.

'They are truly such healers, these Linyaari?'

'Yes, Aziza,' the girl's mother said eagerly. 'Do you not remember that *he*' – she gestured with a twist of her lips to the outer corridor of the ship, no doubt indicating Smythe-Wesson – 'told us of their great medical skills in our briefing?'

'Yes,' Andina said. 'The Linyaari have wonderful healing skills. And, in fact, two Linyaari friends of ours have been following us in Jonas's ship. I could send a Mayday, and I know they would come, even at risk to themselves, if your boss will permit it.'

'He is not our boss!' one of the women hovering in the doorway said. 'We are a team. He is simply someone who had a little job for us to do. And he has not yet paid us!'

From down the corridor came the cry of another woman, 'He is gone!'

As the incredulous cries erupted from her comrades, she reached the group, and said, 'He is gone, the shuttle is gone, the stones are gone. And we are left to take the blame.'

'Well,' Becker said, 'that solves one problem anyway. Better get Acorna on the com unit, sweetie, and arrange a rendezvous so she can treat the kid. Unless any of you ladies are armed and have objections?'

'No, no, please,' said the mother. She turned to Andina, and asked, ''Dina, these horned people, they will not hurt my Layla because we steal from them?'

'Of course not,' Andina said hotly. 'They're not like you. They wouldn't steal from refugees either.'

'Don't listen to her, Fatima,' another of the women, younger but harder-looking said. 'It's a trap. Tell her, Aziza. You are not fooled, surely? Once 'Dina and her man bring those people here, we are lost. As it is, we outnumber them.'

'And Layla?'

The other woman shrugged. 'She will die, I suppose. It would be merciful.'

'That's the most disgusting sentiment I ever heard!' Andina said. 'Poor little girl.'

'But it is true, what Miriam says,' added another woman. 'If the little one is too scarred to dance, to work, then how will she be able to earn a living or support us in our old age?'

Fatima began an anguished wailing.

'Be still!' Aziza commanded. 'She is not dead now, and she is not deaf either! Who would want to live with such vultures as you for aunts?'

Becker shook his head and returned to the bridge, where he put in a call to the *Condor*.

Four

'What do you suppose made Smythe-Wesson jump ship like that?' Rafik asked, now that the emergency evacuation had been dealt with. The two ships had rendezvoused as fast as Becker and Andina could manage it. Acorna used one of Becker's shuttles to board the *Heloise,* where she made short work of healing Layla's burns. Then everyone was transferred back to the *Condor,* while the *Heloise* was towed by the other ship's powerful tractor beam.

'He probably looked at the fuel gauge,' Andina answered. 'It was not a short trip, and I had not yet refueled when he hijacked us. Sloppy of him. He should have planned more efficiently.'

'Yes,' Acorna agreed, 'but his plan, sloppy as it was, worked. He has the stones, and we don't. Besides which, we can't chase him just yet. We need to return to MOO to refuel your ship in tow and let Hafiz deal with these prisoners. Perhaps they will be able to tell us where Smythe-Wesson might go next.'

'The markets for stones of such size is limited,' Rafik said. 'All the potential buyers know we have the chrysoberyls, and that no one has ever seen their like. Whether or not legitimate dealers would buy them from an unauthorized source and risk the wrath of House Harakamian is doubtful. However, there's an additional problem. Partial payment has already been tendered for some of the stones. We will not be able to deliver unless we catch up with the thief.'

'Why'd Hafiz hire that character anyway?' Becker demanded. 'Not only is he a crook, he's not half the security chief Nadhari was.'

'No one would be,' Rafik pointed out.

'True enough. But didn't anyone check his references?'

'I'm sure they did,' Rafik said. 'But who has references that say, "if said applicant found an opportunity to make himself richer than the employer, he would not take advantage of his position to do so"?'

'I see your point.'

Aari listened to all of this with a look of profound concern on his face. 'If this thief was bold enough to steal from the warehouses of House Harakamian, what is to stop him from going to the source of the stones? He might attack the Makahomian citadel of the sacred lake.'

Acorna said, 'Perhaps, except that this particular individual won't know where to go looking. At the time of our return, as far as Hafiz knew, Nadhari was also returning, so he didn't hire a new security chief. As for what would stop him – well, Nadhari would.'

'Would she?' Aari asked. 'I don't have much in my recorded memory about her – except that she was regent high priestess for a time . . .'

'*Is* . . .' Becker corrected him. '. . . *Is* regent high priestess.'

'Oh, sorry, I am looking at the events there from the perspective of recorded history late in the planet's cycle. That is how I knew that Khornya would come and find the shrine the priests made to me for purifying their lake.'

'That's got to be very confusing,' Becker said, shaking his head.

Aari agreed. 'It is, a little. But I was thinking. Perhaps I could record a memory of this event and go into the time device again and return in time to prevent the robbery. Isn't that a good idea?'

Acorna felt uncertain. 'Aari, I know you're more experienced at this than any of us now, but it seems to me still that this is not the sort of thing that should be done casually.'

'Yeah,' Becker said. 'Maybe upsetting the space-time continuum isn't going to destroy the universe, as the people of my home planet used to think way back when, but if everybody uses the way-back machine to go back and change their socks during the day because they don't like the color they picked originally, the space-time continuum is bound to get very chaotic.'

'But it would not be everyone, Joh. Just me. And Khornya, of course, if she would like to come and see how it all works.'

'I've used the machine several times already,' Acorna told him, with a sharpness that slipped into her voice despite all of her good intentions. 'Searching for you.'

'Ouch,' Becker said, giving Aari a sympathetic look.

'I do think the decision for what to do next ought to be left up to Hafiz and to the MOO council,' Acorna said. 'My feeling is that we should see how well conventional means work to recover the stones and catch the thief before we try time-traveling. When you change one event, others are also altered. Perhaps not always for the best.' She shrugged. 'I don't know.'

Aari looked disappointed. 'I suppose I understand your caution. But Grimalkin does it all the time, and nobody seems to mind.'

Acorna gave him a look, and he amended his statement. 'Usually nobody seems to mind. The Friends used time-travel as a tool. I don't see why we can't do the same. You can do lots of wonderful things with it. For instance, Khornya, wouldn't you like to meet your parents?'

For a moment she felt as if Aari had hit her, then she said with careful patience, 'Yes, that would be nice. But I don't see how I could meet them without warning them of the Khleevi invasion. I would have to tell them not to go off on their own with baby me around that time. That way, I could save them. And if I save them, I would be raised by them as a Linyaari. I would never have been rescued by Rafik, Gill and Calum, I would never have helped Mr. Li and Hafiz free the child slaves of Kezdet, and I would probably never have met you. I really would like to see them, Aari, but I like the life I've had thus far.'

'Isn't that rather selfish, when, merely by using a little ingenuity, you could save your parents?'

'Perhaps, but for that matter, couldn't we use the machine to save Vhiliinyar from the Khleevi?' she countered.

He thought about it. 'Well, no. There were so many of them, and they were very powerful. The intervention would require too much for a simple time-voyage by a few selected individuals to affect it. Once the Khleevi came, the doom of Vhiliinyar was inevitable. And, if you had not met the humans, you would not have discovered the plant sap that kills Khleevi. You would have to take very careful notes, and we would have to think it through. That is why we usually do not alter larger events in history. Grimalkin says everything must be carefully weighed and thought through first and that only Friends really have the capacity for such farsight and detachment.'

Rafik cleared his throat. 'That settles it then. We carry through with this in the usual way. Time to face the music and tell old Hafiz what's going on.'

This did not prove as difficult as they all feared. When they returned to MOO with the prisoners, Hafiz sent for them to come to his administrative offices.

In his own office, he sat ensconced in a huge chair upholstered in silks of peacock and flame. To Acorna's surprise, he greeted them with a beneficent smile.

'Good work, my friends. You have captured the miscreants.'

'Yes, Uncle, but we did not recover the stones. Your former security chief used the young girl's injury as a distraction and carried the stones to the *Heloise*'s shuttle. He got away.'

Hafiz fluttered his gem-encrusted fingers dismissively. 'It does not matter. Justice will catch up with him quickly. And the stones are registered to us. Each of them now bears our trademark. No matter who sells them, it will be known at once that they are ours. Also, I have sent relays informing our clients of the theft. Customers willing to pay the great sums the stones should bring are few. They will report to our headquarters if anyone contacts them with our property. This they will do for love and respect of me and for the high esteem in which they hold House Harakamian. Also they do it because they are, deep down, very honest men, however tempted they may be by the prospect of obtaining the stones for a lower price.'

'Uncle,' Rafik said, shaking his head, 'I never thought I would hear you say anything so naïve.'

'I was not quite finished, son of my heart. As I was about to say, *very* deep down they are honest men with a strong sense of self-preservation. I thought to mention to them the curse that was upon these jewels.'

'Curse?' Acorna asked, and she and Becker exchanged looks.

'But, sir,' Aari said. 'I was the one who created the originals of the stones in question. They were produced by a chemical reaction that occurred when I purified the lake. They were actually impurities that bonded together to form pure wholes. That is somewhat magical-sounding, I agree, but certainly there was never a curse on any of those stones . . .'

Hafiz lifted both eyebrows and said acerbically, 'I did not say how old this curse was. It is, in fact, a recent curse, of my own invention. It will fall upon anyone stupid enough to try to cheat House Harakamian. These honest associates who hold our family enterprise in such high esteem understand its nature very well. Smythe-Wesson's betrayal will not profit him. Rather, it shall bring about his ruin.'

'As it has been said, so let it be done,' Rafik said, bowing to his uncle.

The dancers listened raptly. Although they pretended to cower with fear, Acorna sensed it was as much an act as their dance had been. They were very glad that Smythe-Wesson, who had betrayed them as well as Hafiz, would find no reward from his deeds. They were also perfectly confident they could escape again anytime they wished. Acorna gathered from their thoughts that they had done so on many previous occasions.

Before anyone else could bring it up, Aziza, the leader of the troupe, began nuzzling the toes of Hafiz's slippers with her face. 'And what is to become of us, O' mighty sultan of this world? We are but humble entertainers – the man told us that you had stolen the stones and we would return them to the rightful owners who would happily reward us with riches that would allow us to retire and even purchase husbands if we desired.'

'Now, that is a strange tale,' Hafiz said thoughtfully. 'For, although you are each as beautiful as dawn, I did not think for one moment that any of you were stupid. Release my foot, woman, and rise.' He pumped his outstretched hands, palms upward, into the air so that his jowls quivered and the satin linings of his sleeves shimmered. 'Up! Up! Up! All of you up, while I consider what is to be done with you. And uncover your faces, for we have all seen them, as well as a great deal more of you besides.'

At that moment there were scurrying steps outside the office. As the room's occupants listened, the footsteps stopped for a moment, as though someone was recovering both breath and dignity before entering. Finally, the door opened and Karina glided in. 'Oh, exalted husband, do pardon me! I had no idea you were entertaining guests! I so longed for your stimulating company that I chanced coming here hoping to distract you from your duties.'

Acorna lowered her head to hide a smile. If Karina had missed the return of the *Heloise* and the *Condor*, then she wasn't paying her own information network enough *baksheesh*. Her informants would have told her that the crews of the two ships guarded the voluptuous dancers, now all demurely clad in black. Unless Acorna missed her guess, Karina wasn't concerned with Hafiz's abundant charms at this particular moment. No, Karina had arrived in time to protect her own interests and help dictate the fate of the prisoners.

Hafiz patted the divan beside him and gestured for Karina to come forward. 'Now then, my love, we have these women criminals to deal with. Obviously, they are suited for only a limited sort of occupation. Will you not reconsider your argument against pleasure houses here on MOO so these houris may in some measure repay the debt incurred by their crimes against us?'

'Oh, Hafiz, you know I would never ever think to argue with you about the institutions you wish to establish here on this moon you have brought to blossom. You don't think me a prude, surely, my darling?' she purred, snuggling up to him.

'Oh, no, beloved.' He shook his hand and

regarded her with a mixture of awe and lust. 'Not a prude by any means.'

'I only suggest that the children who work here and may grow up here – especially those from Maganos Moonbase, might be traumatized to see that their greatest benefactor allows such establishments. Jana and Kheti, for instance, escaped captivity in such places only through your intervention. I fear it would send conflicting messages to our young ones about our own values.'

He sighed. 'Well, they were but innocent young ones, and these women are experienced criminals and courtesans.'

'Dancers, my darling, however criminal. And that one' – she pointed at Layla – 'is a mere child herself. There is also the opinion of the Linyaari to consider. They are extremely pure and high-minded people.'

'That is so,' Hafiz said. 'You are as always a pearl of wisdom, beloved. But what shall we do with them otherwise? Must I build a prison to hold them?'

'Oh, no, my darling, nothing so expensive! It is much more cost-effective to rehabilitate them, and that is what we will do!' Karina exclaimed. 'The child shall go to school with the other young ones and learn whichever of the skills taught on this veritable university of a moon that appeal to her. I am sure the ladies are capable at least of menial tasks such as cleaning. They do owe dear Ms. Dmitri for the theft of her ship, not to mention the passage she freely gave them from the generosity of her spirit.'

'Oh, no,' Andina said. 'I can't trust them. My people are everywhere on MOO, including the most secure areas, and at times when other personnel are not around. I must know that their honesty is above reproach.'

'Then perhaps some of them are fine seamstresses?' Karina suggested. 'I can always use a new gown or two, and Hafiz's robes are in constant need of repair and replacement.'

'Alas, kind mistress,' cried the troupe's leader, 'we can sew a coin back on or hand-sew a tear in a costume, but we have always ordered our costumes custom-made from a supplier in a distant realm. We know nothing of cloth manufacture or clothing construction, and the new technology for bonding cloth is likewise unfamiliar to any of us.'

'What a pity,' Karina said, pouting down at her current set of violet-and-lavender robes, which were probably at least a week or two old, and in Karina's opinion, soon to be in need of replacement.

'However,' Aziza said, lifting her head and looking Hafiz in the eye, 'you now have a vacancy for a security chief. Who better than an experienced criminal to find the weaknesses in your present precautions? By myself I could improve a thousandfold upon the performance of that pig-dog,' she spat twice on the ground, 'who betrayed us all. My companions and I, in your service, would cleanse your security system of imperfections as surely as a river dampens each rock in its bed. We can immediately recognize those who practice our former criminal profession—'

'Oh, Hafiz, how wonderful!' Karina cried. 'She said "former." She clearly already considers herself rehabilitated!'

'Yes, lady, even so,' the would-be security chief said with a bow of the complicated and dramatic sort that climaxed her dance performance. 'For your kindness and mercy have touched my heart – all of our hearts. Have not these beautiful white unicorn people healed our greatest treasure, our Layla, even when we sought to steal their own treasure? We owe you our gratitude and our allegiance, great lord and lady. Besides,' she said, rubbing her first two fingers and thumb together, 'the pig-dog said that the position pays very well.'

Hafiz laughed, and Karina, taking her cue from him, giggled behind her hand. 'Are you sure you are not a distant relation of mine, woman of infamy?' Hafiz asked her.

When he had finished laughing, he said quite soberly, 'I should not even consider your impertinent proposal. But, as it happens, I find myself wishing once more that my former security chief, also a woman, would return. Since she will not, sentimental fool that I am, I feel inclined to listen to your arguments, gullible though I may be. Besides, I have so little left to steal.' He took a deep breath and continued, his commanding tone lapsing into the voice he used to make a deal, 'And therefore I say to you – yes, normally the job does pay well. But you owe us a great debt, and thus will receive only food, lodging, uniforms, and perhaps a small measure of pocket change to keep you from pilfering.'

'Uncle, should you really trust these women?' Rafik asked.

'I am not sure. I think we must ask for a more accurate assessment. What say you, daughter of my heart if not my loins?' he asked Acorna.

She knew at once what he was asking and scanned the thoughts of the women. To her surprise, the thoughts were indeed full of gratitude and relief. The only plots Acorna discovered centered on what each lady felt she might do to increase her own worth in Hafiz's or Karina's estimation. 'As you have said, so let it be done, Uncle Hafiz,' she answered with a slight curtsy.

Hafiz turned to Rafik, 'Even so,' he said with a sharp nod. 'It shall be done.'

FIVE

Acorna, the crew of the *Balakiire*, Aari, and his family returned to Vhiliinyar. Before Aari's arrival, Acorna, of all her people, had been the one most interested in the time device. Now Yiitir and Maarni, historian and folklorist respectively, as well as several Linyaari physicists, occupied the room containing the time device, while Aari explained its mechanism to them.

Acorna had hoped that Rafik's prediction would prove true, and that she and Aari might come to care for each other again as they had before their separation. But, despite her hopes, it did not seem to be working out that way. Indeed, she found it far easier to talk to Laarye than she did to his brother. At least Laarye did not presume to tell her about her past feelings and thoughts based on a collection of recorded memories.

Laarye and she exchanged thoughts easily. He was very comforting to be around. He knew Aari – or, rather, this Aari, at least – better than anyone.

When she complained that this Aari seemed to feel that everything that had happened before he'd arrived to join them was some sort of light entertainment, amusing but meant to be taken with a grain of salt, Laarye replied, 'It's not just this situation, Khornya. It's his way. He's a good sort really, but he's a bit – um – *naazhoni,* if you know what I mean.'

'I don't, actually,' she confessed. 'That's not a word with which I'm familiar.'

He tried several synonyms, and she understood at last that it meant something like the term 'flighty' in Basic.

Flighty, hmmm? Acorna began to see how Aari and Laarye had ended up in the cave just before the Khleevi attack when all of the other Linyaari evacuated. And yet, when he was captured by the Khleevi, Aari had told them nothing that would help his enemies. Though desperately tormented, he said nothing to his captors about Laarye or about the location of the new Linyaari homeworld. And he had survived afterward and saved Becker and RK. Those were not 'flighty' actions.

However, if Acorna was having more questions and reservations about her relationship with Aari, the reverse seemed to be true of him. The more he watched and listened to her, the more he worked beside her, the more time he spent with her, the more interested, then infatuated, he became with her. And Acorna supposed she ought to be glad that he was feeling that way, but she wasn't. It felt to her as if responding to Aari Whole-Horn would somehow be disloyal to her own beloved Aari – the two felt that different to her.

They worked above ground now, smoothing out the waterways, making sure that they flowed one into the other in a pattern as similar as possible to the one remembered by the elder Linyaari.

Maati and Laarye worked alongside them, though a bit farther upstream.

Aari straightened his back and stretched. He was wearing a simple tunic, and the water flowed around his knees, plastering the feathery hairs to his calves. He shook his long silvery mane and combed it back with his fingers.

Acorna did the same.

Aari then puffed out his chest as he looked around at the countryside, well aware, Acorna thought, of how majestic he looked against the periwinkle waters and soft lavender sky, the blue waving grasses and the newly formed purple, snowcapped mountains defining the horizon. The pure white coloring of space-faring Linyaari was well suited for striking a contrast with the surface of the homeworld. Aari gleamed in the light.

'Every day Vhiliinyar looks less like a disaster area and more like a home,' Aari said with a satisfied sigh.

Acorna nodded. 'The catseyes enhanced the

particle beams so that even the localized surface terraforming we've done yields results almost as fast as if we had evacuated to terraform the whole planet at once.'

'That is good,' Aari said. 'But I cannot understand why the regular process was bypassed.'

'It was because of you,' Acorna said. 'You were missing – or at least, we didn't know where you were. I was afraid you'd return to Vhiliinyar while it was at its most volatile. If you had returned with the planet's surface in complete disarray, I was afraid you would be harmed. Or even lost forever. The council agreed that you had –' she broke off, looking at his perfect horn. 'The council agreed,' she said.

'That I had suffered enough?' he asked.

'I didn't say so, and it isn't polite to pluck thoughts from people's minds,' she reminded him stiffly.

'I didn't need to. I could read your face. And when I returned and hadn't suffered at all, everyone was disappointed in me. Now they've gone to all this extra trouble for nothing. It's a good thing I created the catseyes when I purified the sacred lake, or I doubt you would ever have forgiven me for escaping the Khleevi in this timeline.'

Acorna sighed and sat on the bank dangling her hoofed feet in the water, which was almost bone-chillingly cold at this time of the day. A few fetal amphibians swam over her toes. The *aagroni* already had begun restocking the streams and rivers with life-forms salvaged from the homeworld before the Khleevi attack.

The eastern sky was bulging with bruised-looking indigo clouds. The regularly scheduled afternoon rains would begin soon, according to Dr. Hoa's timetable. The scientist's meteorological manipulations had helped Vhiliinyar bloom again, though the planet's scars were still evident when you knew where to look. Unlike Aari's scars. His perfect surface concealed so many scars that Acorna felt she hardly knew him anymore.

'That isn't the problem,' she said, and felt his surprise. He had expected an instant guilty denial from her. 'Or at least, not all of it.'

'Then what is it?' he asked, taking her hand and staring earnestly into her eyes. 'You have been so distant, and that is not how my recorded memories of you indicate that you behave with me. You are a warm and wonderful female, Khornya, and I was so looking forward to being with you. I suppose I must be somehow unfamiliar to you as I am now, but I thought you would be pleased that I could come to you whole.'

'You were whole before – I mean, in your other shape. It was familiar to me, and your memories of me were not recorded. They were like mine, real memories of moments we shared and glances exchanged, jokes we both laughed at, pain we both felt—'

'And of our joining,' he said, turning her hand

over in his to stroke her palm gently with his thumb. His voice was low and caressing. 'Perhaps if we joined again, if you let me hold you, you would find me more familiar, and we could regain our closeness.'

She withdrew her hand from his, which made him flinch. With renewed patience, she touched his cheek with her fingertips. Mistaking her gesture for encouragement, he wrapped his arms around her and rubbed his hands across her back, allowed his horn to touch hers. She met his kiss halfway, explored it with him briefly, then withdrew, shaking her head and disentangling herself. 'I'm sorry, Aari. Maybe it's because of my human upbringing, but the feelings we shared have to come first, before we can join in that way. Rafik says that since we've fallen in love once, as we get to know each other, we will do so again. Our circumstances before, as your recording will tell you, involved danger and intense emotional experiences. Perhaps that intensity and intimacy of our lives together on shipboard made it easier for us to care for each other so readily, though I confess, I shared similar experiences of danger with Thariinye, and they didn't have the same effect on me. The point is, your memories of that time, of me, you carry only in your head, not in your heart, as you did before you time-traveled. And I can feel the difference.'

He sat back, no longer touching her, his eyes no longer seeking to engage her in intimacy but seeming to evaluate her along with her words.

This was not a side of Aari she had encountered before. 'I see. So, in order to regain our love, we must have new shared experiences and – don't deny it, I didn't mean to read your thoughts without permission, but I couldn't help it – I must somehow prove my mettle to you as I seem to have proved it by heroically undergoing Khleevi torture – and surviving it, of course. I wouldn't have been any good to you had I not survived it.'

'Please don't be bitter,' she said, reaching out to touch him again. But now he withdrew. 'It isn't like that. It will just take time. Maybe it will take a bit longer than it did the first time, because we aren't being menaced all the time as we were before. I'm sure Rafik is right. Our feelings for each other will grow again.'

'Well, forgive me, but I have feelings for you already,' he said, standing. '*I* fell for you simply from the recorded memories of what a brave and beautiful lifemate you were. I thought that you would care for me now as you did when we – I – left. I appreciate you sharing your insight into this phase of our relationship, because you have given me some idea as to what I must do to win you again. At least now if I disappear again for a while, you won't worry. You won't care, really. But I hope to make you care when I return.'

'Aari – please, don't be rash. Disappearing again won't help. Staying and helping me get to know you again will help.'

'I have been here many days already. We have been on a mission together, and yet you are colder than ever. No. I must take action. Farewell, Khornya.'

He ran away through the tall grasses and up over a hill before disappearing from view. Disturbed as Acorna was by the exchange, which so far as she could tell resolved nothing, she was surprised to find that she was not sorry to see him go. In fact, a guilty sense of relief washed over her along with Dr. Hoa's patented rain.

The remorse set in later, punishing her when she tried to rest. She tossed and turned and moaned in her sleep. Finally, she awakened bathed in sweat, her mane stringing into her eyes. Neeva's voice spoke inside her head. (Khornya, dear. Whatever is the matter with you? I strongly suggest you return to MOO and visit with Rafik again. He comes this way so seldom, and I do think from the nature of your dreams you need more time away from here.)

Acorna sighed and sank back onto her sleeping mat. Her aunt was being tactful. (I've been broadcasting again, have I?)

(Yes, dear, you have. And frankly, it was frightening and upsetting to some of the more sensitive among us. Why did you keep imagining Aari being turned into a Khleevi? You know very well that the two of you helped end that particular menace, and yet you had them running amok among us again.)

Acorna winced and rolled over on her stomach, propping her chin up with her elbows as she stared out into the fog that enveloped the lowland area around the stream. (Is *that* what that dream's about? I truly don't know why I would dream such a thing.)

(Perhaps by making him an enemy in your dreams, you can justify the change in your feelings for him now?) Neeva suggested.

(I suppose that could be it) Acorna admitted, though it didn't feel exactly right. And hadn't she had this dream or one very much like it before Aari's return?

(I think you need to at least consider the possibility, my dear. I know it's hard. We all have adjustments to make. Although many of us are separated from our lifemates for great periods of time, true lifemates do not seem to be so significantly altered in one another's eyes when they rejoin as you and Aari have done. But of course, so far in my lifetime, lifemates have only been separated by space. You and Aari have been separated by time, as well. And no one has voluntarily given up their memories of loved ones in my experience. So we *do* understand. But we also would like to get our rest. It is very hard to relax when such a powerful sender as you are is so deeply troubled.)

Acorna smiled wryly. (Therefore, you would all appreciate it if I would take my noisy, scary imagination up to MOO and leave you in peace for a while?)

(Absolutely. But that's not the only reason we'd like you to visit your human family. Rafik would surely like to spend more time with you, dear,) Neeva answered. (And your other friends as well. Much as we love you, we Linyaari are only half of your family and culture. It would be selfish of us to wish to be the only ones to offer you comfort.)

Acorna laughed and stood up. (They didn't make you *visedhaanye ferilii* for nothing, mother-sister. You are the soul of tact and kindness, but have made yourself abundantly clear. I'll put in a call for the shuttle.)

And so she found herself back on MOO in time to have dinner alone with Rafik once more before he returned to supervising the vast House Harakamian empire. Their friends and relations allowed them the time together. But it wasn't as if they had anything particularly private to say. They mostly ate in silence, she munching on grasses and flowers, he on more substantial human fare. They simply treasured being together in dear, familiar company.

With an added romantic and physical element, this was how it should have been between Aari and her, Acorna thought. Time with those who were truly bonded didn't separate them, but deeply reinforced their attachment whenever they shared it.

'You are leaving very quickly,' she remarked.

'I hope to hunt down those crystals soon,' he said. 'Our trademark signature on the stones,

Hafiz tells me, has a homing device in it that should enable me to locate them if I'm in the right place at the right time. Like the markets of Kezdet, for instance. If I hurry, perhaps I can discover them before they are snapped up by black market dealers.'

On the far side of the garden, one of the dancers glided by. Somehow she managed to glide officiously.

'How are the new security officers working out?' Acorna asked.

'Rather well,' Rafik said. 'They are remarkable women. Aziza leads them better than a general could. It has been quite the success story. Karina's been puffed up with pride for suggesting it. Oh, you'll be happy to know that Layla's doing fine. I know Fatima would be grateful if you came to say hello, so she could tell you that she is – ah, grateful.'

Acorna smiled. 'I'll do that. They must be settling in well. You're on first-name terms with them already?'

'We've become friendly, yes. I felt it necessary to get to know them better. I was worried about their hiring. I wouldn't want to be leaving Hafiz's safety to a stranger, would I? I try to learn from mistakes. Smythe-Wesson was someone Hafiz hired in haste when Nadhari left. My uncle knew very little about him except that he was highly recommended by the commander of the nearest Federation outpost. The man kept to himself. I have not allowed Aziza and her troupe to do the same. I've spent enough time with her to learn what those women have been through and what incredible lives they've led. In fact, Aziza reminds me a little of you, Acorna.'

'*Me?*'

'Yes. Like you, she is seemingly a fey, graceful, fragile creature, and yet she is amazingly strong and resilient, with wonderful leadership qualities and, when you get to know her, a charming sense of humor. She has managed to keep herself and the others alive by the use of her wits as well as her talent. These women learned thievery to survive, and learned it so well they have become highly sought after by the criminal world as accomplices. I don't want you to think she or any of them are actually immoral women. They learned their dancing skills as slave girls, and used their less socially acceptable talents to escape the slavers and become independent agents.'

'You really seem to admire them, in spite of their participation in the theft of the catseyes,' Acorna observed.

'What's a little larceny among friends?' Rafik said. 'It's not as if House Harakamian was founded without it. Hafiz admires them, too, but Karina makes sure he doesn't admire them too often or too closely.'

They shared a grin over that.

He laid his purple brocade napkin beside his plate and rose. 'Well, all good things must come to an end. It's been so good to see you again, sweetheart. I hope that boyfriend, or husband, or whatever of yours gets his act together pretty soon. Or we may have to introduce your people to the quaint Terran custom of divorce.'

Before Acorna could answer, three of the security patrol surrounded them, or more accurately, surrounded Rafik. Layla's hair was growing back nicely, and there was of course no sign of a scar on her heart-shaped face. All three women chattered happily at Rafik, who, to Acorna's amusement, blushed a little when Aziza teased him. 'You cannot leave yet! I must have you empty your pockets to make sure you are not running off with the family silver implements for eating.'

'You watch her, Rafik,' Fatima said, batting at him playfully with the tassel from the end of her belt. The women had made rather unique security uniforms out of their black cat-burglar garb. It was practical really, if they wanted to sneak up on some evildoer. 'She told me she intends to do a strip search!'

Rafik held up his hands laughing, 'Ladies, please, not in front of my daughter!'

Layla looked curiously at Acorna. '*You* are *his* daughter?' she asked. 'That's funny. You don't look anything like each other.'

'Sure we do,' Rafik said. 'She has my chin and elegant jawline, don't you see?' He ran a tickling finger along Acorna's jaw.

'If he was wearing his horn, you'd see the

resemblance right away,' Acorna told Layla with mock earnestness.

'No way!' Layla said. Clearly she had been keeping company with the Maganos Moonbase kids.

Acorna gave in. 'Oh, yes. I have his chin and my other father, Gill's, eyes and gift of gab. My third father, Calum, says I get my brains and engineering talent from him and that I must be a throwback to his Highlander ancestors, who were tall like me. Gill says white hair like mine is very common in his family, as the Irish tend to go white early in life.'

Layla looked increasingly puzzled. 'Wait. You have three fathers and you look like all of them. What about your mother?'

Aziza pretended to pout. 'This sounds like a very strange arrangement, Rafik. Three fathers and no mother for your daughter? You don't like women?'

'Of course he likes women!' Acorna said staunchly, twining her arms around Rafik's neck in her best imitation of a clinging vine. 'He *looooves* me, don't you, Rafik?'

'You're getting me deeper in the mire all the time, Acorna.' He laughed. 'I think I've picked a fine time to go. But I'll be back.' Turning to Aziza, he flirted seriously for a moment. Acorna was amused and pleased to see him use his beautiful dark eyes and long lashes to good advantage. Apparently it pleased Aziza, too, who shamelessly flirted back. 'I should make you go with me. I'm going to go find those rocks you stole from us. If Hafiz didn't need you, I'd make you sit on the nose of the ship with the sensor and search for the homing beacon.'

'How grateful I am not to be forced to submit to such a stern lord and master,' Aziza said. 'But I – and my troupe, of course – will wait breathlessly for your return, for in reclaiming your treasures you redeem our honor.'

'Always happy to oblige,' Rafik said.

They all began strolling toward the docking bays, for which Acorna was grateful. The atmosphere in the dining alcove was becoming a bit clogged with hormonal emanations. Being a telepath was not always comfortable. Other Linyaari could send as strongly as she could under certain circumstances, and there were certainly other sentient species with some form of telepathy. Both Rafik and the women, particularly Aziza, were sending unspoken messages back and forth that were more intimate than she cared to hear. At least she felt reassured that the women were sincerely reformed and loyal employees of House Harakamian now. The regular meals, good beds, respectful treatment, and Hafiz's rather lavish idea of what constituted bare minimum pocket money for his security officers had a lot to do with their loyalty.

Acorna felt a little wrench of pain when she hugged Rafik good-bye and he disappeared into his vessel. To her surprise, however, Aziza and Fatima each put an arm around one of her shoulders, and Layla took her hand. 'Come,' Aziza said. 'We three are no longer on duty. You will have tea and cakes with us in our quarters, and you will tell us all about your childhood, yes?'

Six

Former Red Bracelet and former chief security officer of the House Harakamian Moon of Opportunity, Win Smythe-Wesson was well-known to Nadhari Kando. Had she been consulted, she would have advised Hafiz Harakamian against hiring him. In her opinion, Smythe-Wesson was essentially a faithless man and a mercenary to the core. And, as he had so recently demonstrated, even when his allegiance was well paid-for, it was temporary and for the most part imaginary if pledged to any but himself and his own best interests. But Hafiz had been unable to ask Nadhari. And, unlike Hafiz, Smythe-Wesson was quite pleased with the way his recent employment had turned out.

Like other untrustworthy souls, Smythe-Wesson himself trusted no one and nothing but himself, his own cunning, and the proof he saw before his own eyes.

After escaping in the *Heloise*'s shuttle, he had exchanged the shuttle for a ship he had stashed on a desolate planet within range of the shuttle. The battered sphere was one of the worlds the Khleevi had destroyed. It consisted mostly of melted rock, cooled and hardened into a surface stable enough to hold the ship. What little atmosphere it had was pure poison, however, so he needed a repair suit to make the transfer from shuttle to ship.

Once away from the dead planet with a fueled and responsive ship to call his own again, he did not immediately set out to sell the catseye chrysoberyls the Akemilisan dancers had stolen for him. He had heard many claims for the powers of the stones, and he wanted to test those properties himself before he offered the stones up to the highest bidders. He also wanted to develop a capability for the stones that he had seen hinted at in some classified files. The stones, which could be so helpful as particle beam accelerators to intensify lasers for terraforming, could also be used as weapons. If he could demonstrate this use, he knew he could find buyers quite different from the ones who'd planned to buy the stones from House Harakamian. And, if he was right about what those stones could do, the sky was the limit for what he could charge for them.

But he needed somewhere to test the powers of the stones. A dead moon wouldn't work, or an asteroid, or even one of the planets already gutted by the Khleevi. He needed to test the effect of his weapons on living things. He needed to show just how effective they could be as weapons of war.

But he wanted an area far enough from MOO that House Harakamian's ships wouldn't find him, and closer to Federation space than MOO and Vhiliinyar were.

And he had just the right place in mind.

His unconventional 'acquisition' of his new property had been planned for several weeks – since he first learned of the stones, actually. And his careful planning was working like a charm. So far, events had gone just as he had projected.

Back in those heady days of planning, he'd spent a great deal of time finding the right target area. At last he settled on a mustard yellow planet that stank and bubbled with viscous, nasty-looking liquids, eye-watering gases, and volcanoes oozing bright orange magma. It was absolutely full of life of the primitive kind, brimming with it in each fetid breath, and blotched with it all over the bits of land that stood still long enough to let it thrive. Never in Smythe-Wesson's life had he seen a place that so deserved to be sliced and diced.

And he had just the thing to do it. His ship was already fitted with a laser torpedo array, and it took him very little time to adapt it to accommodate one of the catseyes. Once the stone was in place, he trained the weapon on the planet's surface and set out to excise the top of a volcano.

Unfortunately, the slice was so clean that, although he could tell he had done some damage by the small avalanches cascading from the incision, otherwise the top of the cone merely sat there on its base, just as it had previously. He sliced the top vertically into smaller slices and these fell away from the mountaintop with far more satisfactory crashes than his first attack had, spilling boulders to the valleys below. The boulders were rapidly joined by magma newly released from the burning core of the planet.

That was all very well and good, but he couldn't really consider mere rock and boulder as living substance, nor would his prospective buyers. He searched for another target and found a vast forest of strangely shaped trees, occupying the top half of the continent just below the one containing his resculpted volcano. Zooming in on them for a more detailed view, he saw that they were mustard yellow and drooping with gold-brown mossy foliage. Their trunks were lumpy, as if bulging with some sort of growths. With glorious precision he sliced away the lumps on the first trunk, one at a time. He then lopped off the branches before rendering the tree into a stack of wafer-thin slices. Ruthlessly, he excised the extending branch of the nearest tree, which fell against the sliced trunk, toppling it into a sliding pile of slightly overlapping segments.

For a while he refined his technique by vivisecting each tree in a similar manner, but then grew impatient and sliced through the entire forest many times. The results were spectacular, since the upper branches of the smaller trees fell into the diced trunks of the larger, bringing them down. The upper branches of the taller trees in turn smote everything in their downward path. In mere seconds, he reduced the forest to a mesa of wooden disks topped by a fretwork of fallen treetops. The mossy foliage withered and crumpled as he watched, and he shot a fist triumphantly into the air before looking for the next target.

That was all very well, he supposed, but he really wanted to try it out on sentients, preferably people. Perhaps he could find a refugee camp or a pesky guerrilla encampment offending some wealthy government?

Meanwhile, this lackluster planet could provide him with a place to store his booty. If Hafiz caught up with him, he'd just as soon have his loot stored and safe, waiting for the instant he escaped to claim it. Keeping only the stone in his weapon and one other relatively tiny stone, small enough to fuel a devastating hand weapon, he found another forest like the one he had destroyed, jettisoned his carefully packed cargo into its midst, carefully taking the coordinates of the spot where he'd landed, then sliced away the tops of the nearest trees. They covered his treasure as they fell, but since the branches retained their shape, the forest canopy appeared unbroken from above.

Satisfied that he could relocate the hoard at his whim, and that no one else would ever find it without his help, he departed.

But, unbeknownst to him, he left behind the outraged and enraged inhabitants of the planet, a collection of sulfur-based life-forms. They were livid over his unprovoked attack and determined to avenge themselves on the perpetrator. They had been taken so completely by surprise that they had been unable to deploy their own weapons before the flyby massacre of a continentful of their people. But, after assessing the damage and finding the cache of stones left amid the decapitated bodies of an entire clan of Solids, they knew just who had attacked them. They began measures to counterattack.

Though Hafiz had appeared sanguine about the loss of the stones, he was understandably eager to recover them. The docking bay was almost empty by the time Acorna returned from a fascinating tea with the new security staff. The *Condor* was still there, however; the robolift still on the ground.

She saw why when Becker strode into the terminal, and said, 'There you are, Princess! Are you going to join this Easter egg hunt or not?'

'I wouldn't miss it, Captain. Rafik left not long ago on the same mission, though I think he mainly intended to check the black market on Kezdet.'

'Good idea. I can check a few other spots, too, but I have a feeling that our boy won't be showing up in the usual places. He might not have been the brightest star in the cosmos, but he had to know that Hafiz's customers wouldn't double-cross House Harakamian. My guess is he has some ideas of his own about where to sell them. And if his potential customers are the kind of characters I have in mind, our thief'll probably have stashed the stones in a safe place.'

'A place which a ship with superior sensors and scanners might be able to locate while the thief is elsewhere?'

'You got it. The *Condor*'s equipment along those lines may be a bit eclectic, but it beats anything else available right now, even to Hafiz. And your uncle tells me that the stones each have a nanochip embedded within the House Harakamian logo lasered into the girdle of the stones. One homing beacon might be too slight for a ship to detect from space, but if the stones are still clustered together, the beacon's power is magnified exponentially. If anybody can track it, we can.'

So Acorna accompanied them on their search.

'Even with the homing beacons,' she said, 'it will be a bit like looking for a needle in a haystack, although I have never understood exactly *why* a needle would *be* in a haystack.'

'Just leave it up to the *Condor*, Captain and crew, Princess. This is our kinda job, what we do best. Finding stuff. This time we even know what we're looking for. Who knows, maybe that'll make it easier. I've narrowed it down already to someplace in the multiverse. Sooner or later we're bound to find the catseyes.'

While watching the scanners, Becker kept up a

conversation over the com unit with Rafik on his ship *Sinbad*. Rafik's course would diverge from theirs as he headed back for Federation space at some point; meanwhile the companionship was comforting for the crews of both vessels.

While not on watch, Acorna busied herself in the hydroponics garden, with RK's enthusiastic participation, and caught up on Becker's log. She had thought that she would be able to forget Aari, since she had been so relieved when he decided to go elsewhere, but she found she was unable to do so. At least there weren't any active Linyaari telepaths to receive her conflicting thoughts aboard the *Condor*. On Makahomia, she had developed some telepathic communication with Becker, but it worked only when they were directly attempting to address each other.

They were several days out from their starting point when, during Mac's watch, the android suddenly called over the ship's intercom, 'Captain Becker, Acorna, please report to the bridge. There is something on our remote scanners you should see.'

When they saw the faint pulsing light, took the coordinates, and figured out the approximate location, Acorna said, 'We should let Rafik know about this. He's much closer than we are, but the *Condor*'s scanners are far more powerful than what he has on the *Sinbad*.'

They did so, arranging to rendezvous with Rafik at the coordinates from which the beacon emanated.

* * *

'What's to be done about this atrocity?' the spokesman for the Solids demanded. 'Our folk were attacked during a peaceful assembly and horribly cut to pieces. They even had a permit. And then a perfectly innocent wedding party was also attacked, the bride, groom, bonder, and all of their attendants dismembered before being bombed by that horror from the heavens.'

'We are aware of all this, of course,' said the Mutable magistrate in charge of keeping the peace, which was by no means easy with such a volatile population. It was usually the fickle Liquids, always into something they shouldn't be, who started it, but this time they were proving useful. 'We sent several Liquid deputies to seep in under the corpses and determine what was dropped. It is an odd collection of stones. They are not sentient, but do carry a signature and a signal, which indicates that the beings who attacked us intend to return for the stones at some point in the future. We have only to leave the bodies where they are for the time being and wait. When the evil creatures who murdered your kinsmen return, we will be ready for them.'

'We – we will? We who? You're the magistrate. It's up to you to see that the peace is kept. I have no wish to be hacked to pieces by some unseen menace.'

'Nor will you be. Your people who witnessed the massacre will be replaced with Mutables, backed up by Liquids, and we will guard the jettisoned cargo. Our scientists believe the stones are quite valuable. When the owners – this House Harakamian – return for the stones, they will not find such easy targets as those they murdered last time.'

And so the alliance was formed and the plot for revenge upon the horrible House Harakamian initiated.

For many turns of the suns and moons, the Mutables stood around the murdered corpses of the Solids, heedless of the stench of decomposition. At their feet and flowing around them were their Liquid underlings, ready to spray into action at the first sign of trouble.

And now, at last, the time had come. A vessel appeared in the heavens. At first it seemed to be scanning the surface. Then suddenly it homed in on the cache of stones and hovered above the bodies of the fallen wedding party. Trembling Solids watched from what cover they could find, though the force that had beheaded Mount Fumidor and spilled lava over three villages and one ski resort in the surrounding valleys made the idea of cover somewhat questionable.

The Mutables were really awfully brave. You had to say that for them. They gamely stood their ground as Solids, but prepared to dissolve into Liquid before a laser could touch any of them.

However, the vessel was ominously still. Surely it did not understand their plans! How could it?

It appeared to be waiting for something. What? A full-scale invasion force? Egstynkeraht had never been invaded before. Were they to be totally annihilated?

But the Mutables had no intention of staying in one shape any longer than they had to. They considered it degrading, even in the best of causes. They muttered among themselves. Just as they were debating whether or not to turn into vapor and risk dissipating themselves into space by directly attacking the ship, the vessel spawned a smaller vessel, which descended upon them.

Seven

'I don't like it,' Acorna said, when finally they were close enough to make out the planet above which the *Sinbad* and Rafik awaited them. The planet's shifting surface was the brilliant mustard orange of flitter traffic signs on Kezdet.

Acorna hailed her foster father. 'Rafik, please don't move until we arrive to back you up. Becker can use his tractor beam to pull the stones into the ship.'

'Not without moving a lot of foliage,' Rafik told her. 'The payload appears to be buried under the forest canopy. We'd have brush scattered from the surface to deep space if you use the tractor beam, and at the end of it the rocks would still be closest to the surface. Somehow we'd still have to wade through all that vegetation to get at the stones.'

'So what do you suggest?' Becker asked.

'Your guess is as good as mine. There's no place to land a ship near the location of the signal, but I could take the *Roc* down.'

Then, suddenly, he said, 'Well, if that's not the durndest thing! Ask and it shall be given! I didn't notice it before, but there actually *is* a clear space big enough to set the shuttle down fairly near the area sending out the signals. I just spotted it. Funny. I could swear it wasn't there when I started talking to you. I'm going to go suss out the situation.'

While he was on his way from the *Sinbad*'s bridge to the *Roc*'s, Acorna tried to get a feeling for the planet. The molecular base was sulfurous. That much was immediately apparent. But although it was still a great distance away, she felt oddly skittish just looking at it. Perhaps they would discover more as they drew nearer, but she felt sure that what she saw on the com screen was not all there was to this particular world.

'Rafik, I really do think you should wait till we get there,' Acorna said, her voice coming out in a higher pitch than normal. 'I don't like the feel of this place at all.'

'Ow!' Becker said. RK, who had been sitting peacefully on the back of the command chair, sank his claws into Becker's scalp. '*What?*' he asked, then noticed Acorna's expression. 'Rafik, did you read that last message? Belay your landing and return to the *Sinbad*. Acorna is getting bad vibes. Frankly, I'm not crazy about the place either.'

But though they were still too distant to see exactly what was happening, and the *Roc* was now out of visual range, they clearly heard

Rafik's response. 'Mayday!' he shouted. 'Mayday! The shuttle is under attack. No, *Sinbad*, you are not to respond until I understand the threat a little better.' Then he groaned. 'Everybody stay put. I don't know how this is happening but something is shooting acid onto the shuttle's hull. The hull is being penetrated in some areas. Stay the frag away from here.' He started to speak again, but what he was going to say was replaced by a yelp of pain, then the com unit fell silent.

Before Acorna could react, Becker slammed the *Condor* into warp drive, shaking the very seams where pieces of various salvaged vessels married on the outer hull. It was a while before Acorna could move freely again after being shoved violently into her seat back.

But at last the stars quit blurring past the viewport, replaced by a view of the yellow planet with its fungus-crusted, leprous-looking surface relieved by odd puddles and ponds, seas and lakes of thick, polluted-looking liquid. Becker set the com screen for remote magnification.

Acorna set out mental runners, searching for Rafik's consciousness. She found it, and him. She sensed that although he was injured and in pain, he was mostly bewildered about what had hit him.

The *Sinbad* hailed the *Condor*.

'*Condor*, there are only two crew members aboard our ship other than the captain. Rafik took the only shuttle. One of us must remain aboard to maintain orbit. Are you in any better position than we are to help Rafik?'

'Stand by, *Sinbad*. Maintain your position. The cavalry has arrived,' Becker said.

'That's a big relief,' the crewman said, and signed off.

Acorna knew that, in spite of the attempt the crewman made to sound calm, he was desperately worried and frustrated not to be able to rescue Rafik.

But flooding across the emanations from the crewmen and Rafik, from Captain Becker and RK, she felt other presences, heard an undercurrent of other unintelligible thoughts babbling on the planet below.

These consciousnesses were gibbering, gloating, vengeful. And they were closing in on the disabled shuttle, ready to finish it off.

'Captain Becker, Rafik is surrounded!' she said, grabbing the LAANYE and inputting as many words as she could distinguish of the language used by the vengeance seekers. Their thoughts were expressed in sounds that hissed, sizzled, and boomed through her mind.

'How can he be surrounded?' Becker asked. 'There's nothing down there but a lot of really ugly yellow trees and scrub brush.'

'Look more closely,' she advised, glancing at the screen, but mainly relying on the telepathic impressions she was receiving. 'Those are sentient "really ugly yellow trees and scrub brush."'

RK jumped up between Becker and the

scanner most firmly focused on the shuttle. Backing up to the com screen, the cat, ears laid back, eyes slitted and fur bristling, shook his tail spasmodically at the com screen, coating it with smelly essence of tomcat.

'RK, you son of a skunk, what are you trying to do?' Becker bellowed, and smote the cat . . . gently . . . from the console. RK hissed, then turned and looked at him.

The look said, as clearly as if the cat was speaking Basic, 'Pay attention, stupid. You think I did that for my health?'

Acorna wiped the screen with a rag. It still appeared cloudy.

'Jeez,' Becker said, 'Cat spray can ruin anything. I'm going to have to locate a new screen somewhere if he's ruined that one. Can't see anything through it now—'

'But you can, Captain,' Acorna told him. 'The screen is perfectly clear. The cloudiness is coming from the spray the beings are using to attack Rafik. Sulfuric acid spray.'

'Sulfuric *acid*?'

'The beings on this planet are sulfur-based lifeforms. The acid spray is a logical defense for them to use against intruders.' She laid the LAANYE aside. There was no time to learn the language. Mac, approaching the bridge, picked up the instrument and watched his shipmates and the com screen while he nonchalantly connected himself to the LAANYE.

'*Sulfur*-based? You sure?' Becker asked.

'Why should that be hard to believe? You are carbon-based, after all. What's wrong with being sulfur-based?'

'Copy that,' Becker joked, but Acorna, who had less extensive knowledge of obscure ancient communications and record-keeping devices than Becker, shook her head.

'Can we use the tractor beam to pull him out of there, Captain?' Mac asked.

'That ship is dissolving around him,' Becker said. 'If it fell apart as we were pulling Rafik up, he'd have no protection at all from the acid or the vacuum of space.'

Acorna was no longer trying to understand the language of the sulfur beings, but instead was broadcasting a mental image picture of them backing off, ceasing to spray the ship. Of Rafik standing up, unhurt, and his tormentors allowing him to go.

In return she received angry images of lightning bolts from above, attacking a joined pair of beings and the one joining them, cutting them to pieces in front of their loved ones, then dropping something on top of the bodies and dismembering the closest onlookers so that their heads and arms covered the jettisoned cargo.

Acorna sent an image of Smythe-Wesson doing what they had just described – and of Rafik chasing him, trying to stop him.

The spray disappeared from the screen and it seemed to her the sulfur people looked upward, as if trying to see her.

She received an impression that clearly expressed the feelings of the hostile beings.

'You all look alike to us.'

She had no trouble understanding the sentiment whatsoever. Maybe because it was such a universal expression of racism, or speciesism, or whatever.

She sent a picture of herself to them.

Mac, now disconnected from the LAANYE, was peering over her shoulder. 'Acorna, they are saying you do not look like the other two.'

'Mac, you're a wonder. You learned their language in a fraction of the time it would have taken a Linyaari. How can I tell them more clearly that Rafik is innocent?'

'They will not believe you, Khornya. Rafik's ship bears the emblem of House Harakamian, as do the stones. The sulfur beings believe that House Harakamian is the name of the being who slaughtered their people.'

'How can I explain to them that the stones were stolen from us by the person who attacked them?'

'Ahhh,' Mac said, scanning his own data for the answer. Then he gave her a phrase in the hissing, sizzling, booming language.

She let the phrases flow through her mind, transmitting them to the creatures below. Then she asked Mac, 'What did I just say?'

'You told them that we are honorable and superior Mutables attacked by the same lowborn Solid who attacked them, and we too would like to spray acid on the . . . I'm afraid the descriptive phrase does not readily translate, Acorna.'

But she had stopped listening to him to pay attention to the thoughts suddenly bombarding her as thickly as the acid had fallen upon Rafik's shuttle. She opened her mouth and allowed the phrases to flow out so Mac could hear them. She was thankful that, because of her unconventional upbringing, her vocalizations were not as limited in range as were those of her fellow Linyaari. In fact, she was quite a good mimic.

Mac recorded and translated them. While he did so, Becker kept watch on his monitors.

The captain said, 'They're not spraying, and it looks to me like some of the things surrounding the ship have melted away from it. He's got a moat of them around him now.'

Mac said. 'They say they are reasonable beings. They did not intend to kill Rafik – yet. They were going to cause him extreme suffering such as their people experienced. But if we are the enemies of the Solid who massacred them, they are willing to parley with us.'

Becker's eyes flicked from Mac to Acorna and back again as he listened. 'How do we know it's not a trap?' he asked.

Acorna got her revenge for the carbon copy pun. 'We'll just have to take the *acid* test, Captain.'

The little joke did nothing to ease Becker's reluctance or her misgivings. They weren't the only beings on the ship who had reservations.

RK sat on the back of the command chair, growling low in his throat and whipping his tail back and forth.

Only Mac appeared untroubled by their present course of action.

'See there, Captain? They are backing away, clearing a place for us to land near Rafik.'

'Sure, so they can close in and spray us, too,' Becker said.

'Oh, I think not.'

'Well, you're betting your circuitry on this one, pal. Since you understand the language and are the most easily repaired, you go down and parley with them.'

'I think I should go, too, Captain,' Acorna said. 'While Mac understands their words, he is unable to read their thoughts – or Rafik's. If you remain on the *Condor*, you can use the tractor beam on the shuttle in case we run into problems. We will try first of all to rescue Rafik, so he will be with us if we need to be pulled back to the *Condor*.'

She heard a thousand protests go through Becker's mind, but he lost the argument with himself and had to agree it was the best plan they had. Huffing unhappily through his mustache, he said, 'Oh, well, go ahead then. Like I could stop you.'

She laid her hand gently on his forearm, 'Captain, besides the logic of my arguments – Rafik is *my* father, or one of them.'

'Yeah, yeah, I know. I'd feel the same way if it

was old Theophilus. Get cracking before they change their minds.'

She suited up, donning her Linyaari-engineered protective outer garment designed for nonoxygen atmospheres. Hafiz's people had invented a fabric similar to that of the Linyaari garment and called it Ecoderm, a second skin that could open its fibers to admit oxygenated air, but automatically sealed itself in a less congenial environment. It was constructed much like her shipsuit, but fit more loosely, providing air pockets to help maintain ambient temperature. It also featured built-in gloves and grav/antigrav boots the wearer could adjust with a twist of the tiny dial contained with other controls on the inside of the gauntlets. A spacious hood attached to the back collar of the suit flipped up over the user's horn, coming to a V in the middle of her forehead. The front of the headdress was a smooth, masklike, transparent covering that allowed the wearer's features to be easily identified and her expressions easily read, and also allowed a broad visual sweep with the fullest possible peripheral sight lines.

Acorna and Mac strapped themselves into the *Crow,* as Becker had named the *Condor*'s current shuttle, and launched. As they neared the surface and the space the sulfur beings had cleared for them to land beside Rafik's shuttle, they saw that the hull was covered with a thick trellis of solid yellow runners. Acorna realized they were crystallized sulfuric acid, which explained why the visible portion of the hull blurred out of shape, as if melted.

Acorna sent a message to Rafik, 'We're here now. We can talk to these people. They attacked you mistaking you for Smythe-Wesson. It will be all right.'

She felt Rafik's relief, mingled with his worry that she, too, would be attacked. She also felt his pain, which had increased since she last checked. 'What's wrong?'

'I'm burned,' he told her. 'Something sprayed through the hull. I deflected some of it with my hands and arms, but they're burned badly. The suit resealed itself, and I managed to get my helmet on before the ship's oxygen dissipated, but my lungs may be affected, too.'

She turned to Mac. 'We must convince them to let us free Rafik now. He's injured.'

She flipped up her hood, adjusted and attached the mask to the collar of the suit, and nodded to Mac, who opened the hatch.

Mac clapped his hand over his nose and mouth. 'My olfactory sensors are overloaded, Acorna. You are fortunate that your horn purifies and recycles the air inside your hood and suit.'

'I'm experiencing sensory overload myself, Mac,' she told him. 'These are very emotional beings, but their emotions seem to run the gamut from highly irritated to furiously enraged. They are curious about us, and do not view the *Condor* as a threat, or they would not have allowed us to land, but I am at a loss at the moment how to appeal to their better instincts.'

'You must consider the possibility that they have none,' Mac said.

'Perhaps, but that seems so harsh. Surely the couple who were being bonded, the relatives who watched, they all must have experienced other, more tender feelings.'

Mac cocked his head as if he needed to put himself at a slightly skewed angle to process her odd notion. 'Not necessarily. Perhaps their bondings are matters of mathematical or chemical imperative, or for convenience, economic advantage, or even spite. All such motives have precedents in human society.'

'I suppose so, but that isn't helpful in getting them to release Rafik and allow us to take him with us, not to mention the catseyes.'

'Perhaps the logical thing to do would be to appeal to the emotions you do feel coming from them, Acorna.'

'Anger and malice?' she asked, 'Oh, I couldn't do *that*, Mac. That would be unethical. And besides, how could I make it work? Hmmmm.'

As they quietly conversed, the sulfur people moved and flowed in around them again, circling them and their shuttle and cutting them off from Rafik's shuttle.

The front row of attackers assumed a vaguely humanoid form – extruding arm- and leglike limbs, gathering the bulk of their mass into a torso and lastly popping a round head out of the top of the trunk. The liquids flowed toward Acorna and Mac, keeping a deferential distance between themselves and the mutating front row. From time to time, the pools in the back nudged the pools in the front into miniature tidal waves that humped up, seemed to examine the visitors from first one angle, then another, before subsiding again into a puddle.

Behind the puddles and pools, solid forms resembling large oddly shaped yellow trees with some fatal disease slid forward on rootlike lower limbs.

'Tell them it is very urgent that we reach my father, since their mistaken attack has injured him and endangered his life,' Acorna told Mac.

'They know that, Acorna,' Mac reminded her. 'They don't care.'

'No, of course they don't. Well, try this. Tell them that the rocks that form the jettisoned cargo are very valuable. Tell them that House Harakamian would be happy to pay them a reward for the return of its property as well as reparations for the loss of their citizens, but first we must have Rafik back.'

'Appealing to their greed – yes. That is a good start, Acorna. And I have a plan. I will tell them that the fee will be paid only to the Solids, whose people were the ones injured,' Mac said.

He relayed the message.

At once the first row of attackers began thrashing their arms around and speaking loudly. Angrily, they gestured toward their own trunks, then flattened the ends of their extended arm extrusions in a negative way as they pointed toward the Solids in the back ranks.

'My plan worked. The Mutables say *they* are the only ones who should receive a reward, as they are the most sentient beings on this planet, the true leaders. The Solids are so stupid and inflexible they have no idea what to do with valuable items. They have no authority to release Rafik. They are limited to one form and not until their forms break down into their molecular structure for rebuilding are they of any use.'

As Mac was speaking the Solids from the back ranks zipped toward the front, their roots invading the area occupied by the Liquids.

The Liquids began sloshing back and forth, up and down, in an agitated fashion.

Acorna heard their glubbish thoughts clearly, but they were not able to vocalize. She told Mac, 'The Liquids feel that had it not been for their ability to combine themselves with the atmosphere to make the acid, the Mutables, who will not waste any of their own precious molecules, would have had no weapon with which to attack Rafik. The reward would not have been offered. Therefore, the Liquids should share in the reward.'

The Mutables turned to refute the Liquids and Solids. Those Mutables who had turned some of their Liquid essence into the crystallized net holding Rafik's shuttle withdrew the runners back into themselves so that their energies were not divided. The beings between the shuttle and

Rafik's craft joined in the battle, surging out into the crowd to express their views. In the ensuing confusion, Acorna and Mac slipped between the ships. Mac used his laser saw attachment to cut through the melted hatch, allowing them to barge through it. Fortunately, the airlock was not damaged, so they were able to enter without subjecting Rafik further to the sulfurous atmosphere.

Rafik was sprawled on the center of the deck of the small craft. He was in shipsuit and helmet, but his suit was pocked with places where the acid had corroded it, despite its miraculous fibers.

Mac picked Rafik up by the scruff of the neck, carrying him back through the hatch in one hand, just as one might carry a cat. In a moment Acorna, who had stayed behind to make some adjustments to the shuttle's instrument panel, joined him. Together, they sprinted for the *Crow*.

'I'd rather not heal Rafik out here,' she told Mac. 'We might have some unfortunate interruptions if these beings stop fighting long enough to notice what I'm doing. I'd like to get him back into the *Crow* and away from his attackers.'

Mac nodded agreement. But before they could open the *Crow*'s hatch, the angry noises ceased and one of the Mutables pointed an extrusion at them. With that gesture, the creature returned the indignant attention of all of his fellows to the interlopers.

Mac asked blandly, quite as if he were not

burdened with Rafik, 'Have you decided then who will receive the reward?'

'What good is a reward to us?' one of the most sentient Mutables demanded. 'We use no currency and we have no need of alien rocks. We only wish vengeance.'

The others took up the cry with the same guttural word, or their own version of it. The force of their homicidal enthusiasm gave Acorna a horrible headache.

Mac said, 'You shall have it. But this man is an enemy of your enemy, as are we. Therefore, we are your friends.'

The sulfur people turned to each other inquiringly, asking each other, 'Friends? What is friends?'

'Those who are not your enemies, nor your inferiors, but equals who – wish for you to have what you wish for yourself,' Acorna answered, showing the Mutables two Mutables in an amiable pose, the Solids two Solids likewise engaged, and the Liquids peacefully puddling along beside each other. 'Let me heal my father and allow us to leave.'

They were still getting used to the 'friend' concept, so Mac deposited Rafik in the *Crow*, though he himself remained outside. Acorna left Mac to deal with the natives while she took care of the most urgent problem facing them at that instant – healing her foster father. When the airlock closed behind Acorna and Rafik and they could once more breathe oxygen, she removed

Rafik's helmet and her own hood. He had injuries to his hands and arms, a few to his face, and some to his throat and lungs. She tenderly applied her horn to all of the exterior wounds, and to the skin over Rafik's interior injuries for a longer time.

Outside the shuttle, Mac ranted on to the sulfur people. She could not read Mac's mind, of course, since he did not generate thoughts in the same way that wholly organic species did. Still, as she moved from wound to wound on Rafik, during the slight breaks in her concentration she could sense a swell of agreement among the sulfur people and a gradual dwindling of their rage and sorrow – or at least a dwindling of the rage and sorrow they were directing toward Acorna, Mac, and Rafik.

A short time later, Mac joined Acorna and Rafik inside the shuttle.

'They allow us to leave and insincerely express regret over the loss of the *Sinbad*'s shuttle, Mr. Nadezda,' Mac said.

'Never mind the shuttle, just get us out of this hellhole,' Rafik said with a force that showed he was back to his normal state of good health and wished to remain that way.

'No, no,' Becker protested through the com line, which had been kept open between the *Crow* and *Condor*. 'That's great salvage. I'll pull it up in a jiffy. And let's grab those catseyes while we're at it. I'm sure Hafiz wants 'em back just as much as those sulfur critters want them gone.'

'I have another plan,' Acorna said. 'Before leaving the *Sinbad*'s shuttle, I reset the damaged com unit's controls. Though, thanks to the damage it suffered, it cannot transmit and receive as it should, it can still emit a high-frequency signal if its scanner sensor is tripped. When Smythe-Wesson returns for the stones, he'll need to scan the area to find his loot's exact location. I have left the controls set to trip the shuttle's alarm when the craft is scanned, and thus it will notify us when he returns.'

'It should at that,' Becker agreed. 'We'll just have to rig up a few subspace amplifiers and sprinkle them in our path like bread crumbs as a relay between here and MOO. That should do it for the time being. Hafiz can dispatch his security people to patrol the area and intercept Smythe-Wesson when things get noisy. That way he gets his stones back – and the thief who double-crossed him.'

Since they now knew that the majority of the catseyes were buried beneath the remains of the fallen sulfur beings, there was no need for the *Sinbad* to return to Kezdet to search for the stones, so both ships returned to MOO. Rafik remained aboard the *Condor* while his crew guided the *Sinbad* to her destination.

As they set down, the viewport showed the black-clad senior officers of MOO's security force gliding through the transparent-bubbled terminal like a murder of particularly lively crows.

'Good thing Acorna got you healed up and purty again, Nadezda,' Becker said. 'Your harem would have been disappointed if you came back mussed up.'

Rafik grinned. 'Personally, I am happy that Acorna was there to heal me because those burns hurt like the seven pits of the seven hells of the seven devils, but as for my appearance, Becker, you seem to have learned very little about women.'

'How's that?' Becker asked through a bristling mustache.

'They consider wounds in the line of duty rugged and manly. My great personal charm and animal magnetism for the ladies would only have been increased by evidence of my wounds. Probably even your own beloved Andina would have forsaken you for love of me had she seen me in my alluringly damaged condition. Hmmm, maybe I should wear the damaged Ecoderm suit when we dock. What do you think, Acorna?'

'I think you are both – what is the word I'm looking for?'

'Studly?' Becker suggested.

'Charismatic?' Rafik asked.

'Buffoons,' Acorna said with some satisfaction. 'It's an old-fashioned word, but it exactly describes you. You are a pair of buffoons.'

'You need to lay off the Shakespeare vids, kiddo,' Becker said.

Acorna's smile faltered a little. Rafik had only

been teasing, of course, but was there some truth in what he claimed? It was so close to what Aari had accused her of – *did* she care more for *her* Aari because he had been damaged?

Whatever the state of Rafik's charms, they were largely ignored as the security officers swept past with little more than a wink and a wave.

'Wait!' he called after them. 'Aziza, where are you going?'

'To catch that demon spawn when he returns for the stones of course. The master allows me this revenge. Saida and Naima will go with me. Fatima is in charge while I am away, along with ZuZu, Jamila, and Aisha. And Layla, of course. So there will be plenty of us still here to protect you, young master.' And she blew him a kiss and disappeared into the loading chute.

Rafik was still looking vaguely stunned as he, Acorna, and Becker were met by Hafiz and Karina. Hafiz embraced Rafik, followed by Karina, who allowed her embrace to linger longer than was strictly necessary. She gave a deep sigh that caused her draperies to shimmy. 'Did I not foretell it, Haffy? Did I not say that your gorgeous nephew would return to us even before we expected, and bring with him good tidings?'

'I believe so, my flower,' Hafiz said. 'And it was very clever of you to divine our reunion and the news he brings only moments after my heir appeared on our com unit telling us he had found our stones. I confess I am sometimes confused between your predictions of events and the inevitability of the events themselves once you have predicted them, so dizzying do I find your powers.'

More feasting followed their arrival, and ZuZu and Jamila, who were off duty, insisted on entertaining again. As the dancers gyrated around her, Acorna sat next to Maati and chewed thoughtfully on a grass stem. The smell of sulfur had been clinging to her suit when she removed it on the *Condor*, and the odor was so pervasive that it was in her nostrils even as she sat toying with her marigold petals on MOO. The scent brought back memories of her short time on the sulfur planet, along with images of its inhabitants. She remembered how the front lines of sulfur beings changed themselves from trees and puddles into what seemed to be, if not human, at least bipeds. Each time she'd looked, they had seemed to resemble herself or Mac more closely. *Imagine being able to change like that,* she thought. On the whole, of course, she'd rather be able to heal people but still, what a talent . . . She wondered why the Linyaari hadn't received that ability from the Ancestral Hosts as they had received the ability to heal from the Ancestors themselves.

Eight

Somewhere on the Planet Vhiliinyar,
Several Years Earlier

Aari knew where he was long before he awakened fully in the dankness and darkness of the cave. He had come to know this place so well in the time before Joh Becker rescued him.

He held his breath and listened, reluctant to open his eyes. All around him he felt the upheaval of soil and rock, the thunder of erupting volcanoes, a quiver from distant earthquakes and – oh, no. For the love of the Ancestors, no. Could that sound just beyond the range of his physical hearing, a sound he felt more than heard, be the clomping and sliding of Khleevi feet and Khleevi bodies rending Vhiliinyar into slag, trailing their caustic slime as they destroyed everything they touched?

A nightmare . . . he thought. *Surely it's a nightmare.* Though he remembered the agony that had accompanied those sounds for so very long, he was not now in pain. His hand touched his forehead. His fingers slid along the reassuringly solid base of his growing horn.

And then he remembered. He and Grimalkin had returned through time to find Laarye. In the time they came from, his brother had died of starvation in this very cave while Aari was writhing and screaming under the tender ministrations of the planet's Khleevi invaders. But he and Grimalkin were only going to rescue Laarye, who had remained in the cave after Aari had healed him of injuries he'd sustained in that fall. Aari would not need to go for food. Grimalkin had timed them back to Vhiliinyar and sat in the ship waiting for them. All Aari needed to do was grab Laarye and they would reboard the ship, time it forward, and rejoin Khornya and the others. After the many journeys Aari and Grimalkin had taken together, after all Aari had learned of history, with Grimalkin and him such a prominent part of it, this was the time he had waited for. This was the time for which he promised Grimalkin his seed, his genes.

Becker had a peculiar saying about which came first, the chicken or the egg. Aari's friend had explained that the chicken was a sort of a bird and the egg of course what it came from. But on the other hand, chickens laid eggs that produced more chickens. So where did the first chicken that laid the first egg originate, if not from another egg?

The Ancestral Hosts or Friends, as the Linyaari

called them, had a similar situation. They were great scientists determined to create and give races on many other worlds the benefit of their superior genes. They were ageless beings from a possibly immortal race, but they were also shape-shifters whose own forms had become too unstable for them to bear young. And so, unable to have young of their own, they manipulated the DNA of other beings and created new races. Such as the Linyaari. Except they hadn't been able to get it right yet. Their attempts to blend themselves with the Ancestors, a Terran species originally called unicorns, had been disappointing.

This was not the fault of the Ancestors, who were perfectly capable of bearing unicorn foals, though before their rescue from Old Terra by the Friends, they had been in danger of becoming extinct. Earthly hunters had harried them for their horns until the psychic vibrations of Ancestral anguish attracted the attention of the Friends once again. They'd picked the Ancestors up in a space vessel and brought them to Vhiliinyar.

The unicorn Ancestors were willing enough to be bred into a race that would have some of the strengths, such as opposable thumbs, of their former enemies. However, the unstable forms of the Hosts foiled their efforts to breed the race they had in mind – Aari's race. The Hosts changed too quickly and at times too unpredictably. Their first attempts had resulted in the *sii*-Linyaari, a horned mer-people. While a viable race, they were not at all what the Friends were trying to create. Subsequent attempts at creation of the Linyaari, Aari gathered, had been even less successful. They'd resulted in stillbirths and early deaths of the offspring created.

When the destruction of Vhiliinyar destabilized the time network the Hosts had laced throughout the planet, Aari had found himself transported back to those early days, before the true Linyaari were created. The Hosts saw in Aari the shortcut they needed to produce his race. They had not explained themselves very well or bothered to solicit his consent before putting their plan into action. When they restrained him, Aari could think only of his torment by the Khleevi and of escaping from the creatures that were about to experiment on him. Grimalkin had helped him, taking them both forward in time until they could board a space vessel from Vhiliinyar just before the first Khleevi attack.

Once he saw how easily Grimalkin manipulated time, Aari saw the opportunity to save his doomed brother. Striking a bargain with Grimalkin to cooperate with future experiments, he had also agreed to go on the adventures the feline shape-shifter deemed necessary before they reached the cross in the double helix of time that would permit them to rescue Laarye.

Aari had been elated. He distinctly remembered landing, being afraid they would be spotted, though the Linyaari cloaking technology made them all but undetectable even upon descent. And yes, Laarye was there, and not surprised to see him since – from Laarye's point of view, at least – Aari had only just stepped out to find food. His brother had been amazed and delighted that instead of returning with dinner, Aari had found a way off their doomed planet.

Grimalkin brought them both aboard and then . . . Aari couldn't remember. He awakened in the cave. He opened his eyes at last. Laarye was not here, though there was food of a sort, grasses dried to a sort of straw, piled in one corner. Bending down, as he had to in order not to hit his head against the cave's low ceiling, he crept to the entrance. The ship had vanished.

What happened? Had the destabilized time apparatus stuttered again and sent the ship back into space and himself back to the cave? How long would it take Grimalkin to discover the error and return for him?

He waited. And waited. And waited. And finally the straw disappeared and most of the water he had found beside it. And he realized that whatever had happened, Grimalkin, Laarye, and the ship were not returning anytime soon.

In his mind he saw Khleevi patrols passing closer to his hiding place every moment. He shook all over and broke out in a cold sweat thinking of them capturing him again. He had no idea how long they would be there before the planet was so depleted they were forced to leave it, before the *Condor* arrived on its first salvage mission. His ordeal with his torturers had seemed to last an eternity, but it could have been a matter of weeks or merely days.

One thing for sure. If Aari was still here when Joh and Riid Kiiyi arrived for the first time *this* time, Aari would not wait for the second mission to meet them.

The only alternative was somehow to find his way back to Kubiilikaan and the time apparatus and hope that he could manipulate it to take him back to Khornya somewhere close to the moment he lost her.

Another Sector of Space, Another Time . . .

He certainly hoped this plan of his would work. He'd *thought* it would be easy enough, given his skill with time travel, but as it turned out, it required a number of attempts, each of them at the risk of his own life.

Once he succeeded, she had better appreciate all the trouble he'd gone to on her behalf. She had better appreciate *him*.

The main problem was that no one still living knew exactly what had happened during Feriila and Vaanye's last and fatal voyage. Neeva, Feriila's sister, had managed to learn that Vaanye had used a new defense system he'd invented to destroy the Khleevi ship bearing down on his family's small cruiser. For three *ghaanyi*, Neeva and the Linyaari people thought that the entire family had died in the destruction. Neeva had learned of her error only when she and her shipmates embarked on a mission to warn other worlds of the Khleevi menace bearing down upon them and discovered Acorna and her human family.

Which was very nice for Khornya, of course, but the story was quite short on the sort of specifics one needed when trying to do a certain sort of intervention.

Once Neeva had told him all that she knew of the incident, including the approximate times and coordinates, he began to test the waters to find the correct time to intercept his subjects. It needed to be *after* the pod was ejected, *after* Feriila and Vaanye took the *abaanye,* which would put them to sleep forever (unless, of course, the antidote happened to be administered just in time by a heroic rescuer), and *after* the controls had been set to collapse the dimensional space surrounding both the Khleevi ship when it came within a certain range and the little cruiser. And, most importantly of all, his move had to be made *before* the actual collapse took place.

Tricky. Very tricky.

So he simply observed the first time, not making his presence known. When the couple drank fatal doses of the *abaanye* sleeping potion and gave a dilute dose to Khornya in her bottle before ejecting her life pod into space, he lost his nerve and, with uncharacteristic panic, changed his time. Whether he was more alarmed by the prospect of the Khleevi warship clearly visible in the viewport or of the detonation of Vaanye's weapon, he couldn't have said for sure.

But having made careful notes of the times and coordinates, he returned, this time with the remedy for the *abaanye* sleep. He arrived unprotected in deep space. No Khleevi ship, no cruiser. No pod. He returned at once to his former time-space slot, made notes, and pondered.

Vaanye and Feriila stowed their baby in her pod and set the command to eject her before the Khleevi tripped the sensor that would detonate Vaanye's weapon. Then they toasted each other with glasses of sparkling red wine, each mixed with a fatal dose of *abaanye*.

Feriila fought to stay awake long enough to see and hear the signal, and watch the mechanism outside the pod activate. She did not see the pod leave the ship, and her eyes closed shortly after, but she felt she could finally die in peace knowing that her baby had a chance.

But she wasn't allowed to die. Someone dribbled something bitter into her mouth, and said, 'Wake up, Feriila. That was the antidote for the *abaanye* I just gave you. You're safe with me now. You're not going to die today.'

'Vaanye?' she asked, her tongue thick and slurring her lifemate's name.

'He isn't going to die either, though I believe he has a terrible hangover.'

She heard a groan in the familiar tones of her beloved. 'Were it not for you and our child, I'd almost have preferred to take my chances with the Khleevi to this!'

'The Khleevi!' she said, forcing her eyes wide open and half-expecting to see the insectoid monsters studying her.

'They are far away, in another time and place. Khornya – as your daughter is called in Linyaari – and, uh, I, along with many others, have engineered the defeat and destruction of the Khleevi.'

Feriila still felt a bit tipsy. The wine was potent and the *abaanye* antidote had done nothing to counteract the effects of the drink. Above her loomed a familiar but unexpected face. 'I know you!' she said, pointing at the young male standing over her. 'You're Aari! What are you doing here?'

'And where *is* here anyway?' Vaanye asked.

'It is far into the future from the time when the *abaanye* sedated you,' he told them. 'I've brought you forward to be with your daughter. I'm afraid you've missed her childhood – she was found and raised by three human males.'

'What's a human?' both of the other Linyaari asked.

'It's a bit complicated. They are another race of sentients. Once you see one I can explain more clearly. As I was saying, you missed much of your daughter's childhood, but perhaps we can do something about that later. I'll have to think about it.'

'Wait a bit,' Feriila said. 'Why are you doing this, Aari?'

'*How* are you doing this, Aari? Or is this a dream or perhaps a postmortem delusion – some sort of afterlife experience? Were you and our daughter both killed before your time but are here to guide us to the hereafter?'

'Oh, no!' he said. 'As to your question, Feriila, I am doing this because you are in trouble and need my help, of course, but also because I am, or should be, Khornya's mate, and I wish to make her happy. As to how I am doing this, Vaanye, let me assure you that there is more physics than metaphysics behind this process, but it would take as long to explain – even to you – as it would for you to explain your weapon to me. And Khornya and I are both very much alive, as are the two of you.'

Feriila and Vaanye exchanged looks, shrugged, and followed Aari, who, Vaanye recalled, had not been one of the more outstanding physics students in Kubiilikhan.

The Moon of Opportunity, Present Time

Acorna was visiting Maati in the terminal's sophisticated communications room – no longer the humble com shed it had once been – when eerie calls began coming in over the subspace amplifiers.

Shortly after they heard the first of those keening signals, Aziza's face appeared on Maati's screen. 'MOO base, we are receiving transmissions most peculiar from the amplifiers. They do not sound like the utterings of the sulfur beings you recorded for us, nor do they appear to emanate from the planet where the stones are.'

Acorna hailed the *Condor*, which was still in port. Becker's and Mac's faces both appeared on the screen, to be blocked momentarily by RK's as the cat peered straight at her. Becker lifted his first mate off the com console. 'What's up, Princess?' Becker asked.

'We are receiving a weird signal from the subspace amps, Captain,' she told him. 'I was hoping Mac might be able to give us some idea if the sounds being transmitted are actual words of a language, and if so, can he translate them?'

'Oh, sure,' Becker said. 'We'll be right down.'

To Maati's delight, RK came, too, and jumped into her lap, purring. But as soon as she toggled the connection to the subspace amplifiers and the noises began, RK mewed and pawed at the console. Maati petted him, but the cat continued to meow louder and more plaintively with each incoming sound.

Finally, Mac said, 'Would someone be good enough to remove the first mate to an area where his complaints will not interfere with my ability to process those transmissions that we are receiving from space?'

'I can't take him,' Maati said. 'I'm on duty and can't leave my post, even with you guys here.'

Acorna scooped the cat up and took him out of the terminal area. As soon as they were out of earshot of the transmissions, he calmed down and stopped caterwauling. 'You seem to be more attuned to alien utterances than anyone except Mac,' she told him. 'I wish you would condescend to tell us more directly what is upsetting you, rather than insisting that we interpret feline cries and body language. We could use your help.'

He gave a sharp 'Prrt,' and licked her ear. She was reminded suddenly of something Gill had said teasingly when she was little. If she asked a question about anything that she wasn't supposed to know, Gill always looked wise, and said, 'That's for me to know and you to find out.' She seemed to be getting the same response from the cat.

She grazed for a bit in the Celestial Garden, the one closest to the terminal, while RK did his bit for the fertilization and irrigation of Hafiz's prized orchids.

Hearing distinctive Linyaari footfalls, she looked up to see her aunt Neeva stride past on her way toward the terminal, her head bent over a clipboard and her mouth moving.

Acorna called out to her aunt, and Neeva

looked up and smiled. 'Khornya! Are you heading back to Vhiliinyar soon?'

'Maybe,' Acorna said. 'Unless I'm needed elsewhere.'

'I had the strangest dream the other night. It was all about you and Feriila and Vaanye, of all people.'

'Can you tell me about it?'

Neeva stopped while Acorna joined her beside the path, and they both seated themselves on the clover-strewn grass. Hafiz had the grasses of his gardens dotted with the little wild-flower plants specifically for the delight of his Linyaari friends.

'Do you remember I told you that your parents were on their way to the planet where I was posted when they met up with the Khleevi?'

'You mentioned it, yes,' Acorna said. Neeva had not gone into great detail at the time except to let her know that her parents had jettisoned her pod in hopes of saving her.

'Well, I had this very peculiar dream in which Aari came to see me and asked me all sorts of questions about when each event occurred during the last moments your parents were alive. He was very . . . intense . . . about it, insisting that I remember the exact sequence, trying to get me to visualize the chrono on my com screen so that I would see the exact times I learned of each event.'

'Was it Aari Whole-Horn doing the questioning or—' She started to say 'my Aari' but thought better of it.

'Yes, I know exactly what you mean. This was the Aari who brought Laarye back with him. I couldn't understand why he was so interested. Though, of course, as your lifemate, he would want to know a lot about you. But by the time your parents were dead, the evacuation was taking place, and he and Laarye were taking refuge in the cave. Dreams are so odd. I wonder what that one meant.'

'Me too,' Acorna said, though she thought she might know the answer and didn't like to think about it.

(Hey, Princess, Mac's figured it out,) Becker sent her a mental message. He enjoyed using telepathy as a special bond between them, pleased that she could read him when he deliberately addressed her with a thought.

(I'll be right there,) she replied.

RK ran ahead of the two Linyaari as they entered the terminal. The receiver was blessedly silent, but Mac looked quite pleased with himself. If she hadn't known he was an android, Acorna would have said he looked humanly smug, in fact.

'You have translated the strange signals? What sort of language is that?' she asked.

'It isn't a language, Acorna. It is song. Specifically, it is the sort of song known in some cultures as a lament, although that terminology is usually, but not exclusively, applied to vocalizations of actual words.'

'Is it coming from instruments, then?' she asked.

'No – it is vocalized, but uses the voice as an instrument, expressing sounds that have no actual linguistic meaning but fit into a melodic pattern.'

'Oh! Like the Singing Stones of Skarness.'

Becker looked smug. '*Exactly* like the Singing Stones of Skarness, in fact. Mac matched the tonal qualities and determined that they were basically identical.'

'Where *is* Skarness?' Maati asked. 'I know we have some of the stones in Kubiilikhan. Those stones luckily escaped damage when the Khleevi attacked. And Hafiz has some stones, too.'

'The truth is,' Becker told her, 'that nobody really knows the truth about where Skarness is. The stones are very valuable trade items, but the trades take place in such a way that the origin of the stones has never been discovered. I suppose it's for the same reason that your people don't let many others know about your horns. If people knew what they could do, before long galactic hunters would kill the goose that laid the golden egg.'

'Wait!' Maati said. 'What are geese?'

Becker paused long enough to explain the analogy to her. 'It's another of those Old Terran things. Geese were a largish fowl, actually wild at one point but in latter days mostly domesticated. They laid eggs – that's how they had their young. Eggs shaped like your spacecraft.'

'But the Singing Stones aren't shaped like the spacecraft,' Maati said.

'No. And geese didn't lay the stones. Wait a minute. You're confusing *me* now. What it means to say "killing the goose that laid the golden egg" is that if you have something that generates a lot of income, like the goose, killing it cuts off the source of income and is therefore a . . . uh . . . no-no.'

'So the people who live where the stones are don't allow anyone else to know so they won't take all the stones away?' Maati asked.

'You got it.'

Neeva looked pensive, her fingers twiddling at her chin. 'I've never heard of the stones being able to sing loudly enough to broadcast into space, Captain Becker.'

'Me, neither. But ancient Terran lore also tells us that *rock* songs were often very loud and could be heard a long way—'

He was unable to finish the sentence because of the gasping and giggling sounds that Acorna, who was the only one in the room with enough knowledge of ancient Terran culture to get the joke, made in answer to his pun.

'Gotcha,' he said with a pleased grin.

'Indeed,' she said, straightening up and continuing to explain more seriously. 'The thing is, Maati, so far as I know, the people who have actually had the stones only have them in small groups of maybe two dozen. If the stones' song was emanating from their planet of origin, there would be many more stones singing in unison. The sounds are coming from the area we laced with subspace amplifiers. We've never had receivers in that sector of space before.'

The MOO intercom receiver switched itself on, and Karina Harakamian's face appeared. 'I couldn't help overhearing, my dears,' she said. Obviously, she had been using Hafiz's security surveillance equipment, which was separate from the com center's, to eavesdrop. 'And I must tell you, the truth is obvious to me. The blessed Singing Stones might have been singing their hearts out long before this for all we know, but they never tried to sing loudly enough to be heard until the sacred catseye chrysoberyls of Makahomia were deposited in close enough proximity that the Singing Stones felt the emanations from their fellow sacred stones. They are not singing to *us*; they are singing to the chrysoberyls, and the amplifiers are simply intercepting and transmitting the song as we wished them to intercept and transmit other outside signals affecting the chrysoberyls.'

Becker sent another mental message to Acorna. *(I have been in this quadrant entirely too long. She's beginning to make a weird kind of sense to me.)*

'Mac?' Acorna asked. 'Could that be the case?'

'I am not programmed to divine the motivations of stones, Acorna, but it is as likely a conjecture as any, I suppose, though expressed in very unscientific terms.'

'You do what you do very well, MacKenZ,' Karina said somewhat condescendingly, using Mac's full self-chosen name as an adult might use the full given name of someone else's child to indicate that they knew to whom they were speaking and from whence the speaker came, just in case the speaker would have preferred to remain anonymous. 'But you have not the seasoned sensitivities of those of us who have received true enlightenment. No one would expect you to understand. Dear friends, now that we know who is lamenting, the question is, what are we going to do about it?'

Hafiz appeared beside her. 'What is the matter under discussion?' he asked in a businesslike tone.

'It is quite all right, my darling,' Karina said. 'We have intercepted sad sacred songs and I have fathomed the source of the problem and—'

'Please, my curvaceous kumquat, I require an answer phrased in terms that may be understood by those of us who operate on a less elevated plane than that which you frequent,' he told her, offering her a chocolate tidbit to occupy her busy mouth if not her enlightened mind.

Acorna filled him in and turned up the volume on the receiver so he could hear the song for himself.

Large tears fell from his eyes, and he whipped out an exquisite silk handkerchief and blew his nose, waving for them to turn the sound down again. 'Aiee, that is the saddest thing it has ever been my misfortunate to hear. My friends, I think that my beloved is correct as usual. We must learn the cause of the stones' sadness – and their location as well, of course – and relieve their distress.'

As he was speaking, the door to the communications center irised open and Rafik stepped through. 'Any word from . . . ?' he began, but was struck dumb by the sight of his wily uncle weeping to the sad song wailing through the other receiver.

'O, son of my heart, you have arrived in time to undertake a mission of mystery and possibly mercy,' Hafiz said. He summarized the situation as he understood it.

After which, Rafik said, 'I understand, Uncle. A mission of mystery, mercy, and possibly an incidental monetary reward? Possibly an exclusive trade agreement for House Harakamian if we manage to be helpful in this matter to the stones or those who control them?'

Hafiz turned to Karina, beaming. 'Did I not tell you that this boy is astute? Sharp as a saber, keen as a bridegroom on his wedding night.'

Rafik left that line alone and returned to the matter at hand. 'So I am to rescue these rocks, Uncle?'

'Yes, dear boy. Discover their whereabouts – perhaps the excellent Captain Becker and his estimable eclectic scanner array might provide assistance once more?'

'You betcha,' Becker said. RK was pacing quickly and with precise delicacy across the console. For once, he did not set paw to any key that would have disrupted the proceedings. He merely walked from Becker on the one side to Rafik and back again. Maati reached out to tweak the cat's tail and received a stern look warning her that he was working now and so his tail was to be left strictly alone to play its part in his concentration.

'When you have located the source of the stones, you will have the more difficult task of learning the source of their distress and why it is they have seen fit to broadcast it for all the universe to hear. I can only imagine that the cause must be most grave for them to sing so loudly that anyone – even someone unscrupulous who might take advantage of the situation – might hear them.'

Rafik turned his head slightly away from the com screen and with the eye not visible to the screen winked at Acorna. 'The reason for your tears now is clear to me, Uncle. Not only do the Singing Stones enlist your sympathy with their song, but you also fear for their safety. We will mount an expedition at once. Captain Becker, Mac, I, and of course Acorna, if she wishes to go . . .'

Acorna nodded. She did indeed wish to see the home of the famous Singing Stones of Skarness.

'Perhaps it would be wise to have other Linyaari with us as well,' Rafik said. 'The stones may be lamenting some injury or illness that affects them. In that eventuality, the presence of healers would be most efficacious.'

'As it has been said, so let it be done, O son of my heart,' Hafiz agreed.

Which was how the *Balakiire* and her crew joined the *Condor* as it retraced the course to the world of the sulfur beings.

Nine

En Route to the Sulfur Planet,
Present Time

Acorna, Mac, and Becker spent much of the trip modifying their sensors to pick up auditory signals, especially those of the sort made by the Singing Stones of Skarness.

'That way we can backtrack the signal,' Becker said. 'We tune the scanners to the frequency of the songs the amps picked up, and rig our sensor so that instead of someone else telling where we are by bouncing sound off us, we can tell where the source of the stone is by the way the sound bounces back from us to it.'

'You and my new aunt have a gift for scientific discourse,' Rafik said.

'Up your exhaust, Nadezda,' Becker replied.

Traversing the galaxy containing the sulfur world, the *Condor* passed one burned-out devastated husk of a planet after another. Acorna felt oddly cold. The eerie song emanating from the stones didn't help.

'Geez,' Becker said. 'This place gives me the creeps. It's like a ghost galaxy!'

Rafik hailed the *Habibi* and was visibly relieved when Aziza appeared on the screen. Her eyes were wide and a trifle wild-looking. 'Is that nasty sulfur world the only live planet in this galaxy?' she asked.

'Looks like it,' he said. 'The Khleevi passed it by for some reason.'

'Hah!' Aziza said. 'They probably forgot they hadn't been there already, since it looks even more inhospitable than the ruined ones.'

'It is,' Rafik said. 'I can guarantee that. Under no circumstances should you try to land.'

'You did,' she said.

'You didn't see me before Acorna healed me. Those creatures shoot sulfuric acid first and don't bother asking questions later. Just be alert for the signal that Smythe-Wesson is returning and let us know.'

'I don't believe we will be too far away,' Acorna said, checking the scanner array. 'I've been calculating the time it will take us to reach Sarkness, according to the sonar tables Mac provided. It may be the next planet in this solar system, though it could be a moon, I suppose. Still, the impression I'm getting is of a larger mass than that of a mere satellite.'

Aziza and Rafik exchanged a few more remarks, but their usual joking banter was somewhat damped down by the bleakness of this sector of the galaxy.

When Rafik signed off it was with a heavy sigh and a troubled expression. Acorna hailed the *Balakiire* and checked her calculations with Melireenya's.

'It does seem to be rather close,' Melireenya said, scratching the base of her horn thoughtfully with her stylus. 'But I don't see how that can be. According to the readings we've been getting on the surrounding planets, moons, and even asteroids, everything here is completely lifeless – no plant or animal life anywhere. The Khleevi were very thorough.'

'They missed the sulfur world,' Acorna said. 'So they may have missed something else, too. And, as Karina pointed out, we're dealing with mineral-based life-forms in the case of the sulfur people, minerals in the Makahomian catseyes, *and* minerals with the Singing Stones. Perhaps if there was nothing but mineral substance to deal with on a planet, the Khleevi simply ignored it. Minerals, in my experience anyway, don't exhibit the sort of fear the Khleevi use to feed their Young.'

'Maybe,' said Neeva, who had been listening in also. 'But from what you say of the sulfur beings, I would wonder if they wouldn't be more than a match for the Khleevi. Maybe the Khleevi realized it and steered clear.'

'Maybe—' Acorna said, then she, Becker, and Rafik in unison said, 'Naaaah.'

Had it not been for what Becker dubbed 'the

trail of wail,' they would have missed their target altogether. It was, as Acorna had surmised, the next planet from the nearest sun, but it showed no more sign of life than any of the Khleevi-wrecked rocks they had passed already.

Acorna, however, knew at once that it was the right place, for she felt the particular mineral composition of the Singing Stones immediately. And she also knew that this planet had definitely not escaped the Khleevi. It showed the same sort of devastation as the others.

The keening of the stones seemed to escalate as the *Condor* and the *Balakiire* approached orbit, though Becker turned the volume of his com systems down to the minimum. The songs were so loud now that they didn't need Becker's sensitive equipment to be heard.

'All right already!' Becker bellowed, sticking his fingers in his ears. RK, who had begun running wildly around the deck, bouncing off the bulkheads as the volume grew, now burrowed his head into Becker's armpit, his coat and tail so puffed up it caused him to resemble a porcupine more than a cat.

'This reminds me of the stories of sirens luring ancient mariners onto the rocks,' Rafik told Acorna nervously. 'Except in reverse. The sadness dragged me here. But the noise now makes me want to turn and run.'

'We cannot land,' Mac pointed out. 'And we must go no closer. If we approach the planet too closely, the sonic waves it is projecting may fatally damage any organic parts among the landing party. Except for myself, this crew is entirely made up of organic parts.'

'Good point,' Acorna said. The same thought had occurred to her.

Even telepathic communication was difficult, so thoroughly did the wailing fill the air, bombarding not only their ears but also all of their other senses.

'Geez, this is worse than the jungle drums in those old "bwana" vids,' Becker complained.

'Another good point, Captain,' Mac said. He alone was able to maintain a conversational tone in the cacophony surrounding them. 'Studies of ancient indigenous cultures which rely on magical ceremonies have shown that such drumming blocks the alpha waves of the brain, making the listeners far more susceptible to suggestion than they would otherwise be.'

'I suggest they shut up. If they don't shut up, I suggest we leave,' Becker snapped.

Acorna hailed the *Balakiire,* which took some time to answer since all aboard were also preoccupied with the wailing coming from the planet below. Her friends clustered onto the screen, their pained expressions a mirror of her own.

'We need to let whoever is singing – or *whatever* is singing – know that we're here to help, but that we can't come any closer if they don't stop,' Acorna said.

Melireenya nodded, as did Neeva and the other Linyaari.

'Pity we don't know the language,' Thariinye said.

'Send emotions,' Neeva suggested. 'Compassion, a wish to heal, but fear for one's own safety as well.'

Becker, who had been straining to listen, closed his eyes and grasped Acorna's hand with his free one, 'Works for me. Princess, grab on to your daddy. Rafik, take her hand and let's do a thinkathon that would make Aunt Karina proud.'

Acorna had to smile. Becker, like Mac, had begun to consider himself an honorary Linyaari. She joined minds with those aboard the *Balakiire*, lifting the thoughts of her shipmates and transmitting them as well, broadcasting the emotions and intentions as clearly as she possibly could.

She concentrated so totally that she wasn't sure when exactly the singing stopped, but she slowly became aware that RK had withdrawn his face from Becker's underarm and was thoughtfully washing a forepaw. The cat caught her staring, and looked up at her as if to say, 'What?'

Becker opened his eyes and looked to the right and the left, and said, 'Yippee! We did it. They listened. They really did. I guess that means they want us to land.'

Acorna shuddered slightly. She had heard the saying that you couldn't get blood from a stone, but it wouldn't have surprised her if these Singing Stones literally were bleeding from the tone and volume of that song.

The *Condor* set down, the robolift descended, and the crew members stepped tentatively out onto the planet's ruined surface.

A spiderweb of pain seemed to spread itself across the ground. Acorna saw the devastation, as she had on so many other planets, but here she sensed the pain and grief of separation from each fragment of stone. Which seemed odd since normally stones were themselves chipped off of larger deposits and ought to be – well, used to it. But the Singing Stones of Skarness were very sensitive instruments.

Still, it was hard to believe anything on this field of splintered rock could make a noise, much less sing, much less communicate telepathically. And yet, the singing had stopped in response to the telepathic message.

Even so, her mind reeled with the force of the now unsung anguish. Her knees buckled, and she slipped down among the shards of stone.

Once these stones had been formed and tuned in tall columns, each column a family, surrounded by the other columns who were the members of its community, hundreds of thousands of them stretched along the vast coastal areas of the planet. Once there had been a curling ocean, and when individual stones left each family as the result of wind or erosion or simply gravity, they formed stepping-stones leading into the waters. The beach and the floor of the ocean were composed of these individual stones, which in time piled one upon the other, singing new songs and forming new colonies. The colonies spawned harmonic units such as those found in Hafiz's gardens and at the center of Kubiilikhan on narhii-Vhiliinyar. These colonies were harvested from their resting places tenderly, respectfully, and appreciatively by other beings.

'Khornya! Khornya, we are here.'

As the tip of the first horn touched her, the dizziness dissipated, her head cleared, and Acorna sat up, waving away the Linyaari clustered around her. 'I'm fine, thank you.'

'Communing with the minerals again, dear?' Neeva asked.

Acorna nodded. 'But there's another life-form, too – other beings. The ones who harvest the stones for export. We were just getting to that.'

'Sorry we interrupted, Khornya, but you seemed to be in pain,' Melireenya told her. 'Are you trying to tell us that the Singing Stones are sentient? If so, all of the off-worlders who own them, according to what I've studied, are in violation of your Federation's directives against owning sentient alien species . . .'

'I don't know about sentience. It's more of an awareness, rather than thought. They aren't so much communicating as – well, as you put it, Neeva, communing. With each other.'

Becker strolled away from them briefly. The stone fragments under his boots whimpered in harmony.

'They should be reassembled,' Acorna said.

'That would be quite a jigsaw puzzle,' Rafik said.

'Besides, I didn't bring enough Superbond,' Becker said. 'I only brought enough for a fleet of salvaged ships, not enough for a whole planet full of pebbles.'

'We don't have to do the whole planet yet. But we need to reassemble the stones in this region so we can safely tell what lies beneath them without harm to them, ourselves, or what's below,' Acorna said without fully understanding why. She picked up a handful of gravel while trying to figure out exactly what she meant. Idly, she arranged the bits of rock into different shapes on her palm. Two of them seemed to fit together like jigsaw puzzle pieces. She tapped their edges together with her fingernail. And felt an odd tingling in her hand as the two fragments seemed to flow into each other and become one. 'We may not need as much glue as it seems, Captain.' She opened her hand and showed the others what had happened. 'Look here. The oddest thing is happening. Once you line up the fragments correctly, they bond themselves together with only the slightest encouragement.'

Rafik nodded. 'Naturally. These stones are a variant of basalt. They're thoroughly infused with high-quality quartz.' He picked up a largish piece and pointed at little lines of dark coloration appearing randomly throughout the stone. 'These are rutiles of iron. Embedded in the quartz, they form a conductor of a static charge that, when properly aligned with other stones with the same rutiles, forms a strong linkage.'

He was lecturing now. Acorna knew all of this and suspected the information was not unfamiliar to Becker. Mac might have had it somewhere in his data banks, too, but he drank it all in nevertheless. 'But how does that make them go together without a bonding agent, Rafik?' the android asked.

'Like I said, it has a static charge. You know about static electricity, right, Mac?'

'Of course. When there is a lot of it, I can feel rather giddy.'

'Yes, but it can also make certain things cling to other things – and they'll remain there until the link is broken. These stones set up their own bond by forming their own static charge. In other words, if you line them up correctly, the molecules have a kind of memory for where they belong. The same phenomenon is what enables these stones to sing – the quartz rutiles act like antennae and set up harmonic resonances that allow for the range of tones.'

'So,' Becker said, 'they don't need glue. That's good. So we'll have the ships' computers scan the fragments on the surface, twirl 'em in different sequences to come up with matches, feed the data about the location of the fragments into Mac, and he can reassemble them.'

'Meanwhile,' Rafik said, 'we'll probably still need all the glues you have to initiate the bonding. No doubt many of the fragments have been powdered when the stones got turned into gravel. The glue and some of the dust can maybe make up lost pieces. And although it won't take much for each stone, there are a lot of stones here.'

'Sounds like a plan. And it sure beats standing here listening to them wail. So let's get cracking, folks!' Becker said. '. . . Or uncracking, as the case may be . . .'

Acorna and Rafik fed a formula into the replicator aboard the *Balakiire,* then ran the various substances Becker had gathered through it, recombining them into the appropriate bonding agent.

Before they had stored the last batch of glue in the last of all of the containers they used from all of the ships, Mac had taken the first batch of the stuff out and blurred across the com screen reassembling the stones.

The process was tedious, but it seemed to be working. While carrying it out, they took turns sleeping and supplying Mac with sufficient bonding agent.

Although the sleep periods were brief, Acorna was almost too tired to dream. Only once during the three sleeps did the Khleevi/Aari dream intrude, right at the end where it hung unfinished in her mind.

But once she awakened and looked out the viewport, the dream was banished as she rubbed her eyes in astonishment. In place of the pathetic gravel pit that had surrounded the ships when they landed, stacks of whole stone towered all around them. On the ground beneath them, the stepping-stone patterns of the Stones of Skarness were starting to form a pleasing semi-circular pattern. Mac had slowed down so that he no longer blurred across her vision, but he still moved very swiftly, scooping rock from the area beyond the re-formed stones, seeming to juggle the load in midair while applying dabs of bonding agent with the hand that wasn't catching falling stones.

'He should have been in show biz,' Becker said. 'He'd have been a real hit.'

Acorna said nothing. The re-formed rocks were singing again – at least they sang in her mind.

(Do you hear them?) she asked Neeva and the other Linyaari.

(Who, dear?)

(The stones. Listen.)

(I seem to hear something now that you mention it, but it may just be an echo of what you are picking up as I receive it through your thoughts. You do have this way with minerals, you know. Unique among us, so far as anyone's memory extends. Keep listening, dear.)

Acorna turned her attention inward again, hearing the melodious mental whispers of the stones again.

Leaving the ship once more, she walked out across the newly mended stones, each of them striking a tone as her boot touched its surface.

(Come! Make Haste! Seek! Find!) the stones sang.

As she walked, Mac continued to lay newly mended stones on the ground. He didn't appear to be conscious of creating a pattern, but in fact the stepping-stones formed three-quarters of a circle to the east of the ship, farthest from where the columns towered.

Acorna walked toward the center, her heels chiming off the stones as she walked slowly and deliberately, listening, looking down at the stones as if they had faces she could read.

(Underground, under stone, living flesh and living bone,) the stones sang.

Mac, four stones nearer to the center of the circle than she was, suddenly stopped what he was doing and looked down. Acorna caught up and followed his gesture. A deep pit lay within the circle. This was not surprising. The planet was pocked with them. But if this one had a bottom, Acorna could not see it.

She frowned at the stones around her. (And your point is?) she thought. They stopped singing, chiming, or making any other noise either aloud or in her head. Then she could hear the other voices, the ones from underneath, very faint, very weak, but voices.

'Someone is trapped down there,' she told Mac.

'Ah,' he said. 'That explains it.'

'Yes, I suppose it does. The stones weren't singing simply because they had been ruined.

They were sending a Mayday for whoever is below.'

Quickly the others gathered while Becker, Mac, and Rafik deployed the earthmoving equipment the *Condor* carried for particularly heavy salvage jobs.

'Are they right below us?' Rafik asked. 'We don't want to injure anyone.'

Acorna searched, her mind excavating the pit, seeping between the rocks and dust of a collapse, finding open space, another collapse, and, at last, after sifting through yards of boulder and soil, meeting the minds trapped beyond. 'No,' she said, 'they aren't directly beneath. But this seems to be the only opening to the place where they've taken shelter. I will tell them to keep as far back as possible anyway. Their tunnels have collapsed in two places, much the same as happened in Kubiilikaan and the old Ancestral caves on Vhiliinyar. These tunnels are old mine shafts, I think, but when the Khleevi came, the people who could not get off-planet hid down there to escape them. They had no idea of the destructive force they were dealing with.'

'They told you all that?' Neeva asked. 'What I'm getting is far too faint to make sense.'

'No,' Acorna admitted. 'I feel it though.' She tried to explain. 'It's partly the rock. This mineral affinity I have seems to magnify my other senses and make communication possible here.'

'Whatever,' Becker said. 'Tell 'em to stand clear anyway.'

Becker, Rafik, and Mac set up a tripod over the hole, with heavy cables laced across the opening providing a suspension grid for the laser drill. Mindful of the Singing Stones, Becker and Rafik began digging and drilling, Mac working alongside the larger equipment. Suddenly the machinery shuddered, and a noxious gas, redolent of Khleevi scat, boiled up from the opening. Becker and Rafik gasped and coughed. Acorna and the other Linyaari rushed forward to purify the air.

'Before you drill again,' Acorna said, 'let me go down there, Captain, and clear the passage. If the air below is anywhere near as bad as what came out of the hole, it could kill any beings who have respiratory problems.'

Becker coughed and hacked. 'You mean like humans?'

'Perhaps we should go with you, Khornya,' Neeva suggested, with a worried look at her niece. It was as if she was afraid that Acorna was not quite up to such a challenge.

(What is it?) Acorna asked.

(Nothing, really. You are still very upset though. You had that dream again. Do please be careful.)

(Thanks for your concern, but I'm fine.)

'If it's very bad and there's room, I'll call for you,' Acorna reassured her aloud for Becker's benefit. 'But I hope as I get nearer to the barrier I'll be better able to distinguish the thoughts of those trapped beyond. Also, I may see a way to bring the people out again without disturbing the Stones any more than we have to.'

Everyone agreed this was sensible. They attached a mesh basket to one of the cables and lowered Acorna into the pit beside the drill.

Rafik loaned her the helmet with the miner's light he always carried with him. She wished he'd brought hers from her younger days, when she, too, mined with her foster fathers out among the asteroids. Her miner's hat was tailored to fit around her horn. This one kept bumping into it. The light bounced around as a result so she got rather fleeting impressions of the area into which she was descending.

There was the debris, of course, but surrounding it was evidence of the interior columnar structure that on the surface broke into the segments that later became the Singing Stones.

The drill and the basket touched bottom and, since the machinery was very noisy, she sent a mental message to Becker to withdraw it.

Now she would need to listen, to make her way toward the second cave in the area, to try to communicate with the entities trapped behind it.

'Khornya, there you are,' a familiar voice said. She thought for a moment she was hallucinating.

'Aari, how did you get here?' she asked, though she knew already. He was undoubtedly traveling through time and space, using the Ancestral Friends' technology. 'What are you doing here?'

'Looking for you, of course. I only had to check the log on record to know you'd be here about now. And I have a wonderful surprise for you!'

'That's – interesting,' she said, wondering if it was possible for a Linyaari to be insane. Because she felt like she was going what Becker would call 'stark raving bonkers' just about now. Her lifemate's insouciant flitting about through time and space made her more uneasy every time he did it. In that moment just now when he had appeared out of nowhere, goose bumps had actually risen on her skin. She tried to keep her voice level, as she said, 'Aari, right now I'm rather busy, as I'm sure the – er – log recorded.'

'That's all right. You can do this and enjoy my surprise, too. I can return you here and now once I've shown you what I have for you, if you want. But this is probably going to be the most exciting thing in your entire life, so maybe you'll want Neeva or one of the others to come down here and fill in for you.'

His voice was as eager and enthusiastic as it had often been on a new mission, but there was also something . . . well . . . pushy about it, too. And self-serving. In all, what she was dealing with right now was Aari Whole-Horn at his most irritating.

But she said patiently, 'Aari, you know that the others don't share my mineral-awareness. I am down here because I can best do what needs to be done at this moment. I have people waiting on me to do it, both my friends up on the surface and those who are trapped here. These beings may be injured. Some may be dying.'

'You don't get it, do you?' Aari asked, with a smug little smile. She knew he thought his 'Friend' Grimalkin was wonderful, but she was beginning to think the Ancestral Being had been a bad influence on him. Even the way Aari spoke was different now, more flippant and dismissive of other people's, or at least of her own, concerns. 'They won't have to wait at all. I can even make it possible for you to perform your task faster. I can return you here before now if you want me to. Only . . . right now we have to go. Someone else is waiting for you.'

Aari's tone was deliberately mysterious, mischievous, and playful, but she did not share his mood.

'I have to tell the others what's happening,' she said firmly.

'There is no need,' Aari Whole-Horn said.

He shot his hand out of the shipsuit sleeve, and tapped at a rather large object strapped to his wrist. It resembled a watch, but it had a keyboard and a very substantial face. When he stopped tapping, he grasped her hand, and said, 'Here we are.'

'I know that,' she said, almost snapping. They hadn't moved at all, as far as she could see.

'Of course you do. It's the same here, but it's rather different now. It's much earlier in time, before the Khleevi attack, even. Come on. The ship is out here. They can hardly wait to meet you.'

TEN

Somewhere on the Planet Vhiliinyar,
During the Time of the Khleevi Invasion

Aari was about to drink the last of his water when something occurred to him. Water was the conduit for time-sliding on Vhiliinyar. It had been so in the time when Kubiilikaan was great, and it had been so when Aari fell out of his own time.

Could this little bit of water perhaps take him where he needed to go? It wasn't a lake or a river or even an ocean, and it hadn't, as far as he knew, come from Vhiliinyar. It was the last tiny drink he had to see him through to distant Kubiilikhan, or Grimalkin's return, or recapture by the Khleevi. A small risk by comparison with what he might gain. He was unsure how exactly to use the water, but he thought giving it something of Vhiliinyar might serve to connect it to the time-water partnership the Hosts had installed on his poor homeworld.

He bent low and sloshed the thermos a bit so that the water met the gnarled nub of his horn. Maybe it could serve two purposes. Perhaps he could time-travel with it and drink it as well? How he wished Grimalkin had explained more about how the time apparatus worked. If only he could go back to pre-Khleevi Kubiilikaan and examine the time machine, then he would have the whole ocean to experiment with until he could send himself to his own time, Khornya's time. But, for right now, all he had was his last drops of drinking water. It would have to do.

Somewhere on the Planet Skarness,
During the Time of the Khleevi Attack on Vhiliinyar

When Acorna and Aari emerged from the hole, the *Condor*, the *Balakiire*, Rafik, Captain Becker, Neeva, Melireenya, and Khaari were missing from where they had been only moments before. RK, however, sat glaring at them.

Acorna found the cat's presence reassuring. 'Look, he waited for us,' she said, scooping the cat into her arms, which was not an easy thing to do since he stiffened himself into a straight-legged, flat-eared, flinty-eyed scowl of a cat.

'But how?' Aari asked. He did not seem pleased to see RK. The cat hissed at him. Which was very strange. RK and Aari had always been fond of each other. When Aari touched Acorna's elbow to guide her across the stones, RK took a swipe at him with five right hooks.

'What has gotten into you?' Acorna asked RK, squeezing him a little as a reprimand. RK pulled his paw back, looked up at her with a hurt expression in widened eyes, and meowed reproachfully, as befitted a misunderstood cat who had been wronged by someone he trusted.

'He can't come where we're going,' Aari said. His wound continued to bleed, and Acorna wondered why he didn't heal it. She allowed RK to squirm away from her, then she stopped Aari with a glance. Holding his sliced forearm aloft, she bent her head to it and healed the scratches.

'You should know by now that you can't keep a cat from going where he wants to,' she said. 'And, for RK, that's even more true than it is with most cats.'

'That is so. But that cat does not appreciate his opportunities. If I had been in your arms, I would not have jumped down. I know where I want to be,' he replied, and tried to pull her into his arms.

She disentangled herself from his embrace only slightly more tactfully than RK had exited her own.

It was Aari's turn to look wronged. Remorse washed over Acorna again, but she couldn't help it. He kept rushing her.

And yet she remembered how she had longed for him to touch her, ached for him, before he returned. As those memories rushed over her, she tried to smile.

He brightened. 'That's all right, Khornya. You will feel differently when you see what I've brought you.'

He led her to a flitter parked among the restored stone columns. Two young adult Linyaari stood there, waiting. They looked dazed and confused, but when they saw her, their thoughts immediately flew to her.

(Is it you? Is it really my little girl all grown-up?)

(F-father?) Acorna asked, though she knew even as she asked that it was he. Vaanye, her father, the scientist who had used his new discovery to sacrifice himself and his lifemate so that their baby could escape a Khleevi attack.

(My baby!) Feriila, Acorna's mother cried, and rushed to embrace her daughter, as Acorna embraced her. Vaanye joined them, throwing his arms around them both.

Aari cleared his throat. 'She didn't want me to try to find you,' he said. 'But I knew she would be pleased once I brought you here.'

Trouble clouded Acorna's happiness. Her objections, callous as they might seem compared with saving these precious people holding her, were still valid. Seeing the worry in her eyes, Aari laughingly explained how clever he had been to find just the proper moment to whisk her parents forward in time and onto firmer ground using Grimalkin's ingenious devices.

Acorna was overwhelmed by her own emotions. And she was swamped with those radiating from her parents. (Where have you been all these years? How were you rescued? Aari has told us a little, but we have so many questions!)

(I do, too. But right now we need to return to the time I was in when Aari fetched me. One of my foster dads, Rafik, is along on this mission, and I imagine you will enjoy hearing him tell embarrassing childhood stories about me while I try to rescue some refugees who seem to be trapped in a tunnel beneath the planet's surface.)

She looked expectantly at Aari, who was beaming at all of them. He didn't seem to be returning them to her proper time, however.

(Well?) she asked.

'Oh, er, what?' he asked aloud.

'We need to get back to the others. My parents will want to meet Rafik especially, and I have a rescue to complete, in case you've forgotten.'

'Sorry, Khornya, I was just caught up in the moment. It was good to surprise you and make you happy.'

His head drooped ever so slightly, and she wondered why she always seemed to feel like a . . . well . . . she could think of any number of colorful terms Becker might have used to describe her . . . around him. Aari had just given her the most precious thing she could possibly have wished for, and already she had grown impatient with him. Perhaps they had been too quick to form the lifemate bond. How strange that it had been so very strong before his disappearance, and yet it was completely absent now. To Acorna, it felt like her emotional ties to him were all in the past. 'It's not that I'm not grateful. It's just that we have to return. I don't quite understand why if you already time-traveled to bring them here, then traveled to get me, that you didn't come to my time to begin with.'

'I thought your reunion should be private,' he said.

(I was wondering about that myself,) Vaanye sent the thought to Acorna. (Grateful as we are to him for bringing us to meet you, daughter, I cannot help but feel that this time-shifting is somehow – unhealthy.)

Feriila looked pensive, glancing between Aari and Acorna.

RK growled and started to run a paw full of claws down the leg of Aari's shipsuit. Aari looked down at the cat. RK sat back and began washing as though nothing unusual had happened. RK backing down from anything or anyone – but especially from his old friend Aari – would have been remarkable under other circumstances. Among so many incredible events, it went unnoticed.

Aari tapped at his wrist and beckoned for them to follow.

Somewhere on the Planet Skarness,
During the Present Day

Acorna heard Neeva's voice mingling with Becker's and Rafik's.

Neeva stopped speaking to stare at them. An amazed silence was finally broken by her words, 'Feriila? Vaanye? Can it be you?'

'Yes, sister,' Feriila said. 'Did you miss us?'

The hug they exchanged was answer enough.

Meanwhile, while the Linyaari family celebrated a grand reunion, Mac unloaded the drill from the ship.

'I do not understand how it happened, Khornya,' he said. 'You were in the hole a moment ago – I have a very clear record of it in my data banks – but now you are not. I believe you said before that there are people trapped below.'

'Yes,' she said. 'Yes, I did, but apparently you and I are the only ones who remember what went on from before. Once we accomplish our mission here, I think that we need to have a chat, Mac.'

Mac nodded and lowered her once more.

This time she was uninterrupted as she felt her way through the blockage to the cave inside. Her mind met with the minds of the people beyond.

(We're coming. Help is coming.)

(Good,) a thought voice replied. (We still have hydrient, but were considering the digestibility of the most recent corpses when the stones began their song.)

(You have been here a long time?)

(An eternity, it seems. We stocked these tunnels long ago with emergency provisions, but we were thinking in terms of days – weeks, perhaps months. It has been over a year since the Khleevi came to rip this planet apart.)

(I take it that this world is your home, then?)

(We are musicians who serve the stones. Their home is our adopted home. To serve them is our great honor.)

(You serve them? How?)

(We are their agents to other worlds. When an ensemble has reached perfection and is ready to be heard off-world, we select it and take it to a place where it may be chosen for the honor and the wonder of all who hear it. We also help train the newly severed to reach full voice, to blend with others.)

(Fascinating. Your relationship to the stones is what caused them to set up such a racket once they made contact with the chrysoberyls and hence, with us?)

(Is that what happened? All we know is that so many began singing at once – and so badly – that we still have our fingers in our ears. Even so, I fear our perfect pitch is ruined. It's a good thing you're telepathic, or we wouldn't know you were here.)

(You didn't hear the drill?)

(Drill?)

(Well, keep your fingers in your ears a bit longer and we'll have you out. Stay to the back of the space you're in now. Once the opening is visible, come out quickly. We have no idea how stable the walls will be once the rubble is cleared.)

(How many of you are there, anyway?)

(Many fewer than came down here originally,) the voice answered. (Maybe three hundred now? Oh, no, make that two hundred and ninety nine. Fkara's youngest died after the stones' first lament).

(So many!) Acorna thought, (And yet, for the entire – er – nonmineral population of a planet . . .)

(As I said, we are not the planet's inhabitants. The stones are. On this entire world there were only twice our present number. Fortunately, most of us found shelter before the invasion. And, equally fortunately, you have now come to our rescue.)

Using the drill's remote laser guide, Acorna pointed the drill at the blockage from the cave-in. Its laser quickly sliced through the first barrier. Shutting it down, Acorna crawled through the hole and guided the tip once more at the pile of boulders blocking the tunnel. (Stand back,) she told the people behind the rubble. (You don't want this drill's beam to mistake you for a rock.)

When she sensed that there was enough room between the cave-in and its victims, she activated the drill and made an opening large enough for a person to climb through. She fused the edges, withdrew the drill, and helped the first of the cave's occupants scramble toward freedom.

The light on her miner's helmet caught the face of a humanoid female who looked little different than the women of Kezdet, except that her ears were unusually large, long, and pointed at both lobe and crest.

(Send them out to us, Khornya,) Neeva said. (Feriila and I will help them to the area where Captain Becker can use the *Condor*'s tractor beam to raise them to the surface.)

This rescue had become a real family effort for the women of Acorna's line. The thought deepened Acorna's smile as she greeted the rescuees. Not that they could see it, but her smile was there, all the same.

It seemed to take hours to free everyone, and at the end the last few able-bodied people stayed to help those too young, too old, or simply too weak to walk out under their own steam. Mostly the last, since those too young or too old to fend for themselves had not survived the ordeal.

Finally, Acorna joined her mother and Neeva as they watched the last group ascend to the surface. As the soles of their feet disappeared, Acorna heaved a sigh of relief. From the surface came a chiming, a humming, a happy tuneful greeting from the stones. Mission successful.

(Khornya?) her mother asked, rather shyly. (That's what they call you, isn't it? Khornya? Aari calls you that.)

(Yes,) she answered. (My foster fathers named me Acorna because of my horn – no one else has one where we . . . they . . . come from. But when

Neeva and the *Balakiire* crew found me, it seemed impossible for them to say Acorna, so our people call me Khornya.)

(I was going to name you Aliliiya, after your grandam, but Khornya suits you.)

(You must tell me more about my grandam sometime,) Acorna said. (Grandam Naadiina told me a few things, but we had so little time together that I didn't get to ask everything I wanted.)

(I am so pleased you've come to know Grandam Naadiina. How is she?)

Neeva and Acorna exchanged looks in a darkness lit only by the lights on their heads.

'Oh, no,' Feriila said, reading them. (It hardly seems possible. She has always been there, as long as anyone can remember.)

They both sent her the thought-pictures they had received from other survivors of the Khleevi attack on narhii-Vhiliinyar, where Grandam had given her life to save an Ancestor, an *aagroni*, and almost more importantly, the *aagroni*'s precious specimens of the DNA taken from life-forms from old Vhiliinyar.

'I suppose many things have changed since I last saw you,' Feriila said aloud, sighing. 'From my point of view, you are grown now, and mated, daughter, when only moments ago we kissed you good-bye before placing you in the escape pod. Aari is a fine young male, of course. We both find it really remarkable how much he has learned about manipulating time and space.'

'Yes,' Acorna agreed. 'Remarkable. Incredible, really.'

'You are troubled about him, daughter. I sensed great passion from him toward you when he spoke of you, but you seem unhappy. I realize it must be hard for you to think of me as your mother, as someone you can confide in, but—'

'Oh, no!' Acorna cried, reaching out to touch her hand. 'You have always been a part of me, you and Father both . . .'

'The truth is,' Neeva told her sister humorously, 'you are probably the only Linyaari living who is not privy to Khornya's feelings on this matter. She tends to broadcast in a wide band, even her bad dreams.'

'Well, yes, I keep confusing Aari with a Khleevi in my dreams, or Aari bringing the Khleevi or something. It gets all mixed up. Of course, nothing could be farther from the truth, and the Khleevi are all dead now but . . .' Acorna tried to explain to her mother how Aari had come back after his voyages in time changed so much, how he wasn't the post-Khleevi Aari with whom she had shared adventures. She told her mother about this Aari, who never had that experience, whose horn was whole, who was unscathed by torture. 'In order to return as he did, he wiped out everything that happened afterwards, including me. He knew of me and of our bond only by hearsay, really. His friend Grimalkin, of whom he speaks constantly and worshipfully, made him make a record of the old Aari's memories to refer to.'

'Ewwww,' her mother said, as if she had just stepped in dung. 'No wonder you're upset, child.'

'It's almost as if time sent back the wrong person,' Acorna complained. And then listened to herself. 'You know, Mother, Gill (he's one of my foster fathers) used to tell me some of the stories from Eire, where his ancestors lived on Old Terra. His people shared the island with another race of beings who had lived there before them. Those people were magical and lived under the ground. They were mischievous and sometimes malicious. One of the things they did was to steal human children and replace them with one of their children. They would look the same, but . . . they weren't the same. They were called changelings.'

'Oh, that would never happen with a Linyaari,' Feriila said.

'You sound so sure, Mother,' Acorna said with a sigh as she held her female family within the circle of light from her helmet.

'Of course I am,' Feriila said. 'We have our birth disks after all.' She reached into the neck of her shipsuit and pulled forth a double-sided metal locket that even in the dim light reflected several colors. 'This is yours,' she said proudly. 'It's hermetically sealed, but inside is a tiny snippet of your umbilical cord. The design on the edge here' – her broad fingernail indicated looping scrollwork delicately etched along the closure – 'is your DNA code. Should any of us become lost, or should any Linyaari bodies be discovered in a place or time where they were not recognized, the mother or mate of any missing Linyaari would only need to compare the code on the locket to that of the body to know.'

'Oh,' Acorna said, touching the one she wore. 'Aari's mother gave me his. I had no idea there was more than a sentimental purpose to them, though.'

Neeva shook her head in exasperation. 'That Miiri! Such a romantic! She's a scientist. You'd think she'd have imparted the scientific reason for the disks.'

'Okay, below, all aboard!' Becker called down to them.

The three of them stepped to the spot where the tractor beam lifted them to the surface. It was not a particularly pleasant sensation. Acorna felt as if her horn was about to be sucked off and her mane pulled out of her scalp. Her suit rode up around her neck and pulled at the arms and legs where the fabric tried to rise more quickly than the rest of her.

(I should have brought one of Aziza's antigravity belts,) she told Neeva.

When they reached the surface, Mac moved the beam to the edge of the pit and deposited them among the refugees, who resembled large-eared humanoid skeletons, thanks to their long imprisonment, and the crooning stones. The stones sang a song of welcome and joy. Some of the humanoids tried to sing with them, but they were very weak indeed.

(Sorry about the tune, folks,) one of them said. (It's true that musicians are usually hungry, and it only makes their voices finer. But I think we've gone a bit beyond that right now.)

(You poor things!) Acorna said, contrite that she had been dwelling on her own problems instead of focusing on the far more urgent ones of those around her. (We really didn't rescue you from starvation below just so you could starve on the surface.) Aloud she said, 'These people need food and water. How much have we aboard the ships?'

'We used almost all the water and raw materials aboard the *Condor* to make the glue for the stones,' Rafik told her. 'We reserved enough to feed ourselves for the voyage home, of course, but that's about it.'

'We have ample stores for our usual crew on the *Balakiire*,' Neeva said. 'But of course, it is our food, and they may not find it nourishing. Besides, we don't have enough to feed this many people. However, once we harvest we could start growing more. It will, of course, take time.'

RK clawed his way up to Becker's shoulder and sat glaring at Aari.

'Oh, yeah, we've got the c-a-t-f-o-o-d,' Becker said, holding his hand between his mouth and RK's face. 'If they leave enough for the first mate, he'll probably share, as long as nobody tells him about it.'

'That won't be enough to support this many people until we return from our mission,' Rafik said. 'And we may lose some more of them by the time Hafiz can send provisions.'

Becker scratched his perpetually bewhiskered chin. 'Well, the supply has lasted us several years already, but we gave some away to the cats on Makahomia. I've done some fancy navigating out here since I met up with Aari and Acorna and the rest of you folks. I could probably make it out to MOO and back before any of Hafiz's folks that weren't following my course.' He nodded toward Neeva. 'But even with every shortcut I know, it still takes us almost thirty watches to get here – that's what? Seven standard Kezdet days? Then there's the trip back. I don't think the cat food will last this mob that long.'

(Perhaps one of the nearby planets has something we could eat?) the fellow who had spoken to Acorna before suggested when she transferred the conversation into thought-images for him. She quickly returned images of the other planets they had seen. (That bad, huh? Worse off than we are.)

Aari said eagerly, 'But there's no problem, really. I – we can go for the supplies and be back before you come out of the hole.'

'Who's "we," buddy?' Becker asked, his deliberately calm, soft tone indicating he had had about enough of Aari doing fancier tricks with time than he himself could using the wormholes and warpings in space.

'Oh, uh, Grimalkin, of course. He's in the ship that brought Khornya's parents and me here. I will simply fly the flitter back up to our ship, and he can return us to MOO. He could return us there before we left and we will know to load up with many extra provisions this time, enough to feed all of these people for a very long time. And more.'

'There was someone else aboard besides us?' Vaanye asked. 'Where was he? I didn't see him.'

'He was sleeping during my watch,' Aari said. 'And it just happened that you slept during his.'

'But we should have met him!' Feriila exclaimed. 'After all, he was the one who taught you the skills that enabled you to save us. We should have thanked him.'

'Oh, he's – er – very shy about that sort of thing,' Aari said. 'Modest, you know how it is.'

Acorna and Becker exchanged looks. From all that they had heard about Aari's new friend up until now, he sounded anything but modest.

'Do you suppose he'd be shy with me?' Acorna asked as sweetly as she could manage. 'Because I think I'll go with you. I'd like to meet him, too.'

'Maybe when we come back,' Aari said hurriedly. 'We'll travel faster without distractions. Not that it matters how fast we go, really, with the time thing but . . . I'll just be on my way now. These people do look hungry.'

Aari edged away as he spoke. Acorna thought he looked more than nervous. He looked downright shifty. She would need to come up with a backup plan about her lifemate very soon. Something was not right about Aari, and the more he used his time-travel skills to be heroic, the less trustworthy he seemed to her.

'Wait!' she said, and grabbed him for a long horn touch, twining her fingers in his mane as they met.

He finally backed away, gulping. 'I'll be back before you can miss me,' he said, and headed for his shuttle.

Acorna turned back to the others. Becker regarded her with one eyebrow cocked. The stones were singing something that sounded suspiciously like a love song with their humanoid agents trying, despite their depleted condition, to join in over the sounds of their rumbling bellies.

Acorna held out her hand to Neeva and deposited a few white hairs in it. 'Would you ask Khaari to run a test on these for their DNA code?'

Neeva took the hairs carefully. 'Did you get those where I think you did?'

Acorna nodded.

'Then I think that might just be very interesting,' Neeva said, and walked away toward her ship. She looked back. 'Aren't you coming, Acorna?'

Mac, Becker, and Rafik began reloading the drill and other equipment. Becker stood up and stretched his back. 'I think I'd better hail Hafiz and warn him about all this. I'm not sure how this time stuff Aari does works. But I probably need to explain to Hafiz that his beneficence in providing the chow will earn him the undying gratitude of the sole agents and purveyors of the talents of the Singing Stones of Skarness.'

Rafik laughed. 'Becker, are you sure you're not related to House Harakamian somewhere way back in your birth family? You and Hafiz certainly think alike.'

Meanwhile, Neeva, Acorna, and her parents boarded the *Balakiire*. It didn't take Khaari long to run the simple test.

'Hmmm,' she said.

'Hmmm?' Acorna said. 'What do you mean by "Hmmm"?' She slipped Aari's birth disk off over her horn and handed it to Khaari. 'This is Aari's, and those hairs came from his mane just now. Do they – I mean, is he . . . Is there a match?'

'I can tell you that without even looking at the disk,' Khaari said. 'Though I will, of course. But this DNA can't belong to Aari. It's not even completely Linyaari.'

'I was afraid of that,' Acorna said. 'I don't suppose you can tell which species it does belong to?'

Khaari smiled at her. 'Don't worry. It's not Khleevi.'

Acorna groaned. 'Maybe I should wear a horn-hat when I sleep. Of course it's not Khleevi. But whose is it?'

'It bears some resemblance to ours – you see these sequences here. But this – these are feline pairings. And there are many other oddities.'

Acorna shook her head, looking skyward. 'All right,' she said. 'Who are you really, and what have you done with my lifemate?' But she was already pretty sure she knew the answer to the first question, anyway.

Somewhere on the Planet Vhiliinyar,
During the Time of the Khleevi Invasion

Aari wasn't surprised that the water trick didn't work. Mildly disappointed, but not surprised. Very well, there was no help for it but to try to find his way alone, on foot, and in the midst of the Khleevi invasion, back to the underground city. If he remained in this cave any longer, history would show that he, not Laarye, perished there of thirst and hunger.

As soon as he stepped outside the cave, he found food, of course. The small patch of green that marked the Linyaari burial grounds was kept alive by the energy still residing in the DNA of the horns and bones of the dead. He grazed hungrily, then stuffed as many tufts of grass as he could pull into his shipsuit. It occurred to him that he was being foolish to leave what could be the only source of nourishment left on Vhiliinyar, but he felt an increasing urge to vacate the cave where his brother had once died. The skin along his spine twitched with a desire to be away from there.

He had nothing besides the grass to take with him, so he took nothing else. He noted how white he looked against the dark and broken ground of his home planet. When he was out of sight of the green cemetery, he found a nice muddy, ashy place and rolled around in it, blackening his suit, skin, and mane, and rubbing liberal amounts onto his horn and face. It was not much, but it would have to do. If he came across a trail of Khleevi slime fresh enough not to be hardened he might rub a bit of that onto himself, too, repulsive as it was. If the bugs had any sense of smell, their own stench should disguise his.

He was alert, vigilant, always moving, but progressing very slowly, staying close to the ground so he might be below the sight line of a crawling Khleevi. He broadcast no cries for help to Grimalkin, to Khornya in her own time, or anyone else, in case the Khleevi's own sense for the thoughts of their fellows picked up his alien signal. Yet he tried to keep his own senses attentive for their nonverbal communications. He could recognize it, he was sure, though he detected no trace of it so far. But then, neither did he hear any of the *klik*ing and *klak*ing sounds they made with their legs and pincers when in direct communication.

He couldn't dwell on that. He couldn't emit the fear that smothered him every time he let his mind touch on what had happened the last time he was in this situation. He had learned when he fought the Khleevi before that the pheromones he exuded when he was afraid would attract them. They fed on fear and pain.

His mind kept drifting back to the time he had spent with Grimalkin, wondering why the Ancestral 'Friend' who had taken Aari under his wing would betray him and leave him behind here, where his worst nightmares had been born. Now, thanks to Grimalkin, this was no longer merely a nightmare, but reality once again.

What the frack, as Joh Becker would say, was Grimalkin up to? The creature was an empath. As such, the Friend didn't merely know what Aari felt; he actually felt all that Aari had felt during their association, unless Aari shielded from him, which he seldom did. Grimalkin had to know how hard this would be for Aari, had to feel for him. So what could have made him do this?

Aari reviewed all the conversations they'd had. Had he unintentionally mortally offended Grimalkin? So much so that the feline shape-shifter would take such fearsome revenge on him? Surely he'd have noticed something like that. But Aari could think of nothing. Mostly, they'd talked about Aari's life since the Khleevi, and especially of meeting Khornya and how they had become lifemates, joined in spirit and body. That was a joy so intense that he had never imagined it was possible for himself – especially as scarred and tortured as he had been after his misadventures with the Khleevi. Aari missed Acorna so much, and he hated being separated from her, but even so he knew she would understand that he had to try to free Laarye. Certainly

Grimalkin had understood that part of the mission. He had even carried it out while betraying Aari.

Aari could hardly believe it. Grimalkin had seemed so intrigued by Aari's stories of his courtship with Khornya. He'd laughed delightedly at the tale of the silly holograms the children of MOO had devised to finally lure the two of them into each other's arms. He'd seemed touched when Aari told him how he and Khornya helped his little sister Maati rescue their parents. And he'd declared himself thrilled and chilled by the adventures they'd had together ridding the universe of the Khleevi once and for all. But more than any adventures or stories, Grimalkin had seemed to understand just how much Aari loved his Khornya and she him. He'd understood that she was the most remarkable, brilliant, beautiful, kind, insightful, intelligent, resourceful, courageous Linyaari female he had ever met and how privileged he felt that she had chosen him. Grimalkin had even agreed that she must surely be the best specimen of womanhood of her race. Aari began to wonder if perhaps he hadn't dwelled on that a bit *too* long.

But from the first journey they made together, Grimalkin had urged him to make recordings of all of his memories of the time since his capture. Aari recorded his reunions with family members, his rescue by Joh Becker and Riidkiiyi, his healing, his friendships, his adventures, his part in the victory over the Khleevi, and anything and everything to do with Khornya.

When Aari balked at committing his private memories to recorded data, Grimalkin had said in a patient, purring voice, 'I'm only thinking of your own good, son of my sons to be. I am a master of time, but even I occasionally find lapses in my memories from slipping too quickly forward or back. If you miss the synapse in the time-space helix by even a fraction of a nano-second, you may become disoriented and never recover all of the moments of your life. Recording them is the best way to make sure you have them always.'

'Is that what you do?' Aari had asked him.

'Oh, yes, but my device is much more sophisticated. I use it constantly, recording everything as it happens. With visuals, as well as olfactory and other sensory data.'

'You must have had a fascinating life,' Aari said. 'I would like to see these recordings you've made.'

Grimalkin had grinned his sly grin, reminding Aari of RK. 'You're still too young, my boy. Wait until I've shown you a few things; then perhaps I will share certain selected passages that might amuse you. Now, this Khornya of yours, when you mate, what sort of sounds does she make?'

Ugh! Even as a memory, that question was much too personal. Aari had refused to answer Grimalkin, or even to record such intimate information. 'That is for Khornya and me to know, no one else,' he said. 'To speak of these things to others would be a betrayal of our bond.'

'No need to get all stuffy, son,' Grimalkin said with a bored-sounding yawn and a stretch. 'But if you should by ill chance lose that part of your memory in our travels, you'll be sorry. It's your life, after all. I'm just trying to help you, as I have from the start. Does she close her eyes when you touch horns or leave them open, by the way?'

For an empath, Grimalkin could be appallingly insensitive.

And he could be worse than insensitive, as Aari knew. In the right circumstances, Grimalkin could be as cruel as a cat playing with a rodent, a personality trait common to most of the Friends. Aari had seen a great deal of that before he and Grimalkin had left Makahomia. It seemed now to Aari that Grimalkin's empathy apparently extended just far enough to learn Aari's feelings, but only in order to exploit them. And perhaps to develop a prurient interest in Khornya.

But Aari knew that his Khornya would never betray him, just as he would never betray her. While Grimalkin had been busy restructuring the gene pool of Makahomia, making over the population, which was mostly from immigrant Terran stock, into his own image, Aari had recorded not memories, but messages for Khornya, to send across time, to let her know he was coming back to her.

Grimalkin, caught up in a storm of procreation

with anything female on the planet, guaranteeing feline shape-shifting offspring among at least some of them, had urged him to do likewise. 'There's room for two superior species here, my boy. And you are a hero to those females since you purified their lake. You could have your pick. They're a bit scrawny, it's true, but some of them could be quite attractive.'

Aari had declined. Later, exhausted from his exertions, Grimalkin had collapsed next to Aari and sighed. 'It must be restful, being bonded to only one female. When she's away, if you wish you can do something else.'

'We will not be wishing to do anything else for quite a while once Khornya and I are together again,' Aari said, smiling.

Grimalkin stood up, his face shadowed by the walls of the temple that his new friends had built for him.

'Leaving again so soon?' Aari asked.

'I'm suddenly *hungry,*' he said. 'I need to go pounce on something.'

This time, Aari thought, he was the one who had been pounced on.

But not by the Khleevi. Not yet. The ground beneath him shook so often that when it stopped he found himself counting silently, waiting for the next quake.

But, for the time being, he had been spared meeting the Khleevi. As far as he could see in the sun's brilliant searing light, the world around him was bleak and dead. Nothing moved on its surface, though the surface itself trembled, cracked, heaved, and spewed like someone burning with fever.

He had that wonderful Linyaari navigational sense to guide him as he inched through the parched landscape toward the underground city. What if the entrance was blocked by cave-ins from the earthquakes? The city had been above ground when he first saw it, but when he brought the *sii*-Linyaari forward in time, the city had long been buried, abandoned, and for the most part forgotten except in legend and song. But it was a real place. He had been there, and now, if only he could return there and find the time device, he could return to his own time without having to wait for Joh to rescue him again. Or for Grimalkin to reconsider and return for him.

Meanwhile, he kept very low and tried to move as quickly as possible while still maintaining his alertness and strength for the long journey. He wished he had dared to run at the first, when he still had the energy. He could have covered a great deal of ground. Though his people used spaceships and flitters, they all loved to run and could travel vast distances in the course of a day. But with the Khleevi presence, he knew he couldn't make himself so conspicuous. So instead he crept, crawled, and sometimes walked cautiously. As his food gave out, he lost strength. And he was constantly thirsty. His throat felt like the land looked.

He found a place where he and Laarye had splashed in a wide river as boys. The riverbed was now an upheaval of rocks coated with Khleevi scat and husks from the larvae the Khleevi spawned there. Looking at the wreckage from a distance, Aari shuddered. He remembered the voracious Young who frightened even the older Khleevi.

But now the riverbed was scored and stripped of everything but broken stone, which didn't surprise Aari at all. The Young devoured anything and everything of nutritional value to any known species, and only then left to devour other areas. He was fairly sure from his later experience with them that the Young probably also devoured each other as well as their elders when other food sources weren't available in abundance.

Still, remembering the river of his youth, he found it hard to believe that even in a few months, *all* of the water had gone. He found one soft place in the riverbed with less rock over it than the rest and no Khleevi slime. He dug with both hands until he ached so badly he had to run his horn over the parts he could reach to keep digging.

At last he was rewarded by a bubble of stinking, venomous-looking liquid burbling its way into the hole he had made. Cupping some in his hands, he managed to dip his horn into it before it dribbled through his quivering fingers. He drank and repeated the process until he could no longer coax more of the liquid from the ground. Then there was nothing to do but continue his journey.

Once more he counted himself lucky to have arrived after the Khleevi vacated the area. He just wished he had something – anything – to tell him where they actually were so that he could continue to avoid them.

He listened with his entire being for their *kliks* and *klaks*. Their thoughts had been incomprehensible when he first encountered them, but he now understood a great many Khleevi concepts and preoccupations. He heard no babbling of them anywhere near him and had to hope he was safe for the present.

Renewing the coating of soil on his suit, skin, and hair every few hours, Aari dared to walk upright down the riverbed. It was as good a plan as any. Rivers fed into seas. The city had been by the sea. Perhaps this riverbed would lead him to the place where the city was buried.

When he was once more too thirsty to continue, he stopped and dug in the riverbed again. He didn't have to dig as deep this time to find the liquid under the surface. That might mean that he was closer to sea level, he surmised, which was encouraging.

He walked on and on until he found a shallow cave carved into the side of the riverbank. He crawled inside and carefully scooped rubble and rocks toward him so the entrance was somewhat blocked. After his trek through the blasted landscape, he now smelled as bad as any Khleevi. He lay down on his side thinking he could at least try to rest.

Before he dropped into an exhausted doze, he wondered what made Grimalkin think he could claim Khornya, even if the Friend had left Aari stranded and alone?

Eleven

'Captain, we have an urgent message on the com unit,' Mac announced.

Acorna and her fellow Linyaari were hauling huge sheaves of grasses and flowers harvested from the *Balakiire*'s onboard gardens.

Mac, Rafik, and Becker brought out the meager stores of human food remaining on the *Condor* and four large bags of cat food. RK danced around the bags nervously, as if trying to guard them all at once.

Mac continued. 'Chief Security Officer Aziza Amunpul reports that our stones are definitely in the process of being tampered with. She inquires whether or not she and her crew should attempt to detain the suspects.'

'You didn't go near the bridge when you picked up your load of cat food, Mac. How do you know all this? Don't tell me you're establishing mental communication with the hardware on the *Condor*.'

'No, Captain. I will not tell you that. However,

I do have a surprise for you.' He opened the top of his uniform and pressed a spot where a navel might be found on a human being. Aziza's anxious face spread across his chest. 'You see? I have installed a portable com unit modification. I thought it might be useful for just such situations as the one in which we presently find ourselves. Away from the ship when an important message comes in, that is.'

'Mac, you're going to have to add about a foot to your height and get bigger around if you're going to have room on yourself for all those modifications,' Becker said. Rafik was already earnestly in conversation with Mac's electronic belly button.

'How far are they from your position, Aziza?'

The dancer, frowning with concentration, gave him the coordinates. 'That makes them about the same distance from us as you are, but coming from the opposite direction.'

'Stay put. We're on our way,' Rafik told her.

'We can't just leave these people here with four bags of cat food and a hank of grass,' Becker said. 'The way Aari talked, he ought to be back by now.'

'He may not return at all, Captain,' Acorna said. 'The creature who just promised to save these people isn't Aari.'

'You could have fooled me,' Becker said.

'And all of us as well,' Neeva told him. 'But we just ran the DNA and checked it against Aari's. That's not him.'

'It's Grimalkin,' Acorna said. 'At least, I'm pretty sure it is.'

'Where's Aari, then?'

'I'd like to know that myself,' Acorna said. 'I'm hoping he was also on board the ship my parents came on, but there's certainly been no evidence of that. If he was there, why wouldn't he let us know? I'm afraid that I believe that Grimalkin wasn't leaving in order to help us feed these people. I think that he left because he knew he was about to be caught out as an impostor. He has a lot of explaining to do, but I suppose answering questions right now didn't fit in with his plans.'

'All I can say is he picked a lousy time to turn out to be somebody else,' Becker growled. Then he repeated himself, shouting. The refugees were making a lot of noise, what with chowing down on the cat crunchies and the grass. They had descended on the food like locusts and were already polishing off most of it.

'Mac, shut your shirt and let's go use the real thing to call Hafiz.'

'We can remain here to help these people,' Vaanye said. 'The *Balakiire* gardens will grow more food within twenty-four hours.'

(Can your people exist on salad for a while?) Acorna asked the refugees in general.

(It's better than—) one began, but interrupted himself with sudden convulsive vomiting. Several of the others began doing the same thing.

'What?' Becker asked, alarmed. 'The food we

have doesn't agree with them? But I ate those cat crunchies myself!'

'No, Captain,' Neeva assured him as she steadied the nearest sickly refugee, seeming accidentally to touch him with her horn. 'They've simply been eating too fast on stomachs too long deprived of food.'

Acorna and the others surreptitiously healed the refugees with horn touches. As well as curing the starving people of nausea, the healing stopped the hungry people from wasting more precious nutrients.

(You white-horned people are very comforting to have around,) the musician she'd been speaking with in the hole said. (I don't suppose any of you are musically inclined and would like to stay with us?)

(We can all stay with you if you like, until relief comes,) Neeva told him. (Captain Becker has gone to call Uncle Hafiz for it now.)

(I would like to complete the mission on the sulfur planet and return to Vhiliinyar as soon as possible,) Acorna said. (I'm worried about Aari now. Grimalkin must have done something to him or with him to conceal the ruse, whatever the reason for *that* was. And I'm afraid that even if they were friends, as Aari thought, and Grimalkin meant no harm, that creature's judgment just isn't very good.)

(It certainly is not!) Neeva agreed. (He may not be a Khleevi, but it would be just like him to endanger us all by going back in time and finding one just to see what they were like.)

Acorna shivered. (I hope my dreams were only dreams and not a vision of what that creature has done to Aari. I can't bear to think of him back in the clutches of the Khleevi.)

Aari was wrong, Grimalkin decided. His Khornya was a hard-hearted, horn-headed filly who was not worth the effort. No matter how he courted her, she rejected him. He felt distinctly unappreciated and aggrieved. He would have got on better with her if he'd taken over that very territorial ship cat, RK. She cuddled with *him* readily enough.

He supposed he might as well return to Vhiliinyar and fetch Aari from the cave. As for his purported mission to get food for the people of Skarness, as far as he was concerned, that had been mostly an excuse to escape from Acorna's penetrating gaze. Though that last horn touch she'd given him had been almost enough to make him stay, he'd sensed an ulterior motive on her part. Such abrupt changes in behavior, when he did them at least, were usually part of some sort of trick.

But now he was back in space, where he was responsible for no one and to no one. He could go his own way.

He lay on the broad windowsill in front of his viewport. As usual, when he viewed the stars, he wished he could rearrange them to his own liking. They were so *random*.

He really needed to go retrieve Aari. He had one last trick to play before returning to his friend, however. Those chrysoberyls were his by rights. Aari had made them from the contaminants in the Makahomian sacred lake. What nobody realized or at least remembered was that to begin with they had been just unattractive rocks. Fortunately for the planet, Grimalkin had a sense of myth and story. He had rearranged the molecules so that the rocks would always resemble the gleam in his own eyes. And as he and Aari departed their worshipers, Grimalkin had added one more mythic touch, blasting a long valley in each of the planet's moons and setting each slightly off its axis. This gave the moons a slightly irregular orbit so they would align closely enough every so often, and the valleys would fill with shadow while the rest of the moons' surface reflected the red sunlight. It was a lovely and mysterious sight, one that the Makahomians still trembled to see. Grimalkin licked the back of his hand and passed it over his face. His eyes really were, if not his best features, then his favorite among his many attractive personal attributes.

Poor Khornya. The wench had no idea what she was missing. It wasn't as if he meant to take her away from Aari. He'd just wanted to borrow her for a little while to get the species started. If she wasn't so distrustful and particular, she probably wouldn't have known the difference. He had hoped, actually, to feel some of the emotion he drank in from Aari when the lovesick boy talked about her. If his recent experiences were any indication, well, mostly he couldn't see what all the fuss was about. Yes, she was an interesting member of her species, but she was not so special she could really afford to go turning down the advances of interested males, especially a male whom she had every reason to believe was her chosen mate.

Grimalkin would just have to find another way to capture her and Aari's particular genes for the future of their race – the race he would brilliantly create where his fellow scientists had failed.

But meanwhile, there were those chrysoberyls, down there among beings that had no use for them, or any appreciation for them, at all. He decided to lurk back in time a few days and wait to intercept the thief. That was the when. Now he just had to find out where to lurk. Again, that was no problem, except that the spot he needed to occupy was presently filled with Aziza Amunpul's ship, the *Ali Baba*. What to do . . . What to do ...

'Hi, y'all. Anybody hungry?' asked the voice from inside the front of Mac's shipsuit.

Becker stopped in his tracks and in midgrowl. 'Honey-bunny?' he asked. 'Is that you, Andina?'

'You bet your sweet rolls, Jonas. Speaking of which, I have a full cargo of cooking supplies and equipment along with the basic food groups for the ten primary types of alien and humanoid found within the Federation and the immediate vicinity of Vhiliinyar.'

'Don't tell me you're going all psychic on me, too, sweetie . . .' Becker said. 'How did you know we were going to have three hundred extra mouths to feed?'

'I knew you were on a rescue mission. In my experience, there is always *somebody* who gets very hungry, even if it's only the rescuers. I wasn't sure if I was supposed to cook for rocks or not, since it was the Singing Stones sounding the alarm, but I came prepared for all eventualities.'

'Thank goodness someone thought of it,' Neeva said with relief.

The musical refugees happily supplied a list of their normal dietary requirements and preferences. Mac relayed it to Andina, who very shortly set the *Heloise* down on the other side of the *Condor* from the *Balakiire*. Her staff immediately set up a soup-kitchen-type operation, three of them serving, while a fourth staff member handed out dishes and a fifth herded the refugees into line. Andina and her personnel grew a bit sharp with the customers when they refused to allow them to stack up Singing Stones to a height suitable for seating. But, even without handy seating, food was soon in the hands of those who needed it.

'That seems to be well in hand,' Neeva said aloud. (Feriila, Vaanye, as much as I hate to, perhaps I should eschew your company for now. Khornya urgently needs to return to Vhiliinyar. I know you want to spend time with her. So it seems to me that you might want to accompany her on her journey.)

(We will go with her and her human friends,) Vaanye told her. (Until we meet on Vhiliinyar, lifemate-sister.)

The three of them touched horns in farewell.

Becker returned from bidding Andina a fond farewell. 'She is so great. She always knows what people are going to need,' he said, wondering how she did it.

Acorna was wondering about that, too. She was wondering just how, in this particular instance, Andina had known that food would be needed right here, right now.

As an empath, Grimalkin had felt many borrowed emotions, but he had never acquired the knack for guilt. He didn't worry about his promise to return with food or with ships that had food for the refugees. He could always attend to that, if he decided to, later, with a time shift.

He made a slight one now, back to the time of Smythe-Wesson's drop of the chrysoberyls, cloaking his ship to escape the notice of both the thief and the sulfur beings. He watched the whole thing, from when Smythe-Wesson sliced up the first group of Solids to the decapitation of the volcano and the treelike Solids of the wedding party, to the burial of the catseye stones. As he watched, he began to understand

Smythe-Wesson better and to guess at his plan. It gave him an amusing idea.

He had already discarded the notion of retrieving the stones before Aziza was sent to guard them. To do so would negate the mission to Skarness and his coup of presenting Acorna's parents to her. Not that Acorna deserved all the trouble he had gone to after her repeated rebuffs of his affection, but he was justifiably proud of what he had pulled off and had no wish to undo it. Or not right away, at least. The only thing he did while he was waiting for time to catch up with him again took place after the *Condor* approached the sulfur planet and made contact with Aziza. Once the *Condor* was well away, Grimalkin, as Aari, hailed MOO and tipped them off that there were humanoids on Skarness who needed feeding.

Too bad the sulfur beings weren't humanoids. Grimalkin had no trouble shifting his own shape, or that of certain other things, but after he saw the reception Rafik got from the sulfurians he decided that he'd do better to stay off the surface of the planet, if possible.

He zoomed in, extending both the very sensitive monitors on his ship and his own psychic receptors as he watched the sulfur beings attempt to destroy Rafik and his vessel. He plucked up the data Mac gathered on the communications of the aliens and his analysis of it, and 'overheard' Acorna's reception of the sulfur beings' emotional outpourings.

These creatures were a bit too alien, even for someone of Grimalkin's universality. Grimalkin had difficulty figuring them out. He had never met any individual of any race of beings who didn't want *something,* but he was sure these creatures did, too. At least some of them did. They were themselves, at least some of them, shape-shifters, so what else could he offer them? Something. There had to be something.

Ah, yes. The same old godhead thing really, except this time he wasn't about to join with anyone to spread his glory along with his seed. The sulfur people were not a species he cared to mate with. However, he could temporarily make himself over in their image – at least in the consciousness of those he wished to contact. Creating a form that resembled what he gathered from the sulfurous masses below was considered the noblest and most elevated among the Sulfurians, a Mutable, he projected this image of himself to the audience he had selected from among their number.

'Hear me, you Liquids,' he transmitted in a mind voice suggestive of explosions and frantic boiling bubbles as the image of himself shifted from one of the treelike victims of Smythe-Wesson to a rocklike Solid and on through Liquid form until returning to the original. 'Why should you who can assume the form of any container you allow to hold you be bound by the edicts of other forms? Heed my words and I will deliver you from your bondage and give you the form you most desire.'

'What are you? Some kind of container?' the hissing Liquid consciousness inquired.

'I am far more than that. Heed me and you will never again be dependent upon a container for your shape. Never again shall you spend your substance, losing precious molecules as you become acid spray to fight the battles of the Mutables and the Solids.'

'But you are a Mutable,' they observed suspiciously.

'Not *a* Mutable. I am the great Mutator. I have the power to change all beings. I can change you from Liquids to Solids if you wish, and back again, making you as great as any except myself.'

'Prove it. Change us to Solids now.'

'But if you are Solids and Mutables, who shall be beneath you? Who shall spray the acid to protect the memorial of the fallen and the stones that lie under it?'

'It's true. It's true. Only Liquids can do that.'

'Cannot the Mutables become Liquid?'

'They can, but you'd never catch them wasting their drops to spray acid. They leave that to us. But when you make us like them, they'll have to, won't they?'

'I *could* in fact, stabilize their forms so they can no longer mutate. If they should become Liquid, while you become Mutable, your positions would be reversed.'

Malevolent acidic glee bubbled up from the beings below. 'Do it! Do it!'

Grimalkin's sulfurically impressive thought-form gave the local version of a shrug. 'I will change you. Can you change them?'

The Liquids formed a whirlpool of consultation.

'What are you up to? That is not the proper formation for guarding the memorial!' a delegation of Mutables informed the Liquids.

'You know how we are without a container,' the Liquids replied slyly. 'We forget all about the proper form. You had better show us again.'

Whereupon the Mutables turned into Liquids to demonstrate. Grimalkin froze the lot of them, turning them all temporarily Solid, and used his own tractor beam to extract the chrysoberyls from the war memorial. Once he had the stones aboard the ship, he rolled them around and played with them when he didn't actually have to navigate. Then it was time to play with Smythe-Wesson.

Twelve

'Listen,' Becker said, turning the com unit up several decibels and cupping his hand over his ear.

'What?' Rafik asked. 'There's nothing to hear.'

'Yeah. Ain't it great? No rock music. Just nice, empty, silent space.'

And at that moment, Aziza's face appeared on the screen. 'That traitor cur Smythe-Wesson is closing in, *Condor*. Are you detecting his signal yet?'

'Oh, yeah,' Becker said, nodding at the small blinking image appearing on three out of ten of the screens of his current scanner array. 'With these babies I can practically count his nose hairs. I'm not getting any noises from our amps any longer though, are you?'

'We are not. But then, he is not yet close enough to interfere with them. As long as everything is as it should be, we will hear nothing, yes?'

'That's the general idea,' Becker said.

Acorna had been following this conversation with a sense of unease. At first she attributed it to her anxiety over Aari – the real Aari. But as the ship drew nearer to the sulfur world, she realized she was picking up on something else altogether.

'Captain, doesn't it strike you that the Sulfurian planet is a bit *too* quiet?' She indicated the area of the central scanner where once a small red light had pulsed. 'You see? No homing beacon coming from there.'

'Well, I'll be spaced!' Becker said. 'She's right!'

'She usually is,' Rafik said. 'It's a habit with her. But look – the signal is coming from that ship instead.' He indicated an image of the second of two vessels approaching the sulfur planet. Its pale green icon bore a pulsing red heart.

'Smythe-Wesson must have doubled back while we were on MOO and retrieved the stones, before Aziza took up her post here. But I don't see how he got past the sulfur beings this time unless he finished them all off. Are you getting any sense of their status, Acorna, or are we too far away?'

She took a moment to concentrate on the sulfur beings. 'They are exhibiting a new emotional pattern for them,' she said when she had finally decided what the information she was receiving indicated.

'Happiness?' Rafik guessed.

'Peace in the universe and goodwill to all species?' Becker guessed.

'Nothing *that* uncharacteristic,' Acorna told

them. 'They seem to be even more furious than ever. But what they feel now is, in some cases, a *suppressed* fury. But I don't know why they feel that way. All I'm picking up is emotion, not thoughts. I'll tell you as soon as I pick up any specific expressions for Mac to translate.'

She continued concentrating on the planet's inhabitants as the *Condor* came within its orbit. It seemed to her that the Sulfurians had been cheated in some way and were bickering more bitterly with each other than they had before.

She was startled to see two unfamiliar ships occupying a large portion of the viewport's screen, obscuring the view of the planet below.

No, that was wrong. Only one of the ships was truly unfamiliar. The other very much resembled the derelict ships she had glimpsed docked beside the underground lake on Vhiliinyar. Host ships.

'Who's that?' Rafik asked.

'I think it's a Host ship, which means it probably has something to do with Grimalkin,' Acorna said.

'Then all that talk of his about returning to MOO to get food was just talk.'

'Maybe, 'Acorna said. 'But I suppose he could have consulted history, which seems to be his answer to a lot of problems, and learned that Andina would arrive on Skarness in time to feed everyone.'

'But that doesn't explain what he's doing here,' Becker said.

'Perhaps if we hail him, he will explain,' Mac suggested reasonably.

'Or give us some kind of cock-and-bull story,' Becker pointed out. 'I can guess which is more likely.'

Meanwhile, Acorna was sending out a hail of her own to Aari, in case Grimalkin had him aboard the ship. This time her whole heart was in her message. She imagined her own Aari, not changed, not having betrayed her by abandoning their brief life together and all memories of it in exchange for an earlier, more physically complete self. Aari Whole-Horn was a fraud! The thought brought her relief and worry at the same time. Relief that Grimalkin's interpretation of Aari was not the only version of her beloved she was ever likely to see again, and at the same time the fear that if Aari was still missing, he was in some terrible danger Grimalkin had yet to reveal.

Or worse.

'Has either ship identified itself yet, Aziza?' Rafik asked the security chief.

'No, but neither have I. That is why I am cloaked, is it not?'

'You have a good point,' he said.

But Acorna had tuned out of the conversation going on around her. Another conversation on a tight band only her telepathy could penetrate had her full attention.

Smythe-Wesson said, 'The stones are right down there. Under that pile of limbs.'

'You expect me to take that on faith, do you?'

asked Grimalkin's voice, now not even vaguely like Aari's. It was higher and more nasal. 'I do not buy concealed items. I will need to inspect them to make sure they are of the size and quality you claimed. The syndicate I represent doesn't need any more stones of the ordinary variety you showed me. I came out here only because you guaranteed you could deliver something remarkable.'

'Of course. Of course. I will descend low enough to engage my tractor beam. I assure you, you will be not merely satisfied, but astounded.'

'Yes, yes. Carry on,' Grimalkin said. But meanwhile, Acorna picked up on another communication from him.

'O ye Liquids that were and ye Mutables that are, We have returned.'

All of the pent-up fury of the Sulfurians focused on the mental voice.

Acorna had not, apparently, been the only victim of Grimalkin's tricks.

'What? Don't tell me you are dissatisfied with our bargain. Have I not made you equal with the Mutables?'

Acorna suddenly had a vision of translucent yellow puslike substances frozen in place as more solid, foamy-looking yellow substances, also frozen, towered above. Ah, so that explained the rather caged feeling she had received in connection with the Sulfurian rage. Grimalkin had frozen in place both Liquids and Mutables as they transformed to Liquids. She had no way of knowing what the original bargain was. She only knew that the Sulfurians felt Grimalkin had violated it.

In her mind's eye she saw Grimalkin, that cat-man shape she once saw in a dream and later in a petroglyph, lounging on the broad ledge of his ship's viewport, his furred head yellowish from the reflected glow of the sulfur world. Casually, he deployed a low-intensity laser beam that thawed the chemical freeze he'd performed on the Liquids and the Mutables in Liquid form. 'Satisfied now?'

They weren't, of course.

She took in as much as she could stand, then sighed and told the others, 'I hate to say this, but even if he is a thief, I don't think we can leave Smythe-Wesson to Grimalkin and the Sulfurians.'

'Why not?' Becker asked indignantly, but he didn't stop her as she toggled the com unit.

'Smythe-Wesson,' Acorna said. 'This is the *Condor*. We have been deputized by House Harakamian to arrest you for the theft of the chrysoberyls from the Moon of Opportunity.'

'What chrysoberyls?' Smythe-Wesson asked. 'I am in pursuit of the thieves – those belly dancers the cleaning lady so unwisely brought to the Moon of Opportunity.'

Aziza shrieked indignantly, 'Son of a syphilitic she-camel, do you think Lady Acorna is a fool to be taken in by your lies? For the past few weeks we "belly dancers" have been pursuing *you*.'

Both the *Condor* and the *Ali Baba* dropped their cloaks.

'Now that you've caught me, what do you propose to do?' Smythe-Wesson demanded. 'I did save out a few of the chrysoberyls to modify my armaments and, using them, I assure you I could cut you into pieces too small to interest another salvage ship.'

'Pah!' Aziza spat. 'Do you think Lord Hafiz did not think of that? We also have terrible weapons employing the gems.'

'Impossible. I have all the ones you stole from the warehouse.'

'Ah, but we were not so bold as to steal the gems from Lady Karina's person,' Aziza told him. 'And those were of a size and purity that make highly accurate and effective weapons. Shall I demonstrate, Lord Rafik?'

Acorna appreciated the bravado of her companions but, knowing something they had no way of knowing, interrupted. 'Who is your companion, Smythe-Wesson?'

'An ally. A customer.'

Grimalkin, who disliked being talked about instead of directing the discussion himself, interjected, 'An impatient customer. Deal with these people later, Smythe-Wesson. I am anxious to see the merchandise. I will keep them at bay while you retrieve it.'

'Don't do it, Smythe-Wesson,' Acorna felt compelled to warn him. 'The stones are no longer there.'

'Where are they, then? Don't tell me you've retrieved them already? How could you have?'

'It would have been easy, if we'd been in time,' she told him. 'There was a homing beacon embedded in each stone and visible only to ships cued with its code, as we are. That beacon is now coming from your so-called customer's ship. He poses a much greater danger to you than we do.'

'An old ploy, my friend,' Grimalkin said. 'Divide and conquer. Why would I follow you to acquire the stones if I already have them?'

Acorna had no wish to bandy words with Grimalkin or argue with him over his manufactured version of events. Hoping Smythe-Wesson had some smidgen of telepathic sensitivity and sense of self-preservation, she sent him images of what had happened to Rafik in the past, and of what Grimalkin had arranged for him below. She also sent him clear images of the pile of chrysoberyls lying in somewhat scattered disarray on the bridge of Grimalkin's vessel. Some of them were rolling around, and he swatted at them in a rather bored manner.

Her hunch paid off. She got a response to her imaging.

(Why?) Smythe-Wesson wondered.

(Good question. Our current theory is that he's a sociopath,) Acorna replied. (He enjoys manipulating events and people and he doesn't care who is injured by his actions. Compared to him, you are almost an honest man. I suggest strongly that you surrender yourself to Aziza's tender mercies before having any further dealings with Grimalkin.)

To make certain he understood the peril awaiting him, she concentrated again on what had happened to Rafik. However, she substituted images of Smythe-Wesson for her foster father before sending the images to him. She also included some of the sentiments the Sulfurians had expressed regarding the man who had massacred their fellows.

Smythe-Wesson did not scare easily, but the waking nightmare Acorna planted in his head was enough to convince him. Shuddering, he said, 'I surrender.' Acorna picked up a brief impression that as soon as the man was out of danger from Grimalkin, he would probably cease to be so cooperative, but she would leave that to Aziza and the others. She had other priorities at the moment.

'Space your weapons,' Aziza demanded, and when the laser cannon drifted slowly out of an airlock, Aziza locked a tractor beam on the vessel.

'That was no fun at all,' Becker complained. 'I don't know what you did, Princess, but you somehow averted all the burning, bloodshed, violence, and the many explosions that I was counting on to gladden my heart.'

'Yes,' Rafik agreed. 'Good job, Acorna. The sulfur people will never forgive you if they learn you warned Smythe-Wesson away, but good job nonetheless.'

She nodded distractedly and hailed Grimalkin's ship. 'I want a word with you,' she said severely.

'Haven't you said enough already? I was about to see justice done, and you spoiled it all.'

'I have no time for that. I want to know *where* Aari is, and *when*, and I want to know it now, in the present timeline, immediately. If not sooner.'

'Keep your horn on,' Grimalkin said irritably. 'He's perfectly safe back on Vhiliinyar.'

'He'd better be,' Acorna said, sounding positively *ka*-Linyaari, and certainly not pacifistic in the least.

The *Condor* closed the distance to the Host ship. Grimalkin, in his Aari guise, appeared on the screen of the com unit. 'Khornya,' he said in what was meant to be a soothing, gentle tone, 'be reasonable—'

'Take off his face,' she said in the closest to a growl Rafik or Becker had ever heard from her. *'And don't call me Khornya. It's Lady Harakamian-Li to you.'*

Grimalkin morphed before their eyes into the shape of a small and, as he no doubt hoped, adorable kitten with a black spot over one wide green eye. (I'll give you back the stones. I only wanted to help you get them back.) He was using thought transference with her while her shipmates heard pathetic, plaintive mewing. RK, who had awakened from a nap, stopped in mid-stretch and hopped up on the console. He hissed and took a swipe at the kitten on the screen.

(As far as I'm concerned, the matter of the stones is between you and Hafiz. My business with you is more important at this moment. I want Aari back, and I want him back now – or, since you are who you are – sooner. Where is he? What have you done with him?)

'Maybe I'd better lock the tractor beam onto that guy,' Becker said. 'At least until he hands over the stones.'

But the Host ship had already winked out. Acorna caught only a whisper of a thought. (We'll meet you on Vhiliinyar.)

Grimalkin shuddered. Perhaps he had done Aari a favor by leaving him behind. That Khornya! Personally, he would rather have faced the Sulfurians or the Khleevi than that Linyaari female in a snit.

And she had nothing to be upset about, really. He would just go back and collect Aari at the cave. They would return the stones. Aari would no doubt rush back to the arms of his female, and Grimalkin would simply look elsewhere for his DNA samples. He could use Laarye now, and Acorna's parents. All of them had sufficient cause to be grateful to him, and they were close enough to his chosen subjects so as to make no difference in his genetic master plan. Though he thought maybe he should tinker with the material from Acorna's parents and eliminate the factors that produced such unbecoming stubbornness and suspicion in their offspring.

What had she called him when speaking to that criminal, that thief from whom he, Grimalkin, was trying to protect her property? Oh, yes, a sociopath. Ungrateful kit! Why, any of his other females would have been thrilled to the roots of their tails if he had deigned to do them any of the favors he had done for Acorna. *They* would have been pleased if he'd so much as stuck around to inspect his spawn once they bore them. But not her! Some people were so heartless, so unfair. He mewed inside to think of her cruelty. Poor, poor Aari really would be better off in that cave, except . . . well, the fellow didn't actually have enough food to last much longer.

Grimalkin had never intended for Aari to remain there for so long. The Linyaari was a likable fellow, and his companionship had been stimulating. Never in his wildest imaginings had Grimalkin thought it would take so long to impersonate him, seduce the female, then, before she knew what had happened, substitute the real Aari with a few implanted suggestions that would make both of them think Aari was the one who had been carnally reunited with Acorna. It was all Acorna's fault for being so much trouble. Otherwise, Aari would have been free long before this, neither of them the wiser, and no harm done. And, of course, Grimalkin would have what he came for.

He glimpsed Restoration-era Vhiliinyar briefly from orbit before setting his wrist timer and returning to when he had retrieved Laarye. He'd given Aari a mental suggestion that acted as a light sedative, and left him food and drink. Laarye, of course, had thought that Grimalkin was Aari and indeed, Grimalkin's version of Aari was more like the Aari Laarye had known when they found the cave together than was the real Aari, sobered as he was by his ordeal with the Khleevi. Even Aari's parents were fooled.

Oh, well, he never intended to be Aari indefinitely anyway. That would have been a bore. He set the ship down near the green graveyard, put an expression of extreme worry and concern on his face, disembarked, and entered the cave.

'Aari? My friend, where are you? It's me, Grimalkin. I've come to rescue you and take you back to your family and your mate.'

But the cave was empty. The grasses Grimalkin had left behind were gone, the water bottle was empty, and there were fresh scratches on the walls marking off the time. But . . . no Aari.

Flashes of lightning illuminated the cave's dry, dusty interior. Thunder and avalanche rumbled nearby. While he'd orbited the planet, Grimalkin had observed the frequent quakes that split the ground as if the planet were some fragile bit of cloth being crumbled and squashed in the fist of a giant. Rents in its fabric had opened with each cruel dig of the giant's fingers.

Not a safe place to be. Personally, Grimalkin wanted to leave as soon as possible. But if he did, he'd have to make sure and avoid the time he'd just left, or Khornya would have his pelt.

He returned to the ship and hopped into the flitter, after first loading it with the infrared tracking device. Although, with the ground cracking open and magma spilling out of every pore of the planet's surface, he wasn't sure that heat-seeking was a good way to find the boy. He lost the trail only a mile or so from the cave. Thoughtfully, he circled the area, keeping his eye on the scanners for any sign of Aari.

Volcanic eruptions shot fire and smoke all around him, clouds of ash enveloped the little flitter, and the quaking of the world unsettled him. He thought about his options. Really, this was doing things the hard way. He would just slip back a few days to before he left Aari in the cave and this time – not. He already knew that his purpose in depositing the boy there was futile. So they would do as Aari wished, retrieve Laarye, and return to Acorna's timeline . . . well, he would have to backtrack a bit, so that when she and Aari's sister first met him in Kubiilikaan it would be as Grimalkin *with* Aari instead of Grimalkin *as* Aari. All would be well.

Everyone would be the way she liked it, and she'd have no reason to be peeved with poor Grimalkin.

He started to tap his time device when his small craft was enveloped in brilliant white light.

For a moment he was startled, but then he realized that it was only lightning. That couldn't harm the flitter.

And then there was a second flash, a second

boom, and the flitter rocked madly and dived dirtward. Grimalkin was surprised, but he was not alarmed until large pincers peeled back the hatch and a giant buglike bug-eyed alien plucked him from the flitter's interior as if he was some sort of a prize.

Grimalkin looked into the thing's toothy mandibles, then glanced quickly at his wrist, which was waving around wildly as if it had nothing to do with the rest of him. He had gone back a bit farther in time than he meant to. In this time, the Khleevi were still very much present. And he, it seemed, was their latest entertainment. The Khleevi's pincers seized his wrist. He morphed to cat shape, pulled his forepaw free, and ran. But not before his time device fell to the ground at the feet of the Khleevi.

Thirteen

Aari huddled under the riverbank while the ground heaved and caved, rumpling great mounds of soil and rock up, then letting them drop below. He would find no water today, he knew. In spite of the dirt covering his hide, his skin was burned from the light of the sun through the thin atmosphere. His horn, newly grown over the place where it had once spiraled from his forehead, was little more than a stunted knot. But he had used it so often to try to heal his aches and gashes, bruises and sprains, and even fractures that it was depleted. He couldn't actually see it, since it was situated where it was and he had no mirror, nor, more's the pity, a clear pool of clean water to view it in. But he knew it would be transparent with fatigue now. *He* felt transparent with fatigue himself.

And he still had no idea of how much farther he had to go until he reached the entrance to Kubiilikaan, or how far away the nearest Khleevi patrol was.

If he could just avoid them a little longer, he knew he would cease to be in danger from them. But hunger made him feel hollow as an empty seedpod. His thirst made him brother to the cracks in the parched and blighted ground of his planet. Each explosion and rumble seemed to go right through him, so that the marrow of his bones quivered with the vibrations. He knew he was nearer to death than he was to Kubiilikaan. Once, stuck in this time and place, he would have welcomed death, but that was before he knew Khornya. Now his greatest regret was that he would not be able to tell her how much he wished they had their long Linyaari life span to live out together, to raise younglings, and explore new galaxies together.

Acorna had no intention of leaving Aari's fate in Grimalkin's careless hands.

The *Condor* made only one stop on the way to Vhiliinyar, bypassing MOO, though Acorna asked to speak to Laarye on the com unit.

'Yes, Khornya? The news you sent about Aari is very distressing, but I don't see how it could have happened. We were together almost all of the time.'

'It isn't your fault, Laarye, and I know he's glad you're safe, wherever he is, but the – creature – who enabled him to return for you has more layers of motive than Vhiliinyar has layers of soil and rock from surface to core. What I need to know from you is the time – when did they rescue you? Can you recall?'

'My chrono was broken when I had my accident, I'm afraid.'

'The ship's instruments, once you were aboard – or the log. Did you see anything when you first boarded that would have indicated the precise time of day, moons' phases, or rotation?'

'Oh, yes. Our Star had set on the horizon and neither of the moons was up. Of course, it was very difficult to tell, planetary conditions being what they were . . .'

'I'm more concerned with the *enye-ghaanye,* the time of year, the season, the seasonal sector, as near as you can recall it.'

'Oh, now I remember! On the console it said it was the forty-seventh day of Haal, the moons of abundant rain. I remember thinking that was odd, since I don't recall it raining even once after the Khleevi arrived. Does that help you?'

'Yes. Yes, it does. How long would you say you had been in the cave since you and Aari first separated from the others?'

'No more than fourteen sunrises at most. Are you going back to Vhiliinyar? Could you stop for me? I want to help Aari.'

'You just did,' she said. 'And I'm sorry, but time is playing a rather fickle role in this crisis. I'm afraid we may not have enough of it as it is.'

'Where are we headed, the cave?' Becker asked.

'No. I want to return to the time device,' she

told him. 'If you would keep the *Condor* in orbit, I'll take the shuttle down to land outside the entrance to Kubiilikaan. I hope the planet will still support time travel on the surface at the time when Laarye was rescued. The fact that Grimalkin was able to do it is hopeful, but his level of technical expertise seems to transcend the time device's planetside capabilities. With any luck I will find a way to ride the current time flow back that far and include the shuttle in the equation so I have a way to bring Aari out of there again.'

'You'd better,' Rafik said. 'Otherwise, we lose you, too.'

Acorna said nothing, but she set her long jaw. She knew the risks very well but believed she had a reasonable chance of overcoming them. She had to try. There was no other choice, really.

'No we don't,' Becker said. 'If she doesn't come back in a reasonable facsimile of a jiffy, we find Grimalkin and turn him over to RK until he tells us how to bring her – and Aari – forward to our time again.'

'Finding him would be the trick,' Acorna said with a small smile. 'But thanks for the thought, Captain.'

Mac clanked across the steel grid to the bridge.

'Were you able to load the cargo in the shuttle?' she asked him.

In preparation for the *Condor*'s orbit around Vhiliinyar, Mac had taken on his Linyaari persona, Maak, and had attached his horn modification to his forehead. 'Yes, Khornya,' he said. 'Everything is in readiness. Perhaps I should come with you to interact with the time device? It may yield secrets to me it would keep from a purely organic being such as you.'

Before she could demur, both Becker and Rafik enthusiastically endorsed the idea. Rafik said, 'That's an excellent idea, Mac. That way you'll be there when she – uh – travels, so maybe you can keep us posted.'

Well, it *was* a good idea, as Mac's often were. Whatever would help her get Aari back safely was fine with her.

'Thank you, Maak,' she said, giving his name its Linyaari pronunciation, which pleased him.

They landed the shuttle in the shallows of a stream that sank into the ground to feed the underground sea – which was more of a lake these days. Since water was the conduit for time travel, it would be easier to time-travel *in* the shuttle if it was within the liquid time channel.

Wordlessly, she and Mac disembarked and trotted down the short tunnel leading to the entrance of the caves where the Ancestors had once lived with their first attendants. The caves were the foundation of much of the city of Kubiilikaan, and at the back of one of them was the staircase leading into the vast, echoing, self-lighting building containing the time device.

No one else was around. On any Federation planet the place would have been buzzing with people, prodding, disassembling, prying into the secrets of the entire ancient underground city. The Linyaari were not exactly disinterested in the concept of time travel, but neither did they crave it. They simply wanted their planet back to normal and used the time device occasionally as a tool in that quest. Once the process of using the device was understood well enough so that people didn't keep disappearing, other matters took the attention of most of the scientists. Aari was the only Linyaari still missing in action, as Becker put it. Since Acorna was so vitally interested in the time device for such immediate and personal reasons, the other Linyaari left her to it.

Besides, at this time of day most of the people on Vhiliinyar, the terraforming crews and reclamation teams, were grazing with their families, telling each other about their day, preparing to settle down and sleep with the comfort of other warm bodies around them. Things were so peaceful at present with the planet mostly restored to its pre-Khleevi state.

Acorna stopped herself in the midst of that train of thought. No. Now was no time to feel sorry for herself. If she wanted a warm body to sleep next to, she would simply have to go fetch him herself.

The double helix of light and water that flowed upward from the floor of the room to the top of the building twined and curled with unending precision. The wall panels glowed softly with their map of the planet.

Acorna strode straight for the section of the map indicating Aari's cave, tapped in the time Laarye had provided, and concentrated on Aari's image. Two silver-white dots indicated the presence of two Linyaari and a gold dot probably indicated Grimalkin.

The ship's icon was there, too, tiny but discernible. Barely. Had Acorna not known where to look, she might never have found the three dots, two white, one gold, that indicated her lifemate, his brother, and her adversary. Because every other place on the walls around her was crawling with green dots oozing across the surface as if it had suddenly been invaded by armies of insects. Which, of course, was the case.

She suppressed a shudder, suddenly remembering that this image had been part of her recurring nightmare. She had the terrible feeling that she was about to make it come true. Taking a deep breath to steady herself, she returned her full attention to the white dots. Make that dot. The white and gold ones faded, a single white one remained, and then, too, vanished.

'What happened?' Acorna asked.

'The white dot identified on the key as Aari disappeared, Khornya,' Mac told her.

'Uh, yes. It did. But, why? How?'

'I do not know. But perhaps if you board the shuttle and I reset the device you will arrive in time to learn the answer.'

She certainly couldn't argue with that though the swarming icons of the Khleevi made her hesitate. But not for long. If she feared flying into them, how must Aari feel, abandoned again near the cave not too far from where he had been captured so long ago.

'Right. Let's see . . . it looks like the Khleevi are not too close to our present position at that time. And as far as I can tell from the map, the entrance to the cave is still open then. You know what to do, Maak. I will return to the rendezvous point in two Standard hours if all goes well. If I don't return then, keep watch for me at the same point for the next forty-eight hours,' she said.

'Yes, Khornya. And if you are not back by then, I will search for you in the future. If I do not find you, I will return to the *Condor*, we will acquire another shuttle, and follow your path until we locate you. Just as you are doing to find Aari.'

'That's about it,' she said. 'Thanks, Maak. Don't take any chances. The Khleevi would like your organic bits.'

'I will give them no opportunity to enjoy them, you may be sure, Khornya. I will see you in two Standard hours.'

She returned to the surface and boarded the shuttle with one backward glance to reassure herself that her cargo was secure. As she did so, she heard the com unit's smooth beep, and Mac said, 'time transfer beginning – oh, that's odd.'

He hadn't quite finished saying 'odd' when the landscape shifted horribly. The newly reclaimed surface vanished, replaced by a bleak, parched, heaving, burned, and smoking wasteland.

It stank, too. Acorna lifted up from the river's surface and saw the slimy Khleevi trails from the air. Acorna double-checked to make sure her shuttle's special Linyaari cloaking device was activated. Mac had modified the cloak from the Linyaari ships to adapt it to the smaller craft and allow the craft to be virtually undetectable whether in space or within the atmosphere of a planet.

Acorna profoundly hoped that the Khleevi had no means of penetrating the shields. She had nothing that would protect her against the large numbers of them she saw swarming over the surface below. What looked like green foothills tunneled with holes were actually Khleevi colonies housed in a habitat formed from their own hardened excrement. Since this was the first time she had ever been on a planet in the midst of a Khleevi occupation, she had been fortunate enough before to escape seeing this particular feature of the Khleevi's so-called culture.

The instectoid aliens crawled in and out of the tunnels of the mounds, radiating new slime trails from each like the legs of a mutant spider as they destroyed all living organisms remaining in their paths, then digested and excreted them.

Other Khleevi, armed ones, blasted away at anything standing more than a foot taller than the ground. This caused a chain reaction from Vhiliinyar, which, it seemed to Acorna, went down fighting. Mountains were blasted into oblivion but their avalanches buried Khleevi hives. Other mountains spewed lava and magma from their hot centers, while the ground rumbled and shook, fell apart and tried to put itself back together again. The planet's death throes were terrible to watch. The very air was a hellish bruised purple with an overlay of red-violet acrid smoke.

Though the trip via shuttle from Kubiilikaan to the cave was not an especially long one, it seemed interminable to Acorna. She hoped she would arrive before Grimalkin and Laarye left. She planned to give the cat creature a piece of her mind when she rescued Aari. Or rather, another piece of her mind.

When the cemetery and the cave first came within the shuttle's visual range, she thought she'd come in time. The outline of Grimalkin's ship was black against the ruined surroundings.

But as she flew nearer, the ship twisted, and she saw that the blackening really was black, and the ship was little more than the skeleton of a hull.

How could that be? She knew Grimalkin and Laarye had arrived safely in her own time after abandoning Aari. And yet, it appeared that either one of the myriad natural disasters erupting simultaneously all around her had destroyed the craft, or else the Khleevi had intercepted and destroyed it.

Very briefly, she activated her scanners, which she had been cautious about using lest the Khleevi could backtrack her signals as Becker had done with the Stones of Skarness. No life-forms were present in or around the ship, which didn't surprise her, since the Khleevi had been there. However, there was another strong, familiar signal emanating from the wreckage.

The homing beacons Hafiz had placed within the catseye chrysoberyls were calling to her from the wreckage.

Since Grimalkin had acquired the chrysoberyls long after he rescued Laarye and abandoned Aari, the ship had to have been wrecked on Grimalkin's second rescue attempt. Presumably, he had returned to rescue Aari, and the ship had been discovered by the Khleevi.

From the air, Acorna could see no Khleevi patrols nearby, so she risked setting her own ship down beside the wreckage and briefly searching it for remains she hoped she wouldn't find. She was in luck. No people of any species or race had left traces of themselves in the wreckage. The only evidence of what had happened there was that of the stones.

She picked up one, turning it over in her hand, gazing into its slitted eye. Acorna shoved the chrysoberyl into the pocket of her shipsuit. So, Grimalkin and the stones he had stolen from Smythe-Wesson had arrived here from her own time to fetch Aari, as promised. But somehow disaster had overtaken him, destroying his ship and leaving only the stones to identify it.

She immediately discarded the notion of retrieving the other stones, and loading them into her shuttle. No doubt Hafiz would have wished her to do so. But her other task was more pressing.

The trembling of the planet beneath her boots threatened to topple the wreckage onto her head. She kept her psychic ears open for the approach of Khleevi patrols. This was no place to linger gathering mere wealth. If she couldn't find Aari or Grimalkin, she needed to leave as quickly as possible.

It was extremely unlikely that they could have remained hidden from the Khleevi in the cave, but she felt she had to check anyway. Infrared sensors did not penetrate the peculiar mineral makeup of the cave's walls, or Laarye would have been discovered by the Khleevi when they captured Aari. So the fact that she had not seen any sign of them on the scanner meant nothing.

She ducked low, shining a small but powerful pocket torch around the cave. (Aari?) she sent out a mental call. (Grimalkin?) But there was no answer. She found traces of Laarye's recent occupation, but nothing indicating Aari had ever been here, or Grimalkin.

She quickly returned to the shuttle, the ground rolling under her feet as she ran. She jumped into her craft and cloaked it while gaining altitude. She couldn't understand exactly what had happened. Why hadn't she found Grimalkin and Aari? Why was there no sign that either had ever been there except for the ship with the chrysoberyls?

She glanced at the shuttle's console and saw that she had spent forty-four minutes on the ground. Mac would be expecting her in little more than an hour. But she could not now return straightaway.

She had to search, in case Aari or Grimalkin or both of them were running, hiding from the Khleevi who had destroyed Grimalkin's ship. With her scanners activated and her sensors at their maximum sensitivity, she circled the airspace above the cave in an ever-widening spiral. A few miles away, a molten fire pit that had once been a sacred mountain glowed in the darkness.

Acorna ignored the catastrophe all around her and focused on her personal mission. She called to Aari periodically and listened very hard for his thoughts. But she heard, felt, and sensed nothing except for a Khleevi patrol a bare kilometer from her position, moving quickly away.

And then, from the scanners, there was another signal of inorganic origin. She hovered, undecided. The object was not Grimalkin or Aari, and she really should not risk her life, the shuttle, or the precious cargo, not to mention the chance of *finding* Aari, by trying to retrieve the thing. She supposed the sensible thing to do would be note the coordinates and return after rendezvousing with Mac. But the ground lurched sickeningly below her. Whatever the object was, it could be swallowed up before she returned. She had to risk it.

The shuttle's cloak didn't work while it was

grounded. If she had some sort of grappling hook, she could fish for the object while hovering above it, but the shuttle was light on all but essential equipment. She checked the scanner one more time and homed in on the target as tightly as possible before setting the shuttle down.

Cautiously, she opened the hatch and played her torch beam across the barren broken ground. She didn't want to use the shuttle's running lights – no sense in painting the Khleevi a huge sign that said, 'Come and Get Me!'

Rather to her surprise, the beam picked up a reflection from something shiny. As quickly as possible, Acorna climbed out of the shuttle, reached down, and scooped the object up in her fingers.

It looked extremely familiar. Because she was viewing it by torchlight and in an unexpected place, it took her a moment to recognize it. Turning it over, she saw it for what it was – Aari's – no, Grimalkin's – wrist time-changing device, the source of so much trouble for them all.

It had, in fact, been on Grimalkin's wrist when she last saw him.

Her thoughts spun, her nose and brain filling with the stench and smoke despite her horn's attempt to clean the air around her. Grimalkin would not have voluntarily separated from his timer, so he must be either dead or imprisoned. Which probably meant Aari was imprisoned or dead as well. The thought of Aari in the Khleevi's claws again made her almost physically ill. After all he had been through, to be recaptured. It was too much for anyone to bear.

If she could figure out how to use Grimalkin's device, which seemed to be much more flexible and was certainly more portable than the larger device, perhaps she could separate the Khleevi from their prey. But she needed to return to the safety of her own time to study it properly. Perhaps Mac would have some insight.

As she returned to the shuttle, she wondered *where* Grimalkin was? If the time device was here, now, then she knew at least *when* the shape-shifter was. She didn't know where. And if the Khleevi had him, she prayed Aari was not with him.

As she reached for the shuttle hatch, the ground rolled under her, knocking her onto her back and sending the timer flying. She heard a shift and a thump from the direction of the shuttle, but kept her eyes on the timer and grabbed for it instead. Once she had it, she strapped it on to keep it from flying out of her hands again.

She reached for the side of the shuttle to pull herself erect again, but the craft's hull seemed to be in the wrong place. She trained the torch on it. The side nearest her listed toward her as if about to confide some secret.

And suddenly she noticed a sound. '*Klikity-klak-klak-klik-klik.*' Khleevi!

The hatch on the pilot's side of the shuttle wouldn't open – a corner seemed to be jammed against the ground, which was rolling again.

Acorna used the shifting hull to steady herself and made her way to the hatch on the passenger side. Perhaps should could use her own weight to pull the craft upright enough that the hatch would open.

She crawled on top of it and bounced. She thought she felt something move. Clambering down again, she pried open the hatch, which opened just enough to admit her.

But although she was in, the shuttle was not out. It remained partially stuck in the crack. She prepared to launch nonetheless. If the ground shifted just right, she could take advantage of the difference in pressure to escape.

Then she looked up and saw the bug eyes and pincers of the Khleevi staring in at her through the hatch. The things didn't have recognizable mouths, but Acorna could have sworn this one was grinning at her.

She touched the disk at her neck, crying out silently to Aari.

FOURTEEN

'Khornya!' Aari awoke, digging himself out of the riverbed, which had buried all but his nostrils. He had distinctly heard her voice crying out to him. 'Khornya, where are you?'

He knew she was in terrible danger from the Khleevi. But that must mean she was here, somewhere in the past, at some time close to this one. But where and when? He had to get to her, had to help her somehow. She had faced the Khleevi before with cleverness and courage, but that was with a great deal of backing from their own Linyaari people and House Harakamian. He knew somehow that she was all alone this time. If she wasn't actually frightened yet, she should be.

He sat up and looked around him at his thoroughly alien – and alienated in the most literal sense – homeworld.

He ought to be nearing Kubiilikaan now. Grimalkin had told him the entrance in his own time was through the Ancestors' caves. His

Linyaari navigational sense told him that was just about – *here*. He had seen an image of it in Grimalkin's mind when Grimalkin spoke of it. But where the entrance to the Ancestors' cave should have been he saw nothing but a mountain of rubble. While it didn't look as if the Khleevi had found much to interest them here, the earthquakes and avalanches – and a tsunami, no doubt, from the inland sea, had thoroughly wrecked the entrance. If he had equipment half as heavy as his heart felt at the sight of the rubble, he could have moved it all out of the way, but as it was he would never reach Kubiilikaan by this route.

He had come so far to reach this place that he was at the end of his strength. But the memory of Khornya's dream voice spurred him onward. She needed him, and he had made it this far. Several tons of dirt were not going to stop him from reaching his goal. He could find Khornya if only he could get to the time device, and somehow he would reach her. What he would do after that was unclear.

He eyed the obstacles between himself and the tunnel's entrance bleakly. However, if one upheaval had caused the cave-in that prevented him from entering here, perhaps that other catastrophe, the one that had blasted another hole through to the underground city, had also occurred by now.

He took several deep breaths. On hooves that felt as if they had been filed down to the quick and held over a slow fire, and muscles that were so sore they burned with the aching, he tottered forward, bypassing the cave's entrance and heading for the sea upon whose shores he had played as a child.

The sight of the sinkhole where the waters had been ought to have depressed him, but instead filled him with hope.

He walked out onto the mudflats that stretched for miles in every direction. They were not actually mud any longer, however, since mud implied dirt and water. The seabed held no more water than a desert, and much less nourishment. He dropped to his knees, feeling as though he could go no farther, but after lying still a moment or two, fearing he might sleep, or pass out, and make easy prey of himself for any passing Khleevi, he crawled forward.

Mac made a note to himself to invent a communication device that would cross time as well as space barriers. It was most inconvenient not to be able to continue instructing Acorna after she left the present time zone.

No sooner was she in the shuttle than he noticed that the Aari icon had unaccountably blinked off the screen, as had the icons for the ship, Laarye, and Grimalkin. He tapped cautiously forward but found no trace of them. He returned to the moment when the ship landed and watched it all over again, but this time continued to watch for a moment after the icons disappeared.

Abruptly the ship and Grimalkin icons reappeared, but this time neither Aari nor Laarye was present. However, a great many Khleevi converged on the ship's position. The Grimalkin icon disappeared, but a moment later, it reappeared. It was immediately swamped by Khleevi icons.

He tapped forward in time, and the Grimalkin icon blinked on and off again. The Khleevi icons moved away. They were so thick that Mac could not tell if Grimalkin's icon was among them or not. A light tap forward again and there was Acorna's icon and that of her ship. The time device apparently was not deceived by Linyaari cloaking.

Even Mac's excellent analytical programming could make little sense of all of this. He kept tapping forward at the same site, looking for signs of Aari so that when Acorna returned he could tell her when to search next.

'So, Mac, is she back yet?' Becker's voice hailed Mac from his chest modification.

'No, Captain, she is not. However, I have looked forward in time, and I am now at the point where the Khleevi are leaving Vhiliinyar.' The slime green icons were disappearing in droves, blinking out while he watched. In another tap they were almost all gone, but he saw no white Linyaari icon, nor for that matter did he see the golden one that signified Grimalkin.

One more tap. No icons of any kind appeared on the part of the wall he scrutinized. He set his visual sensors so they minutely scanned the rest of the massive screen inch by inch. However, he detected nothing, no life signs whatsoever.

Most puzzling.

He tapped three more times, lightly, and on the third time, he saw Aari's icon reappear inside the cave. 'Ah! There he is.'

'There who is?' Becker asked. 'Aari?'

'Yes, Captain. I wish Khornya was here to see this now. She would be extremely relieved. Grimalkin did not abandon Aari to the Khleevi. While everyone was on board, Grimalkin apparently shifted the ship forward in time until it and the people aboard were out of danger from the Khleevi. *Then* he abandoned Aari to the cave.'

'Oh, hey, that was real nice of him,' Becker growled. 'Guess I'll only have to break him into two pieces instead of a dozen. What about Acorna? Where is she?'

'I will return your hail when I have ascertained her geographical and chronological position, Captain. It will take me somewhat longer if we remain connected and I answer your questions while conducting my search.'

'I can take a hint. You let us know immediately when you find her, though. That's an order.'

'Yes, sir. Of course, sir,' Mac said, but he was already tapping a new sequence.

* * *

The sinkhole was wide and deep. Aari had no idea how far he would fall before he landed in the water below. He didn't know if there was enough water to break his fall or if the distance was so great he would be killed on impact. But there was no other way, so he closed his eyes, stepped forward, and dived head-first into the abyss.

After a couple of nanoseconds he hit something solid that then gave, quickly covering his eyes and filling his nostrils and mouth. He jerked his head upward, shaking it from side to side, as he continued to slide down the slippery slope of – mud! His descent was slow enough now to allow him to bring his hands to his eyes to free them. His elbows dug into the surface and further slowed his progress. His eyes adjusted, and he could tell he was sliding down a mud hill as tall as a small mountain. This was the surface debris that fell into the great inland sea upon which Kubiilikaan was built. He had hoped it would be here now – the sinkhole had indicated that it would, but he had never approached it from the surface before.

He turned so he slid on his backside the rest of the way into the water, entering with such force that he created a personal tidal wave that washed ten feet or so up the mountain, muddying the water. His horn, of course, unmuddied it as soon as it touched the liquid.

(Hey, be careful, Cousin!) a thought-voice complained. It was a familiar thought-voice at that. It sounded very like someone who couldn't possibly be here now.

For no *sii*-Linyaari should be occupying this stagnant sea, he knew. He had transported the aquatic folk, pre-Linyaari experimental genetic blends of Ancestral genes with Host genes, from their original position to a post-Khleevi future.

(Upp?) he asked. (What are you doing here?)

(You should know that very well, Cousin. You brought us here. For that dubious boon I owe it to you to tell you that a female of your kind came seeking you.)

(A female. Khornya.)

(Could have been. We told her you and that cat-father had brought us here, then left in one of the old ships. She was not happy about it.)

(When was this?)

(Maybe one swim around the water ago. Speaking of that, why are you back so soon? Where is the cat-father and where is your ship?)

(That, my friend, is a very good question.)

Aari was trying to swim, but he was very weak from his long ordeal. Upp regarded him with scorn on his ugly horn-studded face. (You are in very poor shape in such a very short time, land cousin.)

(More time has passed for me than it has for you,) Aari said, realizing Upp probably wouldn't understand.

(That troublesome device of the Parents, eh?)

(Yes, something like that. I . . . must . . . get . . . to . . . shore. Must . . . find . . . Khornya.)

(Oh, very well. Hang on to my tail, then. You're never going to make it the way you're going now.)

It took all of Aari's remaining strength to comply. He allowed himself to be towed to shore. Letting go of Upp's tail, he crawled out of the water and up onto the road leading down into it. Then he rolled onto his back and for a moment lay there gasping. As his breaths deepened and his heartbeat slowed, he began crawling up the hill, past the constantly changing facades of buildings lining the street.

This part of the trip felt almost as if it was longer than the entire journey leading up to it. As he reached the entrance to the building containing the time device, he cursed Grimalkin. There was no adequate expression in the Linyaari language to express his feelings, so he borrowed a few choice phrases from Becker's repertoire.

Aari reflected bitterly on the riverbeds he'd slept in, the foul-smelling Khleevi stench he'd wallowed in to throw them off his own scent, the caves he'd crammed his body into. And all for nothing! He was never in any danger from the Khleevi at all. Grimalkin had brought him forward in time before dumping him. Of course, Aari was glad the Khleevi hadn't been there to recapture him, but he would have been gladder if he'd known about it before he took such elaborate precautions to dodge them.

Sparing little more thought for the cat-creature, Aari entered the building. The walls lit instantly.

He picked his way down the incline that had once been a moving staircase and found the room containing the time device. Fortunately, after traveling with Grimalkin for what would have been several years in linear time, he was familiar with the workings of this sort of device. He knew the time he was in now, and the zone he and Grimalkin had been in when they landed to rescue Laarye. But how would he know *when* to find Khornya and expose Grimalkin's deception? He was wet enough now that he could leave from and arrive in the time machine room without going back to the lake, so *where* to go was no problem.

He began tapping the screen. Pain shot up his hand, and his finger felt as if it had entered orbit on a particularly heavy-gravity world. He bent his horn to touch it but was able to make it only slightly less painful. His horn had been depleted by continually trying to purify the tainted air, water, and soil on his journey, as well as healing his injuries along the way. He was exhausted. But never mind that. He had to find Khornya.

And he did. With only a few more taps, her icon appeared in the space on the screen indicating the room in which he now worked. That was better luck than he had any reason to hope for. His sore hand felt better just from touching her icon.

Everything in him told him to go to her here, now – then. But if he stepped back into her time before he and Grimalkin rescued Laarye, Laarye would not be saved. He had to reenter after Grimalkin had returned Laarye safely to their parents.

He sighed and leaned against the panel where Khornya's icon appeared. His head was spinning, and he realized that part of what he was thinking was rational, part of it mixed with senseless dreams. He had to sleep, and soon. His mind was too weary to work the equations that would tell him when to go. And yet she had cried out to him. She was in danger. He would lean this way just a while longer, touching her icon, feeling her presence across time, if not space.

Mac continued his search, tapping ever more rapidly so that the Aari icon seemed to jerk across the screen from the cave southward along a riverbed until he came to . . . until he came to the same room in which Mac was now standing. Well. There should certainly be something Mac could do about that.

It was true that Aari was probably not standing in water, and perhaps he was trying to travel to some other when. But Mac felt the highest probability was that Aari was looking for Khornya. So, the android reasoned, Aari should come to the present time with him. Mac could use his help.

He wasn't one hundred percent certain that what he planned to do would work, but he performed the same operation he had performed to send Khornya back in time, reversed it, and hoped that was how one brought someone forward again.

He felt himself shoved aside as Aari's body suddenly appeared almost on top of him. Aari appeared to be unconscious. If it were possible for an android to be shocked, Mac would have been shocked by Aari's appearance. He dimly remembered, back when he himself had been a simpler being, how Aari had looked when Becker first rescued him from the cave. It wasn't quite the same. Nothing was broken or missing, but this Aari was so thin he could practically have crawled out the neck hole of his shipsuit without unfastening it. He was filthy, and Mac's olfactory sensors were not happy with the aroma wafting from the thin, bedraggled body.

'Aari, my friend, I am here. Please awaken. I desire your help to find Khornya. I regret that she is not here, because if she was, I know she would wish to hover over you in your current condition, speaking soothing words and caressing your fevered skin with her beautiful horn.'

'What's going on down there, Mac?' Becker demanded from the area where Mac's fourth rib would have been had his construction been as shoddy as that of the average organic man. 'Who are you talking to? Did you find Acorna?'

'No, Captain, but Aari is here. The authentic Aari. But he is extremely weak and sick and very dirty. His horn is lying to one side and is the color of new oil.'

'In other words, he's no use to her or us in his

current condition?' Rafik asked, an edge to his voice. He didn't know Aari well. All he had seen of Acorna's lifemate was the false version presented by Grimalkin.

Becker said, 'There's got to be someone with a functioning horn nearby. Let me call Terraform HQ and see who's in the vicinity.'

'Other Linyaari?' Aari asked in a raspy voice.

Becker's voice returned in a minute. 'Well, I suppose her horn is better than no horn at all. Liriili is taking inventory of new plantings near the cave entrance. She should be meeting you there in a few minutes.'

'No – time,' Aari said, and pulled himself up the wall, starting to tap at it.

He and Mac were at it when Aari heard Liriili's thought-inquiry, (Are you there? I hope this is as important as my work. I quite lost count when I received that peremptory summons.)

'She's here,' Aari told Mac, between taps. 'She seems lost. I got her message, but my horn – too weak. Can't send.'

'I will go to the doorway and call to her then, shall I?' Mac said, striding away.

Between his first footstep and Aari's next tap, Aari saw Khornya's icon, inside that of her little shuttle. As well as the icons of dozens of Khleevi surrounding her.

Aari, still wet from the sea, did not hesitate. With a shaking hand, he scribbled the time signature and coordinates on the screen for Mac.

Then, with a horrified visualization of what must be happening all around her, he focused on Khornya, dived into the time stream in the middle of the room, and went in after her.

FIFTEEN

Greedy Khleevi eyes watched Acorna through the clear shuttle hatch while their pincers scored and gouged at the little vessel's artificial carapace. Fortunately, it was every bit as tough as the Khleevi's own covering. Tougher, in fact. Since her attempts to free the shuttle from the crack in Vhiliinyar's surface had failed, Acorna turned in her seat and fumbled with the webbing holding her cargo. She didn't think she would be able to save herself with it, but she could at least relieve Vhiliinyar of a few plundering Khleevi before she died.

Despite Mac's modifications, no Linyaari vessel contained gun ports. Instead he had equipped the shuttle with high-powered fire-extinguishing rifles with the anti-Khleevi weapon. Acorna was glad now that they had taken the time to stop on the sentient plant world Becker referred to as PU-#10. The sap secreted by these plants when they were in a state of agitation had been the secret weapon Acorna and her allies used with good effect against the Khleevi during their last invasion.

Now she hoped she could open the hatch and fire quickly and in a wide enough pattern to buy herself a little time. Perhaps her movements and those of the Khleevi would be enough to free her little vessel and allow her to escape after all. Perhaps she would simply have the time to destroy more of the Khleevi. At least she would not simply sit in the shuttle and wait to be taken.

She finally cut the webbing loose and freed the weapons – there were only a half dozen of them from a stock Becker had taken in trade for some Huicholian welded circuit boards he'd salvaged from a freighter called the *Zapata* out of Nuevo Guadalajara. Before she strapped two of them across her chest and back, bandoleer-style, she held another one of the rifles with the barrels pointed at her, took a deep breath, and fired, covering herself and the command chair, but not the console, with the odious-smelling sap.

The sap! She had a momentary flash from her future dream of the dripping green stuff covering her, Aari, and the Khleevi. It was the sap. Was the dream in the process of coming true? It could not. It simply could not. And yet, this was the only possible course of action open to her if she was to survive and rescue Aari.

At one point during the trip back to Vhiliinyar, she'd confided her dream to Becker, and her concern that it could be a premonition of things to come.

That was when she suggested the side trip to PU-#10 to pick up the plant sap.

Becker had approved. 'Makes sense. Any Khleevi that tries to take a bite out of you will want to take a bite out of something else to take the taste out of his mouth. But by the time he does, it'll be too late because he won't have a mouth anymore.' The sap was corrosive to the Khleevi carapace, then it destroyed the inner tissue. The worst thing any non-Khleevi being had experienced from the sap so far was a slight allergic reaction.

She cleared her nostrils, eyes, and fingers of the sap, strapped the guns across her body, and picked up two more, one for each hand. The Linyaari were pacifist by nature but fortunately for Acorna she hadn't been raised in her own culture. Her mentors growing up had been three rough-and-ready human asteroid miners, all of whom had a nice streak of violence when it was necessary to survive. Besides, she considered this not so much destroying Khleevi as saving whatever lifeforms these few Khleevi would destroy. Maybe even herself.

After taking another deep breath, which she regretted almost at once, she once more looked up to face her attackers.

They goggled down at her for a split nanosecond, then suddenly turned away, looking at something, lumbering toward something that she couldn't see because the Khleevi in front of her blocked her view.

Then, to her horror, she found out what it was.

(Khornya! I am drawing them off so you can escape!) Aari's thought-voice, the real Aari's thought-voice, spoke to her mind.

(Not without you!) she said, standing with her head lowered and throwing her shoulders and back against the hatch. It gave more quickly than she dared hope, and she stood with her torso exposed, dripping slime and pointing her water guns at the Khleevi clustered fifteen yards from the bow of the shuttle. She fired into them. The Khleevi broke, emitting high-pitched squeals along with frantic *klik*ing and *klak*ing. Their defection exposed Aari, who was being held in the pincers of three more Khleevi.

Acorna fired the contents of her other water rifle, aiming first to cover Aari, then waving the firing weapon so it spread its contents over Aari's attackers as well. They dropped him.

(Quickly, love, before the others replace them,) she said. But he was very weak, and could only stumble toward her. Staggering forward, he tripped and fell over a fissure in the ground.

Without another thought for her own safety she pulled herself out of the hatch, discarding her discharged weapons and tossing the rifles strapped over her out onto the ground so they didn't catch on something as she ran. She leaped to the ground, slid in the sap, but reached Aari and pulled him to his feet as the other Khleevi advanced. There were far more of the bugs than she had realized – perhaps the patrol she'd seen at first had called for reinforcements?

She dragged Aari to his feet and pulled him back as far as her abandoned rifles, which she snagged, keeping one for her own use and handing the other to him. The damaged Khleevi were being trampled as their comrades advanced on the two Linyaari. Acorna knew that the sap covering the downed Khleevi would eat into the feet of the tramplers, but by the time the attackers realized they were injured, it would probably be too late for her and Aari.

Then the ground convulsed beneath her boots and knocked her, Aari, and the Khleevi off their feet. She kept scuttling backward, pulling Aari with her, then, suddenly, she felt air beneath her scrabbling hand and heard a crunching, rending noise. Turning, she saw that the crack holding the shuttle was opening to a chasm into which the shuttle tumbled.

Aari's hand caught on her wrist. He went still, then he grasped her wrist with his other hand and rubbed away the sap. (Grimalkin's timer?) he asked.

(Yes. I found it out there, which is why I stopped.)

(Using the timer, we can leave,) he told her, radiating excitement and the first hope she had sensed in the emotional bleakness he'd been broadcasting.

(How?) There was no time for caution, but she felt an awful sinking inside her, a sense of the inevitability of fate. *My dreams*, she thought. *They could come true* . . . The risk was unimaginably horrifying, but the other way lay certain death for both of them.

(Input the desired date, time, and coordinates. Simple.)

She made a quick decision. Predestination and the inevitability of fate were not concepts she embraced. Thrusting her fears aside so they would not distract Aari, she sent a practical thought instead. (Maybe it would be if I could see the timer, but it's dark.)

He touched something and the timer illuminated.

Meanwhile a wall of Khleevi feet, mandibles, and pincers crushed in on them.

(You know how it works. You use it,) she said. (I'll try to keep the Khleevi off us.) She started to shove the timer off her wrist to him, but he stopped her.

(I need to touch you so we can both go,) he told her. (Just a—) His fingers were busy.

Acorna opened a half circle around them by attacking the surprised Khleevi with the most sap-saturated parts of herself she could while still allowing Aari to retain her wrist. The Khleevi tried to touch her, but quickly retracted their pincers and jaws, *klak*ing and making high-pitched squealing sounds of pain and shock.

Khleevi telepathy alerted the rest of them that the prey wasn't palatable. The giant bugs backed away from the Linyaari.

Acorna felt hope rise within her heart. They were going to get out of this!

Then the Khleevi hordes around them opened to permit two new pairs of Khleevi to approach. Each pair of the Khleevi held something between them.

(They've got nets! Hurry, Aari, hurry!)

(Almost got it—)

The first pair of Khleevi threw their net. Acorna ducked, but still she felt the metal strands drop onto her head and shoulders. Aari grabbed her close to him as the Khleevi grabbed the net edges.

Acorna shut her eyes tight. All she felt was the warm pressure of Aari's arms beneath the net, holding her neck and back, and the touch of the cold steel net tightening around them.

She dimly heard Mac's voice calling, 'Mayday! Mayday! Captain Becker, please assist at once! Implement emergency plan B and dispatch all available personnel to lend immediate aid! As we feared, Acorna and Aari have returned, but I cannot discern their condition because they are covered with a net of some sort and are surrounded by Khleevi.'

Grimalkin screamed as the Khleevi pincers snipped at his tail. He felt the rush of air and actually lost a few hairs before he could jerk his treasured appendage into the hole after him. The Khleevi simply ate the rock and soil around his hiding place until he was exposed again. As one leaned forward to grab him, he bounded over its head and landed behind it, facing the feet of another Khleevi. He zipped between those legs, and several other pairs of legs as well, running through them like he was speeding down a slalom course until suddenly he faced open mandibles instead of feet.

He screeched to a halt, then turned to flee in another direction. But other Khleevi were also bending down, grabbing and snapping at him with those cruel pincers. Once more Grimalkin leaped, but this time the Khleevi in back were ready for his move so he had to stay aloft. He did this by landing on the nearest bug's skull, then leaping from that bug head to the next and the next.

If only there weren't so many of them, he could get behind them, outrun them, and return to where he lost his timer. Once he had that again he would be safe. Even in feline form, he could work the controls.

But no matter how he leaped and turned, hid, or skittered among them, the Khleevi always surrounded him. There were so *many* of them. He had hoped they might tire of trying to capture one small feline, which was why he had shifted to his alternate shape as soon as they laid hold of him in his two-legged form. But the bugs were relentless, and as stubborn as only the deeply stupid could be.

It looked as if he'd have to backtrack to his timer while totally surrounded by these tiresome creatures.

No sooner had that thought occurred to him than he suddenly felt the hunt cease. He ran without interference past the forest of Khleevi legs and feet into an open area of rock and rubble. He looked over his shoulder but the Khleevi weren't watching him. Their antennae were all pointing in another direction.

He heard it then. It sounded like a high-pitched whine – but it was mechanical, not animal, in origin. Could it be an engine? It sounded like a small vessel – maybe a shuttle or a flitter. What was it doing here? Or more precisely – what was it doing *now*? Grimalkin was sure that non-Khleevi vessels weren't present in this time. Vhiliinyar was completely conquered, with no non-Khleevi alive on the planet except himself. And . . . maybe . . . Aari? But Aari should be somewhere in the post-Khleevi future. Of course, he should have been in the cave when Grimalkin arrived, but he hadn't been. Grimalkin thought that was probably because he was trying to land the ship at the same time it had left with himself and Laarye before. There was always a bit of temporal distortion in that kind of situation.

He scampered up the highest mound of rock and hardened slime to get a better vantage point. In cat form, seeing in the gloom presented him with little difficulty. The ground shook under his paws, though he was uncertain whether it was because of the stampede of Khleevi feet or from one of the monotonous earthquakes that periodically rocked Vhiliinyar.

The Khleevi were bearing down on a large egg with wings on either side. Grimalkin recognized it as the Linyaari shuttle Captain Becker carried aboard the *Condor*. A Linyaari, though he couldn't be sure exactly who it was from this distance, squatted beside the vessel. The Linyaari seemed to be staring at something.

His timer! The Linyaari . . . Aari, surely, or maybe Laarye . . . or perhaps even Acorna . . . had found his timer! Joy! Exultation! He could leave here and take whoever it was with him. He was beginning a leap to the plain where the Linyaari was kneeling when the ground bucked up and knocked him onto his tail. When he stood up, cautiously, on the trembling earth, it felt as if he was trying to ride some large and unhappy animal. He could see that the little egg-like vessel had wedged one of its wings in the crack. The Linyaari became aware of the Khleevi bearing down on the ship. The creature pried open the hatch and crawled inside with barely a centimeter to spare between the hatch and the first Khleevi pincer.

Grimalkin made his leap and pelted toward the ship, once more dodging between Khleevi feet. Grimalkin to the rescue! As usual, he was landing on his paws. He would get his timer from the Linyaari and save both of them!

Then the situation got more complicated. Suddenly Aari appeared in the midst of the knot of Khleevi farthest from the ship. Grimalkin was surprised to see that Aari did not look at all well.

However, Khleevi were converging upon him, so the poor fellow was apt to look a lot worse before too long. Too bad Aari was the one who was closest and the one with the timer – Acorna? Grimalkin still couldn't be sure – was inside the shuttle.

Before he could decide what his next move would be, the hatch of the shuttle burst open and a monster, glistening wetly with something so foul-smelling that Grimalkin nearly swooned, climbed out.

A second glance revealed that it was Acorna, though where she got that rotten slime from Grimalkin couldn't imagine. She emptied the weapons she carried in her hands at the Khleevi. The evil-smelling, wet-looking stuff erupted from the ends of her guns and coated both Aari and his enemies with the same glop coating her. Grimalkin realized this must be the sap Aari's recorded memories spoke of – the sap that had helped the Linyaari and their allies to finally destroy the Khleevi.

It was working again. Khleevi fell screaming to the ground – or rather, *klak*ing and *klik*ing, which was much the same thing for them.

But everything happened very quickly after that. Grimalkin tried to break through the line of Khleevi feet but had no luck. He would have switched to his other form, but then he would surely be captured, and, unlike Acorna and Aari, he had none of the sap. Even so, he would have risked it if he'd seen his timer on Acorna's wrist, where Aari feverishly programmed it. By the time Grimalkin saw the device and realized what was happening, it was too late. The Khleevi had thrown a net over Acorna, Aari, and, alas, the timer. Before Grimalkin could blink, both the Linyaari couple and the Khleevi clinging to the net had vanished from the clearing leaving the shuttle, more Khleevi and . . . oh, dear, himself . . . behind.

That was when someone picked him up by the tail and started swinging him in a long arc. He changed to his biped form, which had no tail, to escape. Unfortunately, that form lacked not only a tail but also the grace, speed, and agility of his cat form. Two more Khleevi blocked his path at once. Each took one of his arms, not caring at all if they dislocated his shoulders. He suspected from the way they responded to his screams that they would prefer it. They carried him between them. He went limp and stopped struggling. Before long they entered one of the large mounds of hardened slime. He found himself in the center of an amphitheater-like space with a single furnishing at its center – the torture machine that had played a starring role in so many of the Khleevi's propaganda vids.

Sixteen

Acorna struggled to free herself from the net and the Khleevi hanging on to it, trapping her and Aari.

As she unsnarled herself, pincers snaked out to grab her wrist. Just when she thought she would lose her head Maak charged in and chopped the pincer and the net away with his hand, or rather, the laser cutting tool he'd replaced it with. So precise was his cut that it maimed the Khleevi and opened a hole in the net big enough for Aari and Acorna to escape from its tangles. But the Khleevi wouldn't give up.

Another pincer reached out, and Acorna grasped her wrist with her other hand to protect the time device. If the Khleevi got that, as they seemed to have realized, they and their kind could travel through time as well as space. Not only would their race be reborn in a time beyond their extinction, but they could travel back and forth in time ravishing the same planet, killing and torturing the same people, again and again.

They seemed to be everywhere, their stench filling the room as they poured waste into it. Their mandibles snapped as they rampaged around the time lab *klik*ing and *klak*ing and making high-pitched squealing sounds.

Acorna slid away on a floor covered with fresh Khleevi excrement and the stinking green blood, as well as the noxious sticky plant sap. The monsters were covered with sap, just as the Khleevi in Acorna's dream had been.

Despair ate at her heart as surely as the sap ate at their cells. Now she realized that her dream hadn't been a premonition or predestination. It had been a memory, bleeding through the veils of time to warn her that this would happen. Yet she had been powerless to prevent it. Even if she had sacrificed Aari by not returning for him, the Khleevi would have found the time device. The sap was gone, and now it was all she, Aari, and Maak could do to stay alive while the Khleevi seemed to fill the time lab.

Maddened by the sap's caustic effect on their carapaces, they thrashed about wildly, gouging huge holes in the walls as they flailed against them. Panels fell dark as their controls were destroyed. The Khleevi's snapping pincers and jaws tore at the inner workings of the room.

Mac made *klak*ing noises, too, using the bits of the Khleevi language he had learned on previous encounters. 'It's no good,' he called finally, his voice strangely calm and reasonable, though pitched loudly enough to carry over the *klaks* and squeals. 'They are beyond understanding at this point. However, there are only four of them, and they are much damaged by the sap. Perhaps we can contain them before they do further damage.'

Only four? Acorna's spirits suddenly pulled out of a nosedive. No more Khleevi seemed to be appearing. So the dream was wrong in that respect. The time door was not yet open to infinite numbers of the monsters. 'Too bad Maak ruined that net,' she said, dropping and rolling out of the way as a Khleevi charged straight for her, missed, and fell into a wall instead. It stayed there, sagging as the sap finally ate into its vital organs.

'I am sorry that I rendered that resource useless. In the future, I will add a net to my attachment arsenal,' Mac said. 'There is a net on the *Condor*, but it is too far away to be of any use right now.'

Another of the creatures lumbered toward Acorna, snapping and *klak*ing for all it was worth. Mac was busy with another one, but Acorna dodged, dropped, and rolled again, this time between the thing's legs. It was not a wise move. The Khleevi anticipated her and pulled its feet together.

Aari lowered his head so his knobby horn pointed straight out and ran straight into the Khleevi, butting and goring at its center.

The Khleevi fell back, tripping partly on Acorna and partly on its own feet. It landed hard on the side of the pool from which the DNA helix rose to penetrate the entire building. Mac's Khleevi also backed into the pool in its haste to escape Mac. This time it broke through the side of the pool and fell into it.

The helix vanished as a geyser of water shot up then splashed over onto the floor, flooding the room and spilling out into the hallway. The remaining Khleevi, its carapace vanishing in a stream of green ichor, took one step toward them and fell forward, narrowly missing Aari, and lay motionless.

Leaving the Khleevi carcasses to wash back and forth in the water spilling from the ruined pool, Acorna, Aari, and Mac quickly fled to the trapdoor leading to the Ancestral caves. Mac sealed the door with his laser attachment to prevent the tunnel from flooding, too, but water still seeped through and first dripped, then dribbled, then spurted down after them.

With a collective sigh of relief, they reached the portion of the caves that led upward to the restored surface of the planet.

'Captain, this is Maak, Captain Becker, please respond. Mr. Nadezda? We must relay an emergency situation to the Linyaari High Council. The time device has been damaged by some Khleevi who came forward in time with Khornya and Aari. The Khleevi are now dead. However, the chamber and possibly the entire building, maybe the caves, perhaps even the city, will be flooded by an underground spring flowing beneath the DNA helix in the time chamber. Repair and containment must be immediately initiated. Is that an accurate assessment of the situation, Aari? Acorna? Perhaps we should return . . .'

Acorna, dizzy with relief to have lived through her worst nightmare without damage to her loved ones or herself, sagged against Aari.

He met her halfway, and the two collapsed, panting, into each other's arms.

Mac continued sending his Mayday along with instructions and coordinates, but Khornya and Aari didn't seem to hear him. Instead, each of them gazed at the other as Mr. Harakamian had looked at the catseye chrysoberyls, as if they each had discovered, or rediscovered, a treasure beyond price. Neither seemed to notice that the other was, despite the floodwater dripping from them, still covered in sticky sap and the stinky slime they had inherited from the now deceased Khleevi.

They were horn to horn, nose to nose, their eyes wide, as each of Mac's very untidy Linyaari friends drank in the sight of the other. Aari's hands cradled Acorna's head and back, and hers did the same to his. It seemed to Mac that deafness was a side effect of the interesting mental condition they both shared.

Mac continued trying to reach Becker. He was somewhat distracted by the verbal murmuring sounds coming from Aari and Acorna, subvocalizations that were almost purrs. They didn't seem to care about the disaster or the ruin of the underground city, an ancient relic full of amazing artifacts that no doubt would hold much valuable knowledge for, not only the Linyaari, but many other races who might learn through them.

'Maak, this is Melireenya aboard the *Balakiire*. We received your transmission to Captain Becker and are relaying it to the Council. A team is on its way.'

Immediately Melireenya was replaced by Neeva. 'Maak? Is Acorna with you? Did she find Aari?'

'Yes, *visedhaanye ferilii* Neeva, they are both here. They appear to be uninjured, though they are extremely messy. And they are behaving in a peculiar way that I believe may be attributed to Linyaari preliminary mating rituals. Or . . . at least . . . is that what it means when they lie on the ground together, heedless of their surroundings, horns touching and . . . ?'

'Oh, yes!' Feriila, Acorna's mother, now appeared on Mac's chest screen. Vaanye, his face partially obscured by Mac's left nipple, nonetheless seemed to be smiling indulgently as his hands rested on his wife's shoulder. 'The dear children!' Acorna's mother seemed almost to weep with joy.

Khaari's voice said, 'Everyone prepare for landing. We'll be joining them soon!'

'I am very relieved that you are coming,' Mac

told Acorna's relatives. 'I had received no response to my prior communications.'

'That's because Becker and Rafik had to make a detour to rendezvous with Aziza and her crew. As they were entering orbit on their way to join your crew, they picked up the homing signal from the stolen catseye chrysoberyls and located them in the ruin of a ship heretofore undiscovered outside Aari's cave.'

'Curiouser and curiouser,' Mac said, using a literary quotation from a classic children's book he had discovered in Becker's library of salvaged hard-copy volumes.

'We have all been trying to reach Khornya by thought-talk,' Neeva told him, 'But she didn't respond. I understand now that she has been too preoccupied . . .'

'I apologize, Mother, Father, Neeva,' Acorna said, taking Aari's hand to rise to her feet and giving herself a little shake, which was meant to settle her clothing about her but instead only redistributed the sap and slime. Aari stood with his arm protectively around her shoulders. 'We were in another time zone, being attacked by Khleevi, and then the Khleevi followed us to the time chamber with the results I believe Maak has mentioned, and then – well, this is the *real* Aari.'

'Indeed,' Vaanye said.

'Perhaps you'll want to tidy up a little before any of the other teams arrive, Khornya,' Neeva suggested with a not-quite-suppressed smile.

'Oh!' For the first time, Khornya seemed to

notice that she and Aari were looking less than their best. No doubt she only noticed that she and Aari had seemed beautiful to each other. 'Oh, yes! Perhaps we could use the *Balakiire*'s sonic cleaner when you land?'

As she finished speaking, the *Balakiire* set down in the clearing reserved for ships bringing equipment and provisions to this sector of Vhiliinyar.

(You go clean up, *Yazzi*,) Aari told Acorna. (I have one more thing to do before I do the same.)

Acorna sighed. (I suppose this something will require the use of Grimalkin's timer?)

(I fear that is so.)

(Then my shower will have to wait, too. I haven't gone to all this trouble to find you just to lose you again. It is very good of you to put his fate above your shower, under the circumstances. After all, he left *you* to the Khleevi.)

(Not really,) Aari said, and explained the time shift to her.

By that time the *Balakiire*'s crew, including Neeva and Acorna's parents, had joined them.

Acorna looked at them a little helplessly. She longed to embrace her parents, but knew she would soil them with the sap. Besides, she needed all of the sap still clinging to her as protection from the Khleevi. (I'm sorry, Mother, Father, Neeva. But Aari and I need to return for Grimalkin. We can't just leave him to the Khleevi.)

(How do you intend to get him away from

them?) Vaanye asked. (It seems to me you will most likely arrive to find him beyond help and yourselves captives again.)

(And for goodness sake, you can't go against a Khleevi invasion force armed with only a few patches of sap on your bodies. You've got a time control device. Use it! At least take the time to go back to PU-#10 and get more sap.)

(There's more aboard the *Condor*,) Acorna said. (And you're right, of course.)

(In that case, I think you should take more people with you.)

(More Linyaari would probably just get killed. Our people hesitate to use a deadly weapon, even against Khleevi,) Aari told her. (Thanks to our past experiences, Acorna and I don't have that problem. Besides, I don't know exactly what the limit is on how many people can use the timer at once. We did bring back two Khleevi with us so apparently four can travel with it so we could probably take Becker and Maak. But I see no reason for them to endanger themselves. For that matter, I wish you would keep Khornya here. Instead of directly confronting the Khleevi, I thought I might time it so that perhaps I meet Grimalkin just before he loses his device, warn him, and both of us return here. I am assuming he went looking for me. If he finds me, there is no reason for him to remain.)

(He would want to take you back to the ship where the catseyes are,) Acorna said. (And you'd both be captured, as would the timer. With the underground time device disabled, you would never be able to come back, and no one would be able to save you. You're right that we mustn't let the Captain endanger himself or Maak – if anyone can put the machine back together again, it will be Maak.)

Vaanye harrumphed. (Really, my dear, I do have a bit of experience in that line myself – not with time machines, but other devices of a similarly complex nature.)

'So I've heard, Father,' she said.

The *Condor* landed beside the *Balakiire*. The robolift descended, bearing Becker.

'Aari!' Becker cried. 'Well, looks like Acorna made a sap out of you, too!'

Aari looked puzzled.

Acorna said, (It's a joke employing an idiomatic expression. In Basic speech, the word 'sap' refers to the blood of plants, such as the material we currently wear, as well as to a person who is a fool. It is a comradely insult in this case, made for the sake of wordplay. It indicates that Captain Becker is happy to see us together again.)

(Ah! I thought so. Joh is not *that* hard to read.)

'I would greet you properly, old friend, but then I would make a sap of you also,' Aari told him. 'We would like to clean up aboard the *Condor*.'

Becker glanced at the *Balakiire* and raised his right eyebrow inquisitively, but said only, 'Sure. Maybe you kids want to share a shower. I know it's been a long time. I guess I can wait until you and Acorna have – uh – debriefed each other before I get any answers from you.' To Acorna he said, 'When we got the *Balakiire*'s relay that you were okay, Rafik stayed at the cave to help Aziza's crew load the catseyes.'

Acorna and Aari tried to hide their impatience and act as if they were going to do exactly what he expected. At last he stepped off the robolift, and they stepped on and were carried up into the *Condor*, and the remaining supply of the precious Khleevi-killing sap.

(Khornya,) Aari said, turning to her and taking her shoulders in his large slightly trembling hands. (Please do not come. You have no idea what they could do to you if we are captured. If they get their claws on you, that would be worse for me than anything they did to me, even the second time.)

(And how do you think it would be for me, love, waiting and waiting again, not knowing if you were coming back until you did?)

He quirked one side of his mouth up and gave her a shrewd look. (Actually, the waiting wouldn't be a problem. If we are not back at approximately the same moment I leave, you'll know we aren't returning. Ever. In which case you'd better prepare everyone for a second invasion because the Khleevi may just extract the secrets of the timer from one of us and come forward themselves.)

(Now I *know* I'm coming with you,) she said.

(If we are captured, I will find a way to destroy the timer before I let that happen.)

(Easier said than done, *Yaazi*.)

RK mewed a greeting and hopped down from his perch atop the command chair of the bridge. Both of them gave him lingering strokes for a few precious moments, then turned their backs on the ship's cat. His paws clattered on the grid behind them.

As they reached the cargo hold they heard the robolift descend once more.

(The Captain is returning,) Acorna said. (Or Maak.)

(We'd better hurry,) Aari said.

(I suppose – but in a way there is no hurry. With the timer, as you pointed out, we can retrieve Grimalkin before he is captured and bring him back so he won't have known suffering at all. On the other hand . . .)

He caught her very *ka*-Linyaari thought of what she half wished would happen to the manipulative Ancestral 'Friend.' He shook his head, smiling very slightly. (Khornya, annoying as he is, he has done neither of us real harm. He certainly doesn't deserve what the Khleevi have in store for any prisoner.)

(I suppose not,) she said. (But if he had had his way, I might be having kittens by now.)

(No, because he would have made sure the Linyaari race sprang from your loins, so you would have only been your own multigreat-grandmother.)

(And that's better?)

They pulled forth the plas skins of sap and stared at them, wondering how they would fight a planetful of Khleevi.

(We could open them up, throw them to the ground, and jump on them, squooshing the sap on anyone who comes near.)

(I hate to say it, but that's as good a plan as any. I am changing my mind. We must wait until we can acquire a better means of distributing the sap.)

Footsteps approached, and Acorna felt the unfamiliar but wonderfully welcome presence of her father.

(Daughter? Aari?) Vaanye said, when he stood beside them surveying the sap in and out of the cargo hold. (I have been pondering our problem. You two are just beginning your life together, as I understand it, and after a very long interruption. Aari has already endured a long and painful ordeal with the Khleevi. And, Khornya, your mother and I could not bear losing you again after finding you, so beautiful and strong and ready to begin a new life and another generation of our clan. I owe Grimalkin my life and your mother's. It is fitting that I should attempt his rescue.)

(No one will be able to rescue him the way things stand now, Father,) Acorna told him. (The plas rifles we used to shoot the sap at the Khleevi were all lost when the quake took the shuttle. We will have to wait until Hafiz can send more from

MOO. Besides, even though you made defensive weapons for our people before, you have not actually used offensive ones before. Both Aari and I have learned that we are capable of doing so when necessary. It is not a common trait among our people.)

(I wasn't thinking of using an actual weapon,) Vaanye replied. (Actually, the tool I have in mind is better suited for distributing the sap over a wide area than a plas rifle. We brought several fertilizer sprayers aboard the *Balakiire*. I could load more than a single charge with one of those, carrying a container that will feed into the sprayer.)

(We thank you for the information, Vaanye,) Aari said. (But I will go. Khornya should stay here with you.)

(*Aaaarrri!*) Acorna's thoughts were not kind.

(She will not, of course, but she should,) Aari said. (I would have her do so.)

(You two don't be so *male,*) Acorna told them. (After all, Aari, when we faced the Khleevi, neither of us would have escaped except for the other one.)

(All the more reason for me to go. Also, if I cannot persuade you two to stay here . . .) Vaanye said.

(. . . You cannot,) Aari and Acorna assured him.

(Very well then. I can carry three of those containers.)

They returned to the robolift, followed by RK who was bawling his protest at being left out of the excitement. When they stepped onto the robolift, each burdened with as much of the sap as it was possible to carry, the cat jumped onto the lift with them.

All of them were trying to think what to tell the others – especially Acorna's mother – but they need not have worried. Ships and shuttles from all over Vhiliinyar were landing, and the Ancestors had also made an appearance. The reverse of a bucket brigade seemed to be taking place, with a line of people from the tunnel entrance to the river bearing a number of hoses from a series of pumps working to clear the passages.

Acorna, who still possessed the timer, stayed below with the sap while Aari and Vaanye boarded the *Balakiire* to fetch the fertilizer sprayers.

RK ran to the river, no doubt to examine the stuff coming out of the hoses to see if there were any fish for him in it.

When the men returned with the fertilizer sprayers, they each transferred three of the easily expanded sap skins into one and strapped it on, attaching a feeder hose to the sprayer. At Acorna's insistence, Aari gave her and Vaanye a quick lesson on how to program the timer. If only one of them survived, at least that one would not be stranded among the planet's past and the swarming Khleevi for lack of knowledge.

Once they were ready, they all joined hands. Aari programmed the timer with his free hand, as one of Acorna's hands rested in his and her other hand rested in Vaanye's. Acorna took in a last deep breath of clean, fresh air . . .

. . . And exhaled it amid the hot, acrid fumes of Khleevi-occupied Vhiliinyar.

Vaanye gasped. (Feriila is fond of saying that I go looking for trouble, but I never imagined anything like this! It's horrible! Horrible! Are you certain we are still on Vhiliinyar?)

(Yes.) Aari's thoughts were full of even darker images than the one before them.

The ground shook, and all of them stumbled.

Acorna pointed to the fissure that had swallowed the shuttle.

(I do not see any Khleevi here now,) Vaanye said, clearly trying to look on the bright side of things.

(True,) Acorna said. (But we must go looking for them if we're to find Grimalkin. I suppose it's possible that he escaped them . . .)

(No,) Aari said. (Not without the timer. If he was able to escape at all, he would have returned for that. I know what that is like, to be stranded here with the Khleevi, hiding from them and in fear every moment for my life.)

Acorna felt Aari's hand growing stiff and icy with cold sweat despite the heat. (I saw mounds from the air with Khleevi coming and going from them. Is that the sort of place where you were when they had you, *Yaazi*?)

(I think so, yes. I don't remember seeing the outside. I was unconscious when I was captured, and the torture chamber was destroyed when the Khleevi evacuated and I escaped. But it had a domed ceiling I looked up at a lot when I was able to see, and trying to focus on something other than pain.)

(I saw one from the air as I flew to your cave and back,) she said. Her mineral sense was overloaded with foul smells, poisonous tastes, and the sinister rumbling from the tormented planet beneath their feet. But she let herself blend with the hellish landscape, felt the fissures and mountains of gravel, and finally found the right shape – the mound of slime she had noticed a mile or so from their position. (It's this way,) she said.

Sparks and ash rained down on them. Acorna's right foot sank to her knee in something sticky. She was able to pull it out only when she mired her left foot as deeply.

(Horn it all, what is *this* stuff?) her father asked.

(Khleevi slime trail,) Aari answered. It was hard to see, but he and Acorna were both well informed of its substance by the stench.

(Try to pull free and walk through it as quickly as possible. It hardens fairly rapidly. The fact that it is still liquid means one of them has passed this way quite recently.)

(They don't always leave this goo behind them though, do they?) Vaanye asked, thinking of the vids he'd seen and the reports he'd heard from those still attempting to escape the planet after the invasion began.

(Only when they're feeding,) she replied. (I do hope this isn't Grimalkin we're wading through.)

(They don't eat sentients, Khornya,) Aari reminded her. (Not at first, anyway . . .)

A tense silence fell after that remark.

Except for the sparks and the distant glow of the volcanoes that had once been Vhiliinyar's sacred peaceful mountains, the night was very dark as they moved through the blasted landscape.

It was not still, however. Though she had scarcely been aware of it beneath the groaning and grumbling of the planet in its death throes, Acorna suddenly heard the *klik*ings and *klak*ings of the Khleevi sending staccato messages to each other. She heard something else, too, among all the Khleevi chatter. She heard the yowling and howling, hissing and snarling of a cat in great fear or pain. She had only known Grimalkin in his disguise as Aari. Hearing the feline cries of terror twisted her heart.

(If he's in cat form, they will destroy him quickly,) Aari said. (Though that would be a good thing, of course, if we were not here to save him.)

Acorna saw the movement before she saw the mound; Khleevi were gathered round to watch and listen. They were peering in, *klik*ing their mandibles appreciatively as the yowling increased. They were having so much fun that they appeared unaware of the approach of the three Linyaari.

(I believe our target is now within range,) Vaanye said. (While I bow to the previous experience that I'm told you two have in anointing the Khleevi with sap, may I suggest that we aim low? If their feet are affected, they will not be able to give chase easily, and laying down a good coat of sap on the ground should make sure they are all affected, as anyone within range will be. After the initial volley, perhaps we should reserve some sap so there is enough remaining to cover our retreat, however far that may need to be until we can use the timer again.)

Acorna had learned something of her father from Grandam Naadiina and Neeva, but until that moment she had not realized that he really was the closest thing the Linyaari had to a military strategist. What he was not mentioning was that once the Khleevi's feet were damaged, the rest of their bodies would follow as they wallowed in the sap. Acorna began to feel a bit better about the entire mission.

Aari lifted a hand from his gun to scratch at his neck, face, other hand, and a bit of his leg where his shipsuit had been torn during his journey.

(What's the matter, *Yaazi?*) she asked.

(I am not a Khleevi, but I do get something of an allergic reaction to the sap. Are you not feeling it?)

(*Now* I am,) she said. She wondered if she dared to lean over and touch his itchy spots with her horn.

At that moment, a Khleevi turned around from

the entertainment happening inside the mound and saw them.

(Spray!) Vaanye said.

Acorna opened the nozzle on her sprayer and pulled the trigger on the pump sprayer. It squirted a glob of sap onto the middle of a Khleevi at the end of the spray nozzle. The Khleevi clutched itself and bent over in agony. Acorna adjusted her nozzle so it pointed down and laid a cover of sap between them and the Khleevi.

Aari forged his way toward the entry to the mound, pointing his nozzle at the feet of first one Khleevi, then another. The Khleevi parted around him and tried to scale the walls of the mound to escape the sap. He could clearly see the torture machine in the center of the room now. He ignored the rush of memories of his own time in such a chamber and ran inside. (We're too late,) he told Vaanye and Acorna. (He's gone. They must have killed him off in his cat form. There's no one here but Khleevi now.)

Seventeen

As soon as the Khleevi clamped his wrists, legs, and head to the torture machine, Grimalkin resumed cat form, shrinking himself out of the restraints. He felt the first nauseating wave of energy rise from the machine as he shot straight into the air and onto one of the many ledgelike protrusions pocking the inside of the mound.

The Khleevi surprised him by swarming up the wall after him. As they climbed up, he dropped down and dashed for the opening. Pincers snapped at his tail and he screamed and resumed biped form, thus removing himself from the Khleevi's grasp.

If only he hadn't lost the timer! If only Acorna hadn't found it and taken herself and Aari away without him. He would have been far, far away from here and now.

A Khleevi caught his arm and he shrank to cat form once more, but he knew he couldn't keep this up forever. There were other forms in which he could hide if only he could elude the Khleevi long enough to change unseen, but his two principal forms were the ones that required no concentration to shift from one to the other. He needed time to concentrate if he was going to try for something fancy.

A Khleevi caught him again, this time with its pincer encircling his head. There was no escape from that. The Khleevi tenderly put just enough pressure on his catty cranium to carry him, not enough to injure him seriously or kill him. His paws were once more strapped tightly to the chair by something that was at first sticky and foul-smelling, then rapidly hardened. Even his tail was immobilized by it. Finally, something slid under the pincers to circle his neck. As the princers pulled apart so he could see once more, he yowled over and over again, until the hardening Khleevi slime cut his wind short. What he saw now was a solid wall of Khleevi vastly entertained by his struggles and protests. Some of them crawled on the ground, and some stood. Some even hung overhead. His rapid changes had conditioned them to be alert for his shape-shifting.

The one nearest him *klik*ed its mandibles and lifted its pincers so they were about an inch from his face. They snipped, and the tip of his longest whisker fell away. He yowled with indignity and they *klik*ed and *klak*ed appreciatively. They probably thought it hurt him. He was sure that before very long, as they snipped away at him, they would be right.

His superb sense of smell in this form was totally bombarded by Khleevi stench and the fire and brimstone atmosphere of the planet, but suddenly it seemed to him that the ill wind was blowing a current of comparatively fresh, sweet air to his sensitive nostrils.

His second whisker tip fell, and he lost himself in loud, piercing caterwauling. If they thought this really hurt, they might linger over it. He just hoped his voice would hold out.

Suddenly, the wall of Khleevi surrounding him thinned. Those kneeling stood and turned away from him. Those who were tormenting him swiveled their heads to look toward the entrance.

The plant stink grew stronger, and the stench of Khleevi slime increased as several of those who had been facing him extruded it behind them and tried to climb the walls, using only their pincers. They emitted high-pitched squeals along with chatters of mandible *klik*s and *klak*s.

Grimalkin couldn't see what his captors were looking at, but he could see that the ceiling was crawling with Khleevi, clumsily swarming over each other as more and more of the beasts avoided contact with the floor.

The inevitable happened. The new ceiling crawlers bumped off the old ones and they started dropping like the dead bugs they were. Which was all very well until two of them crashed down on him.

Fortunately, the weight of the first one landed on the top of the torture machine and tipped over the chair, breaking the hardened Khleevi slime holding him. He darted to the side, avoiding catching the second Khleevi in his tender feline mid-section. Then he had time to change into the only safe form he could think of.

When he had transformed so successfully that he hardly knew himself, he scuttled forward to see what the fuss was about.

(Where *is* he?) Aari's thought images were increasingly, sickeningly violent. He imagined what had happened to Grimalkin was much the same as what had happened to him. (I heard him screaming a moment ago.)

(Yes, I did, too,) Acorna said. (You don't see him? Perhaps one of the Khleevi snatched him up.)

But as she was trying to see past the squirming, squealing Khleevi, she heard another sort of noise behind her. She had heard that noise all too recently.

(There's no time. Reinforcements are coming. You hear?) she said.

A new horde of insectoid invaders marched into the light cast from the interior of the mound. The light was greenish and vaguely glittering. Acorna thought it must be some sort of bioluminescence. She had not noted it before in connection with the Khleevi, but then, she had never been among them in a habitat of their own manufacture until now.

She stepped forward to take a position

between Aari and the oncoming force, standing with her back to his so that the containers strapped behind them were shielded. By now the interior of the mound was a mass of flailing, writhing, slipping, sliding Khleevi. They screeched so shrilly and *klak*ed so constantly that it was a good thing the Linyaari were telepathic or they wouldn't have been able to hear each other. The ceiling of the mound was covered with climbing bodies but as the sap took effect on the injured, they dropped from their high perches like overripe fruit, often taking others of their kind with them.

Aari said, (Vaanye, we have to leave! You come and watch Khornya's back. I'm going in to search for Grimalkin.)

(You can't do that. What if they're armed?)

Acorna examined the oncoming Khleevi even as she began laying down a barrier of sap between their feet and hers. (They're not,) she told her father.

Aari added, (They didn't expect us, and I think they're too dangerous to each other to carry weapons when they're not engaged in battle. I don't remember my captors ever being armed with anything but their pincers and jaws.)

(In that case, you and Khornya cover me. I'll go in.)

(*No!* Father! I cannot stand to lose you when I've only just found you.)

(I have no intention of being lost again – especially when Aari – I suppose I mean

Grimalkin – isn't available to prevent my death a second time. But I have not seen one of their mounds before or seen them vulnerable like this. I want a closer look.)

The vanguard of the reinforcements paused to sniff at the sap before stepping into it. Acorna wondered if the others had communicated with them about their previous encounter with the sap? They would have had to do so while they were dying. As far as she had been able to tell, Khleevi didn't appear to form emotional attachments, friendships, or kinships of any personal significance to them. Given that, she wondered who the dying Khleevi would warn first? As the squeals of the reinforcements joined those of the Khleevi in the mound, she found her horn itched to heal them, even despite all she knew about them. She decided it was simply her sap allergy, shook off the feeling, and shot a large gob of the sap onto the three Khleevi now dancing backward to escape her weapon. Meanwhile, others were edging around them. She shot a semicircle of the stuff around the bugs closing in on them, but her bursts were getting weaker and weaker. She was running out of ammunition.

She turned to see how Aari and her father were doing, and if their sap containers were as depleted as hers. Aari stepped forward, but she saw her father wave him back. (Stay, I tell you. Take care of her.)

Vaanye waded forward, picking up his feet and setting them down again ponderously as if he were walking on a heavy-gravity planet. Streamers of sap clung to his hooves no matter how high he lifted each foot.

(I begin to understand where you get your courage, *Yaazi,*) Aari told Acorna.

She turned and fired as a particularly hardy Khleevi crossed the narrow sap line to her right. But her weapon was sapped in more ways than one. The emerging substance extruded from the nozzle and hung there. In desperation Acorna scooped it up on her fingers and flung it at the intruder, hitting it squarely between the eyes.

It retreated.

She turned again. (Please, we have to leave. Have you received any message from Grimalkin, anything at all to show he's alive?) she asked Aari.

(He could be alive but so crazed with pain and fear that he doesn't realize we're here and that he could reach us,) Aari told her, his thought bleak with his own memories.

From the inside of the mound, a Khleevi waddled toward them, its progress through the sap even more labored than Vaanye's.

(Watch out, Father!) Acorna cried. The Khleevi seemed unaffected by the sap and ignored it. The alien homed in on Vaanye, simply ducking out of the way of its fellows as they fell from the ceiling, Vaanye fired sap at his attacker but the Khleevi wiped it off and kept coming.

(Could one of them have built up an immunity to this substance already?) Aari wondered.

Before either of them could rush to Vaanye's aid, the Khleevi snagged him with a pincer and dragged him with it, trampling its fallen fellows to get at Aari and Acorna.

Acorna fired at it point-blank, but nothing emerged from the nozzle. She backed away, toward the onslaught of Khleevi. One of the newcomers backed away, then ran forward, and she realized it would attempt – and probably succeed – to jump over the narrow channel of sap separating it from her and her companions.

Not realizing the danger from that quarter, Aari dashed forward to try to extricate Vaanye. The creature dodged him quite adeptly for one so large.

(Khornya! Watch out!) Aari warned. Failing to reach Vaanye, he now tried to block the creature from reaching Acorna. Its free limb brushed him aside and grabbed Acorna's arm, shaking the fertilizer gun out of her hand.

Three of the relief Khleevi patrol hopped across the sap barrier and bore down on them.

Aari shot a slug of sap at them, then dropped his own nozzle and shoved at the Khleevi. It focused its big bug eyes on him but did not release Acorna.

(What are you waiting for?) it demanded. (That is no mere bauble on her wrist, but I can't program it with pincers. Punch this sequence. 1800-46-788-minus 56389 and get us out of here!)

Eighteen

Acorna tore the timer from her wrist and thrust it at Aari, who was more experienced with the device. He made several quick jabs at the cool blue light of the faceplate.

All of the Khleevi except one disappeared, as did the devastated darkness of Khleevi-occupied Vhiliinyar. The remaining Khleevi turned into a cat, jumped onto Vaanye's shoulder, and disappeared. So did Vaanye. So did the timer. Acorna and Aari exchanged glances, rolled their eyes, and shrugged. There was no telling what Grimalkin was up to now.

But the acrid air was also gone, replaced by the moist perfume of sweet grass after a light rain. The rush and tinkle of a fast-running stream filled their ears, and they saw its gleam through a stand of trees a short distance from the opening of the pavilion in which they stood. Instead of darkness, they were bathed in a soft lavender-to-violet rose-to-purple twilight as the star set over the sacred mountains.

(Amazing!) Aari said, turning to her. (I had no idea so much had been accomplished with the terraforming.)

(Nor did I. But I've spent most of my time either off-world or underground with the time device. Maati told me there's been remarkable progress, but I had no idea!)

(Good of Grimalkin to bring us to such a lovely spot and discreetly vanish with your father so we can be alone – at last,) Aari remarked.

(Yes. Though I must say that I have learned to be wary of Grimalkin's goodness.)

(You have a point. But he's not really so bad. I thought so when I believed he'd abandoned me to the Khleevi, but now I realize he was just curious about you. I must be more careful about singing your praises to other males, no matter what species they are.)

(What praises are those?) she teased. (I haven't heard them sung in quite some time – at least not by you.)

(Oh, you know. How beautiful you are ... Grimalkin can hardly tell the difference between one Linyaari and another – can you imagine? How brave you are, how clever . . .) He broke off to give himself a vigorous scratch in several places. (Do you suppose you could get my back? The sap itches so much I feel like leaving my body to get away from it.)

(I have a better idea,) Acorna said. (Let's go bathe in the stream. We'll find some soapweed on the way and do a good job.)

The soapweed grew conveniently near the stream banks. They stripped off the awkward containers that had held the sap, then their ship-suits and boots. Even in the moonlight, she saw that Aari's skin and her own were red and bumpy where they had been exposed to the sap.

'Me first!' Aari said, and jumped into the stream feetfirst, splashing droplets that glittered like amethysts and rubies in the dying light.

Acorna waded in after him. To her surprise and pleasure, the water was not cold, just pleasantly cool. It felt soothing on her irritated skin. She pulled soapweed from the banks and handed Aari some. Then she helped him find all of the hidden places the sap had invaded, and all of the hurts and bruises, and she soothed and healed them.

He did the same for her, lingering where her skin was the most tender or sore, following each cleansing with a touch of horn and a light kiss. She needed no birth disk to tell her that this was truly Aari, *her* Aari. The smell and feel of him were just right, the tension of muscle beneath his skin, the cording of the veins in his forearms and neck, the beloved stunted knot of horn that was in its very imperfection all the more beautiful to her.

When he finished his exploration, she felt every cell of her being vibrating with the longing for closer touch and guessed he felt the same.

But, to her disappointment, Aari dragged

himself up on the bank and lay down in the grass, where he fell asleep.

Sighing, she plucked their shipsuits from the bank and scrubbed them, laying them and herself on the bank beside Aari to dry. Then she joined him in slumber.

Soon she was dreaming that she was being lifted and carried in strong, familiar arms, her head resting against a well-loved shoulder. She didn't need to open her eyes all the way to know that it was true. He carried her back to the pavilion and laid her upon the feather-soft sleeping mat. He started to rise and roll over to sleep again, but she kept her arms around his neck and pulled him down into her embrace again. (*Yaazi,* I am so glad you are finally home. Now I need you to come all the way home to me. All the way home.)

Grimalkin leaped down from Vaanye's shoulder. Immediately, the wretched ship's cat landed on him with all talons extended, sharp fangs sinking into his head.

(Scum-sucking phony, I've had enough of you!) RK growled, rolling over with him to try to get at Grimalkin's underside. (I knew you were nothing but a flea-bitten mite-eared, worm-tailed moggy from the first time I saw you.)

(That's no way to treat one of your ancestors,) Grimalkin squawled in protest. (What is it with you anyway? You're a cat, I'm a cat, what's the problem?)

(This is *my* turf, and those people you've been upsetting are *my* people. Give them back *nyow* or I'll gut you and go fishing with your entrails.)

RK's back claws gouged hunks out of Grimalkin's hindquarters. The ship's cat twisted to bring himself onto Grimalkin's exposed belly.

Grimalkin changed back to his Linyaari form.

RK still clung to him.

Grimalkin batted at him ineffectually with both his hands, screeching, 'Someone get this monster off me!'

Someone did. 'Cut it out, you fuzz-butted fraud. Let him alone!' Becker thundered as he pried RK's claws loose.

'Thank you,' Grimalkin said, trying to regain his dignity. Unfortunately, his dignity was in shreds, along with several others parts of him. 'I don't know what he has against me.'

'I do. And I was talking to you, not RK. What did you do with Aari and Acorna?'

Grimalkin ignored him and backed up to Vaanye. 'Please. I am in pain. Heal me.'

'Please answer Captain Becker first,' Vaanye said.

'But you were with me. You know they're fine.'

'I did not see where we were. You changed times so rapidly I saw nothing except that they were gone, and you and I returned here. I cannot believe you continue to be so devious and secretive when the three of us just risked our lives and worse to go back to face the Khleevi and save you.'

'Devious? Secretive? Me? I was simply rewarding my dear friends by taking them somewhere beautiful and peaceful where they could finally be alone together and enjoy each other before returning to yet another disaster.' He motioned to the lines of people from ships to the cave entrance, the pumps, the mud, and the air of urgency. 'I have been trying to help them all along, and for my trouble have received only distrust and anger. Not from you, of course, Vaanye. At least, not until now. I am an empath. I suffer when you suffer. I suffered when *they* suffered. When this crisis is done, I will fetch them back. Meanwhile, they have earned a little holo day, don't you think?'

Vaanye sighed, misunderstanding as Grimalkin had figured he would. 'Yes, yes, of course they have. It's just that Feriila and I have had so little time with Khornya ourselves. But what time we've had we owe to you. We can be patient a bit longer.' His posture had relaxed, and his voice softened, but it hardened one more time as he said, 'Just so they return as you say they will. Meanwhile, I think it might be a good idea if I keep the timing device for you, in case you are tempted to disappear again.'

'Good thinking, Acorna's Dad,' Becker said. He stood with his feet slightly apart, his fists balled at his sides as if he wished they were holding wrenches, crowbars, or other blunt and weighty objects capable of inducing trauma.

'Very well,' Grimalkin said, and removed the

timer from his neck, where it rested when he was in cat form and could be programmed with touches from his hind foot. As he feinted with it toward Vaanye, he pressed the preprogrammed tab, then popped the device back around his own wrist. He had to laugh at the looks on their faces just before they vanished from his timescape.

They'd probably accuse him of deviousness again, but he was only thinking of everyone's greater good. He could not surrender his timer. He had events to arrange, histories to shape, fate to engineer. If people were occasionally resentful of his power, it was because their understanding of the cosmos was too limited to encompass an understanding of his responsibilities.

Like the one he must discharge now, knowing even as he did so that somehow or other it was bound to cause him more trouble.

He arrived at the healing center three days after he deposited Aari and Acorna in the holo suite there. The center was seldom used, now that the unicorns were on Vhiliinyar and could so readily heal any injuries or illnesses. The holo suite was relatively new, and spacious enough that occupants could go for a romantic walk and never guess they were within a single room. Before he rescued Aari the first time, he had seen to it that the suite was especially tailored to contemporary Linyaari tastes. Whether it was intuition, or a memory from time he had spent in the future, he had known even then that the suite would be needed, though not exactly how or why.

The pavilion had appointments their people found comfortable. The grasses were those they favored. The climate was carefully controlled to be pleasant and relaxing. Rain would patter down only when the occupants were near enough to the pavilion to enjoy a few refreshing drops before seeking shelter. Dramatic storms occurred only while the occupants were snug inside the pavilion. It was always twilight, or dawn, when the world was at its most beautiful, and not incidentally, at its most indistinct. Even the temperature of the stream was chosen with Linyaari pleasure in mind.

It turned out to be the perfect place for – what had the humans called it? A honeymoon. This was the perfect place for their honeymoon, where Aari's and Acorna's union would be repeatedly consummated and where they could bond in peace.

Grimalkin stopped by his own den, which changed the spots and stripes of its upholstery, floor, and wall coverings in slow rotation, a cosmic cat joke.

He checked the observation screen and saw that within the suite it was night. Aari and Acorna slept tangled together in each other's arms. He gulped, feeling an unfamiliar ache in his upper thorax. They were very beautiful together. Maybe even more beautiful than they were separately.

He checked the readings from the suite's internal monitors. What they told him was more definitive than he had hoped or imagined. It was a perfect opportunity. Much more perfect than what he had planned to do. Yet it also made him sad. They would never know, of course. There was no need for them ever to know, and what they didn't know could not hurt them. And it would be beneficial to the project, the race, and ultimately the universe. He was, of course, overjoyed to be the bearer of such a gift.

He wished he did not have to – *betray* was rather a loaded word, wasn't it? *Trick,* then. He wished he did not have to trick them again. But he did.

And he would only feel worse the longer he delayed, so, gathering what he needed, he entered the holo suite.

It was time.

NINETEEN

Acorna awoke quickly, though she felt uncommonly drowsy and stiff. But she was aware, even before her eyes opened, that they were no longer alone. Beside her, Aari sat straight up.

'Grimalkin,' they said together.

'Hello, lovebirds!' he said, looking even more smug than usual. Becker would say he had that 'cat who swallowed the canary' look. Grimalkin was in cat-man form now, standing on two feet but wearing an orange-and-cream-striped tail, an inhuman amount of body fur in the same colors, and ears on top of his head, twitching in all directions. Though his face was more or less human, his pupils were unnaturally wide and round in the dim light of the pavilion, and his eyes glittered with the nocturnal brightness of a cat's. The mustache under his human nose was composed of very long individual whiskers that drooped like the mustache of one of those Fu Manchu villains in old vids.

'I hope you have all of *that* out of your systems

and are ready to rejoin your people. I have other things to do than ferry you around, you know.'

'Yes,' Aari said lazily. 'Now that you're alive and away from the torture machine to do them, I'm sure you do.'

'Don't think I'm not grateful,' Grimalkin said in a way that told Acorna that although he thought he *ought* to be grateful, the cat creature could not quite get his mind around the concept. 'This little vacation was in part my way of thanking you.'

'What was the other part?' Acorna asked, instantly suspicious.

Grimalkin's eyes grew even bigger and filled with kittenish innocence. He was as difficult to read as ever. But he hesitated slightly before answering, 'Why, to allow you to rest, of course. Both of you were completely exhausted from your travels, and I felt somewhat responsible . . .'

'You *were* responsible,' they said in unison.

'Hmph, I said *somewhat*. Nothing interesting was happening in your usual haunts . . .'

'Except for floods and mass destruction,' Acorna said. 'But I don't suppose a little thing like that concerns you.'

'All of that is under control. Don't you think there are others who can deal with that sort of problem? And you two didn't need to take on any more trouble just now. You needed to relax. So I brought you here.'

'Where – or should I say when – is here exactly?' Aari asked.

'Never mind that. It is time for you to go back to your dreary workaday existences.'

He grabbed their hands, but first Acorna snatched up their shipsuits and tossed one to Aari. He looked regretfully at it. The Linyaari had no moral issues or societal mores concerning public nudity, but Acorna had been raised by humans. She had her share of rules about clothing. She pulled her suit on before taking Grimalkin's hand. Aari shrugged resignedly and did likewise.

One moment they were inside the pavilion holding Grimalkin's hands and the next they were in the field outside the cave entrance. But Grimalkin was gone.

They stood beside the *Condor*, watching the emergency crews remove their flood control equipment. Feriila ran up to greet them. 'Khornya! Aari, you're back. I will let Vaanye know. We have so been looking forward to spending time with you! Vaanye is in the old city inspecting the damage to the time device.'

Behind them, the robolift descended, and Becker yelled, 'Hey, kids! Good to see you finally got out of the sack and came back to work!'

RK and Mac were with him. Feriila disappeared into the tunnel. Acorna hugged Becker and lifted RK for a kiss, but the cat immediately squirmed to be released. Mac, his horn modification attached to his forehead, patted her carefully on the shoulder and, just as carefully, shook hands with Aari.

'I'm not even going to ask what you've been up to,' Becker said, winking at them, 'but we have been real busy here. The flood messed up a lot of the old city. I have some of the most interesting salvage of my career aboard now. Can't wait to get out of here and find me some buyers. It's the durndest stuff you ever saw. And I can pack a lot of it aboard because its molecules are so loosely bonded it keeps changing shapes all the time. I literally was able to fit an entire hospital building into Bay 7.'

'But the waters have receded?' Acorna asked.

'Not really. We pumped them up and dumped them into the rivers and what's left up here of the sea. The surface still needs the water. There's an artesian well down there underneath the time device apparently. The people who used to live there regulated the flow, but the Khleevi you brought back with you busted the regulator. Your dad and some of the other engineers were able to fix that, but so far, they say it looks as if the time machine itself is toast.'

(Our people have made remarkable strides in trusting *this* outsider at least,) Aari said. (Remember when they didn't want him to step onto the surface of narhii-Vhiliinyar?)

(Yes, and even when the Council decided he could be permitted to land here in an emergency, at first he couldn't leave the *Condor*, then he wasn't to know about the ancient city or the time device.)

(Perhaps we should have an artificial horn

made for him for his natal day?) Aari suggested playfully.

(Don't mention that aloud, or he'll want one,) Acorna said, smiling.

Becker looked from one of them to the other, grinning uncertainly. 'Okay, what are you two thinking at each other? It's about me, right?'

'We can't tell you,' Acorna said. 'It's a surprise.'

'Oh!' he huffed into his mustache. 'Really. Well, okay, then.'

They strolled toward the tunnel mouth as they talked, reaching it just as Vaanye and Feriila arrived, followed closely by Laarye and Maati.

Vaanye embraced them both. 'I confess I was a little worried about you two being somewhere known only to Grimalkin.' He spoke aloud for the sake of Becker and Mac, and the others followed suit.

'We worried about it, too,' Aari said, putting his arm around Acorna's shoulders. 'But we finally resigned ourselves to the inevitable and made the best of it. Fortunately for us, for a change Grimalkin proved trustworthy and came to get us.'

'I still don't trust him,' Maati said. 'He's a very shifty kitty.'

'But he has done great good along with all his tricks,' Laarye argued. 'We are all back together again because of him. And not dead. I certainly count that as a positive development.'

'True,' Maati said. 'But he only did it because it

suited him to do so while he was doing something else. Still, I'm glad. I know I should feel grateful to him, but I guess I'm still waiting to see what else he's up to.'

'I suggest we forget about Grimalkin and what he might do and concentrate on the problems we currently have at hand,' Vaanye said. 'Khornya, Aari, you two are more familiar with the time device than any of us. Perhaps you would care to examine the damage the Khleevi inflicted yourselves and make some recommendations?'

'I, too, would like to see it,' Mac said. 'As a fellow device, in a manner of speaking, I might have some helpful suggestions. Before the Khleevi returned with our friends, I collected and processed considerable data about the mechanism. It may help me analyze its operation and participate in its possible repair.'

Becker accompanied them since he needed to pack up some more salvage. 'Pretty nice of them to give me the concession on all this stuff they're tossing out, seeing as how I didn't even know the city was there until a few weeks ago.'

As they slipped and slid down the passageway's mud-slicked rock floor, he remarked, 'This is the cleanest-smelling flood site it has ever been my honor to visit. No smell of mold, no old sewage mixed with the water. The Linyaari horns took care of all that, I guess. The place is pretty well wrecked, of course. But instead of being a filthy mess, this place just looks like it got put through a too-enthusiastic rinse cycle.'

Acorna saw that Becker was correct when they traversed the freshly washed tunnel. She was glad to see none of the cave's paintings had been damaged. Instead, they were brighter than ever, gleaming as though they had just been painted. Small pools of water glistening in the indentations of the cave's floor were the only indication the place had been flooded.

The time device building was the worse for wear – though the damage seemed to be from the struggling Khleevi rather than the floodwaters. The walls no longer lit when they were touched. Panels had come loose, littering the hallway and leaving openings into the various rooms.

But the room where the time device had been was the worst. The Khleevi had done more damage than she realized, gouging great holes in the planetary maps within the walls, leaving circuitry exposed. The huge double helix that had once dominated the center of the room was gone. It left behind only the hastily patched container to hold the now placid pool.

Acorna knew without further examination that the delicate device was damaged beyond *her* ability to mend it, at least. But she went through the motions of looking at everything, just in case her intuition was wrong, though she was sure it wasn't.

Then she heard the footsteps – not single ones, but important, impatient ones, steps of beings with two-hoofed feet and also the steps of beings with four.

Thariinye, looking very important and impatient himself, stood in the entrance, and announced, 'The Linyaari High Council and a Delegation of Ancestors has come to inspect the premises and make a determination as to its disposition.'

'Whoa there, big boy,' Becker said. 'I think we agreed that I got whatever was to be disposed of.'

With the Ancestors in the front, the Council members paraded soberly into the room. The Council questioned each of those who had come to fix the time machine. Then, without comment, the Council departed to tour the rest of the city. Acorna climbed after them to the upper level. Crude stairs had been inserted into the hill-like barrier between the lower floor and the upper.

From this level she could see clearly into the street beyond. It was not a pretty sight. Many of the structures had already been cleared. Some that remained were little more than partial frameworks with bits of façade clinging to them. Others continued to shift their shapes – but each disconnected piece shifted at a different rate into a different sort of building from all of the other parts. To Becker, at least, it looked like the nightmare of an architect who had had far, far too much to drink.

Thariinye acted as the guide, marching the Council up and down streets. The only place they paused at for any length of time was the shore of the little inland sea at the foot of the incline on which the city was built. The *sii*-Linyaari lived there now. Maati said the reclamation efforts would have been far less successful without the help of the aquatic people placing pumps and hoses and helping to shut off the artesian well. The sea churned briefly, then was full of horned heads, smacking tails, and gesticulating webbed hands. That consultation continued for some time before the Council performed an about-face and marched back to the time device building.

'Please be so kind as to follow us back to the surface,' *Aagroni* Iirtyi said. 'There we will advise everyone at once of our decision.'

Once they were all aboveground, the ships' communications officers returned to their posts and hailed other crews at work on Vhiliinyar's surface as well as Linyaari on MOO and narhii-Vhiliinyar.

Mac returned to the *Condor* on Becker's behalf. Becker remained at the invitation of the Council.

'What we have to say concerns you, too, Captain.' The *aagroni* was the speaker now. 'The items you have already salvaged from the city below you may sell abroad, as is your practice. However, there is one condition.'

'Name it,' Becker said.

'You must never let anyone know where you obtained these things.'

'Of course. I never reveal my sources even without conditions.' Becker sounded mildly offended, but very relieved.

'Very well. Out of courtesy, we felt we should

address your concerns first. For the rest, we will be brief. On the advice of the Ancestors we came as a body to inspect the city following the recent calamity, with a view toward abandoning the site.'

'Abandoning it?' Maati said. 'I don't understand. There's so much to be learned, to be done down there . . .'

'If one chooses to pursue it, that is true. However, the Council and the Ancestors feel that our energies and resources would be more usefully employed in the continued rejuvenation of Vhiliinyar.'

'But, *aagroni*, you yourself have used the machine to bring back specimens of lifeforms lost during the Khleevi invasion. Our terraforming crew has used it to model the planet's new face. It has been extremely valuable in this work.'

'Yes, it has. I put forth the same arguments myself. But this was not my decision alone. Even while acknowledging those contributions, the Council – and the Ancestors – feel that there is too strong an element of danger involved with the use of the device. For instance, when Acorna and Aari brought Khleevi back into our time again, however accidentally. At present they are blessedly extinct. We very much wish to keep them that way.

'The only issue for the preservation of the underground city that is equally compelling, in our estimation, as the argument for abandoning the site is that it has become a habitat for the *sii*-Linyaari who have been brought forward to our time. We propose, therefore, that the *sii*-Linyaari be brought aboveground along with as much of their watery habitat as it is possible to bring. They may live among us and we may learn from each other as the siblings we are. Otherwise, the Council has decided that the city is to be sealed off once more. It is too expensive and time-consuming to attempt to repair the damage done to it, even assuming we felt that was the best course of action for our people. And, without those repairs, it is far too hazardous for anyone to continue the studies of the Ancestral Friends' mechanisms. The usefulness of the time machine is also no longer an issue, since that has been destroyed. Of course, if a large enough percentage of our people petition a change in this decree, we will reconsider. But for the time being, except for the reintroduction of the *sii*-Linyaari to the surface waterways, the underground city – and the matter – are closed. We trust this will facilitate the progress of our more urgent work on our planet. Thank you.'

TWENTY

Karina's voice over the com unit was breathless, though she tried to maintain her deep mystical sonorous tones to lend authority to her words. Her chins and bosom trembled with emotion as she spoke, and her hands moved with fingers extending upward in both offering and benediction. Behind her, Hafiz's chins trembled with emotion as he watched Karina's chins and bosom. 'I see a large gathering of people of diverse species and origins. Despite these superficial differences, many of them are related to each other through a single connection. Important life passages are taking place at the gathering. Two females, of different species, and yet, soon to be related, will become formally attached to their mates according to the rites of their indigenous cultures. There will be beautiful gowns, sumptuous fabrics, fine jewels, and rich and delicious foods to please all palates.'

'What my beloved Karina is trying to say,' Hafiz interjected, 'is that we wish to have a party celebrating the marriage of my beloved nephew and son of my heart to the woman he first met in her previous capacity as a thief. This pretty thief has stolen his heart it seems. Additionally, Karina, Rafik, and I would all like to formally celebrate the reunion of the daughter of our heart, you, dear Acorna, to your mate. We realize that the custom among your people is to make the forming of the lifemate bond under less formal circumstances, but we hope you will indulge our barbaric love of pageantry when such events occur in the lives of our loved ones.'

Acorna thoughtfully stroked RK's proffered tail and turned to Aari, Becker, and Mac. 'We can hardly say no after all Uncle Hafiz has done for us,' she said. And, as she said it, she heard in the lilt of her own voice how very much the idea pleased her.

'Ask them if I would need to braid my mane with flowers and ribbons,' Aari said, wrinkling his nose.

Acorna laughed and conveyed his concern to the com unit. Rafik poked his head around the portly forms of his elder relations. 'Tell him I certainly don't intend to, and that we bridegrooms should stick together.'

'Bridegrooms?' Mac said. 'An unusual word. But, Khornya, from my research into the sociological patterns of wholly biological bipeds, it seems to me that when the principal person involved in a rite of passage is from two cultures, the rite is frequently celebrated according to the customs of first one, and then the other. Since you were raised in human culture, it would not be inappropriate for you and Aari to wed according to human custom.'

'There. See? Mac says it's okay, so it must be okay,' Becker said. 'I'll haul out the dress uniform. Weddings are good for business. You can do a lot of valuable schmoozing at the receptions, and you know Hafiz will invite a lot of his business buddies.'

'Do you think Calum and Gill will come?' Acorna asked Rafik wistfully. She hadn't seen her other two foster fathers since the defeat of the Khleevi.

Rafik grinned. 'They'd better. They're the groomsmen. They started wrangling about who would be best man at my wedding, so Hafiz took matters into his own hands and declared that *he* would be the best man. Then they sulked and neither of them were going to come until we told them we planned to get you and Aari hitched at the same time – uh – according to our quaint native customs.' He grinned evilly. 'Now *you* get to decide which of your daddies gets to give you away.'

'But I don't want to be given away,' she said. 'I want to keep all of you.'

Mac said, 'I think this is an opportunity for you to forge some new customs, Rafik. Perhaps a committee formed of yourself, Mr. Baird, Mr. Giloglie, Uncle Hafiz, Vaanye, Captain Becker, and I should see Khornya safely to Aari's side at the ceremony.'

'Sounds kinda like a posse,' Becker suggested, with a twinkle under his heavy brows. 'Too bad Aari doesn't have as many people to make sure he gets to the altar on time. He's the one who's done the most disappearing.'

'Actually,' Hafiz said, 'we will be entertaining a state visit from Makahomia at that time, led by Regent Nadhari and the Mulzarah Miw-Sher. I believe they feel they have a very strong claim to our Aari, who is widely celebrated in Makahomian history, legend, and myth.'

RK's ears pricked up, and Hafiz noticed. 'The original purpose of the visit,' he continued, 'was to deliver two of the new litters of kittens as a planet-warming gift to the Linyaari from the people of Makahomia. It seems to me that things are falling together nicely. Leave matters in my hands, and all will be well.'

Thus it was that a remarkably short time later, amid much fanfare and confusion, a double ceremony was held on the Moon of Opportunity, uniting Rafik and Aziza in holy matrimony, and also uniting Aari and Acorna as lifemates.

The double-wide wedding canopy, with ample room for expanded wedding parties, was adorned with red silk and garlands of brilliant orange-gold flowers, which incidentally happened to be delicious to eat for the Linyaari. Aziza wore a gold-gilt-filigree-trimmed gown of sheer silks layered rose over orange over rust over red over wine. Her hands, feet, and face were painted with intricate reddish designs, which was an ancient practice among her people.

Acorna's gown, ordered for her by Karina, was of a similar style to Aziza's, though it was more flowing than draped and tucked. The gown's skirt and long, bell-shaped sleeves were a waterfall of brilliant aqua over deep emerald, all over deep blue, and trimmed in silver to complement Acorna's complexion. Grandam Naadiina's belt was the perfect finishing touch to the outfit. It served as the 'something old' Mercy Kendoro told Acorna she needed as a charm for good luck and happiness.

Mercy, Judit, Calum and Gill had all arrived a week before the festivities so that the ladies could help with the preparations. Of course, there were several hundred staff members, relatives, and friends already there to help, but Mercy and Judit had recent knowledge of the wedding customs that Calum's and Gill's people followed.

'Let's see, Grandam's belt is the "something old." Your gown is the "something blue." Calum wishes you to carry a kerchief in the tartan that's related to his family. So you'll be borrowing that. Something new? Hmmm. We could say you're getting a new husband, but you and Aari have actually been together for some time.'

'The dress can be blue and new, too, can't it?' Acorna asked.

'Well, yes, I suppose so,' Mercy agreed reluctantly. It was clear that she felt that they really should be separate items.

Karina, who had been circling Acorna as she tried on the wedding gown, snapped her fingers, and said, 'I know what it is!' She looked meaningfully at Acorna's hand, then at Mercy's and Judit's. However, they looked back at Acorna's three-fingered, single-knuckled hands.

'Oh, well, perhaps not,' Karina said. 'But something! I must go see to it at once! And talk to Aari, of course.'

Feriila, who had been sitting quietly in the corner, out of the way of the cyclones created by the human women, suddenly giggled. '*I* know what's new, daughter.'

Baffled, Acorna turned to her. 'You do, Mother?' It was so nice to have someone to call 'Mother.' She had many fathers and uncles and even an aunt, but it pleased her deeply every time she reaffirmed the presence of her own actual mother, who was once again in her life. Of course, her mother looked to be about the same age as she was, but that was to be expected. The Linyaari aged very slowly once they reached adulthood, and then there was all that time-shifting to confuse the issue. 'What?'

'You mean you don't know yet? Hasn't she spoken to you?'

'I don't understand what you mean.'

'Your daughter. The one who caused you to loosen Grandam's belt a notch just now.' She shook her head in amazement, staring at first her own abdomen, then at Acorna. 'It seems only a few weeks ago you were *my* baby daughter.' Her mouth quirked wryly. 'That's time travel for you, I suppose. It *was* only weeks ago in my life. And now I will be a grandam, and you the mother of a daughter.'

'I'm having a daughter? When?' She didn't know what to ask, and instead of addressing Feriila, asked her question of her own mid-section, which gurgled. Not in answer to the inquiry, but because she hadn't grazed all day long, having been so busy with meeting and greeting the steady stream of arriving guests.

'Soon. Our children grow quickly, you know. You'd better finish this rite of passage in short order and brace yourself for the next one.'

'Really? Oh, I can't believe it! How wonderful! Our own child already! I have to find Aari . . .'

Mercy and Judit laughed and held her back as she tried to jump down from the chair on which she was standing while they pinned up her dress to just the right length. They insisted that laser stitchers just weren't accurate enough since they needed measurements input instead of using a keen bridesmaid's eye. 'Whoa, Acorna! Not in that dress! It's bad luck for the groom to see the bride in her gown before the wedding.'

'You're joking! He's seen me in nothing at all! Why should it be bad luck for him to see me in this pretty dress?'

'It's just a human superstition, but *I* think the

reason is it spoils the surprise. We're done here for now. Change and then go find him. Please?'

She laughed at them but did as they asked.

She found Aari seeking sanctuary from the wedding chaos in the laboratory with his parents and Laarye. His human friends had been bombarding him with their plans and expectations, too, she knew. Judit said males were programmed not to enjoy their role in these ceremonies as much as females.

But Acorna's news had nothing to do with ceremonies and everything to do with love.

After Acorna told Aari her good news, the others had to make their wedding preparations without them, as they were too busy taking long walks through the gardens, grazing, gazing at the holo sky at the top of the bubble, and thinking of baby names, planning for the new arrival a variety of childhoods and careers.

The ceremony, when it finally arrived, was very lively. MOO's security chief was accompanied down the aisle by her trusted lieutenants and kinswomen. They had traded in their black uniforms for new dance costumes that were even more colorful and revealing than the ones they'd first worn. From the way each dancer made eyes over her veils at the men seated around the center aisle, Acorna guessed each of them was thinking that the next such ceremony could be hers.

Rafik looked . . . well . . . beautiful. Instead of

his familiar shipsuit, he wore an outfit that might have been in the closet of the Arabian Nights' sultan, Harun al Rashid. His clothing was in the same colors as that of his bride, with the addition of a dollop of yellow-orange, his shirt. Standing beside him, Aari looked skittish, as if he was about to bolt, as if he would almost rather be facing the Khleevi than this.

But then Acorna followed Aziza and the dancing girls up the aisle, and Aari turned and saw her. His face lit up in a grin that almost, but not quite, bared his teeth. The rest of the ceremony was a blur for her. She felt as if she were wearing one of the dancers' antigrav belts, as if she were floating a foot off the ground. Words flew around and through her like so many bright birds. She could only hope they said them in the correct order. All of the other faces were a blur. Only Aari's eyes held hers and her hand gripped his, which gripped hers back as if separate tractor beams were trying to pull them away from each other.

When Rafik and Aziza exchanged rings, Aari slipped a bracelet onto Acorna's wrist – Karina's idea of something new, Acorna realized. Rings were impractical for the Linyaari, but this bracelet bore in its center a teal blue catseye large enough that she could carve out a home in any wilderness if she so desired. Carve out a whole city, in fact. Aari smiled apologetically and winked. They both knew that there was no saying no to Karina, who only meant to be kind and generous, after all.

At the end of the ceremony was the reception. More merry-making ensued, with the wedding garden suddenly terraced with banks of edible reeds, flowers, vines, and plants. It was all too much.

Then there were the gifts. The Linyaari, unfamiliar with these customs, mostly brought bouquets of edibles, but the humans lavished both of the couples with all manner of things. The agents of Skarness brought a set of stones for Aari and Acorna. When the agents learned of Acorna's condition, the stones were retuned for lullabies.

Becker was far more excited about the news of their incipient offspring than he was about the wedding. He gave them a set of children's vids and some rather decrepit hard-copy volumes of stories about an odd-looking ursine creature who lived on a planet populated with a braying, depressed equine with long ears and a very energetic feline not unlike Grimalkin. It seemed to possess an unusually flexible set of antigrav-technology-equipped paws. 'I think he's confused the wedding reception with the baby shower,' Andina said, smiling as they opened her set of cleaning supplies.

Even RK got into the act. Acorna thought there was something odd about his fur when she first saw him at the reception, then realized that parts of it were blue and part had red designs on it rather like those on Aziza's hands and feet. 'Cat got himself painted by a Makahomian cat painter from the planet's delegation. That hot jungle cat Haruna came with them, and she had a dandy paint job, too. It's something the cats do on special occasions, and RK didn't want to be left out. He brought you these.' Becker hefted a dead rodent and one of the large bags of cat food with which he'd replenished the *Condor*'s supply. 'Well, the kid will need a kitten. The kitten will need food. We're thinking practical here. The – uh – dead rat is a customary cat gift. Feel free to heal it if you want to.' Acorna and Aari looked nervously toward the Makahomians. Instead of the rumored litters of kittens, they had brought with them only Grimla and Haruna and one of the kittens, now almost fully grown, from the orphaned litter Grimla rescued in the steppes. Acorna couldn't have been happier to see her old friends.

Mac apologetically said he was making them a gift. He had not had time to finish it yet.

Hafiz's gift was a new space vessel of their very own.

(Good,) Aari told her. (It will give us someplace to put all these other things. What do we do with three portable kaf replicators anyway?)

(Perhaps we can trade one of them with Aziza and Rafik, in case they got three of something we might need one of.)

(We don't need any of these things! We need a name for our daughter! We need good teachers, we need . . .)

(Excuse me, Aari. I hate to break in like this,

but I cannot make myself heard otherwise.) That was Feriila. The crowd around them parted to make room for her and Vaanye. (I have something for you. Miiri gave Khornya your birth disk.) She pulled a silver chain from around her neck, and the little disk winked with rainbows from the party lights. (I thought this was an appropriate time to give you Khornya's.)

Aari's family smiled across at Feriila, as Aari ducked down to receive her gift.

(We will, of course, arrange for the birthing assistants and physicians, if needed,) Kaarlye told him. The Linyaari were all using thought-talk now because it was very difficult to make themselves heard over the noise of the party.

(And we have employed the best artisan among our people to create your daughter's birth disk,) Miiri said. All of the Linyaari relatives smiled.

When they finally caught up with him, Grimalkin was batting at a shiny silver disk and watching it spin.

'Give us the specimen, Grimalkin,' the eagle said as it landed in the tree where he had been hiding and changed into a beautiful woman. 'You know you can't escape us. We got your timer.'

'Yes, I know, and I'd like to make a formal objection about that . . .'

'I'm sure you would. Return the specimen, and we'll discuss this rationally. That is, if you are still capable of rational thought, words, or deeds.'

Grimalkin sulked and palmed the disk. 'I am. More than you are. Why should you censure me when I exceeded all of you in obtaining what we need?'

A man who was still folding his long tail into his rather simian body answered. 'It's your attitude, and you know it. Exceeded all of us indeed! Without authorization, you released a valuable subject of study.'

'You were scaring him to death. Besides, there was an easier way. I thought.'

'This led you off-planet with him for how many time twists? And the rest of your story, about the brother and that cultural half-breed mate of his.'

'Khornya. Acorna. And it wasn't a story, it was true.'

'True or not, it was quite a story. You cannot simply go chasing your tail through time because the potential donor of some useful genetic material believes himself to be frightened of us. Look what you led him into when it suited you to become better acquainted with his mate! You are not fit to carry a timer, Grimalkin. You lost it, and it could easily have fallen into the hands . . . no, pincers . . . of those monsters. As it was, they ruined this time facility for all future generations. Besides which, three unauthorized subjects used your timer without supervision. It could very well have been lost to you then. You are too irresponsible to continue carrying it. You are certainly not reliable enough to retain possession of the specimen.'

'It is not a specimen, it – she – is a child in progress. The child of your subject and the cultural half-breed. They are friends of mine—'

'Which is why you took it?'

'They have another one.'

'Why did you not bring it as well, then?' the woman demanded. 'Their sort enjoy making more.'

'I saw no reason to be greedy. Starting the Linyaari race from one individual from the future race is *truly* chasing our own tails, if you consider it, as you say, rationally. Taking a second female with the same DNA and genetic structure would be pointless.'

'Not at all. We may need a backup. Zygotes are fragile. Something might happen to it.'

'Exactly,' Grimalkin hissed, his eyes narrowing. 'Which is why I decided not to give her to you after all. That and – she is lonely. She misses her sister. I had no idea she'd feel that way. I couldn't wait to get away from my littermates, myself.'

'Be that as it may, you cannot care for the specimen – for the incipient infant – and it will soon outgrow the collection womb. You will need our facilities to preserve its – her – viability.'

'I plan to return her to Aari and Acorna.'

'I see. And Acorna can simply put it back where it came from until it is born?'

'No – no, I believe it is too old at this stage. But something could be done.'

'Something has been done, Grimalkin. We have taken your timer so you cannot return the specimen. It will die unless you give it to us to preserve. In doing so, as you well know, you will have provided the missing link between ourselves, the unicorns, and the Linyaari.'

He could not argue. The beings surrounding him, known to the Linyaari as the Ancestral Hosts or Friends, were shape-shifters as powerful, maybe even more powerful, than he. They were excellent at political intrigue, whereas he considered himself merely tricky. He brought forth the collection womb and stroked it with the pad of his hand that was rapidly turning into a paw. (Don't be frightened, little one. No one will hurt you. And the unicorns are rather nice.)

(?) The thought was small and indistinct – probably inaudible to the telepathy of those around them, but it twisted something inside him with unexpected pain.

The woman reached for it.

He pulled it back. 'I'll just carry it as far as the laboratory, then I will relinquish it.'

'You'll relinquish it now or risk its destruction,' she told him.

'Oh, very well. Don't fret, little one. Daa will come and visit you often.'

The woman took the womb and handed it to a swan-woman, who flew away with it.

'I'm afraid that won't be possible, Grimalkin. You see, we've decided to banish you.'

'Banish me? You can't do that!'

'Oh, but we can. We have your timer, but we can send you whenever we wish. Since you are so concerned about this family, we suggest you return to them if they'll have you. You'll have a lot of explaining to do. I'm afraid you'll have a difficult time doing it.'

He was shrinking into his smallest cat form as she spoke, literally shrinking away from her.

She held out her hand, and the simian man slapped an instrument into it. Grimalkin tried to change again. She pointed it at him, and he felt something tight and cold, so cold, enter him.

'Just as you froze the forms of the acid creatures you mentioned, we can freeze your form. Perhaps this will be beneficial to your fickle nature. Good-bye. Good riddance.'

Grimalkin could only mew and vanish.

Twenty-one

As Feriila predicted, the baby began communicating before she was born. She knew the thought-form for mother – '*Lalli*' and the one for father, '*Avvi*.' It delighted Aari when he picked up on it, though at times Acorna felt a bit foolish talking to her own abdomen. But often the baby seemed restless, more than just the restlessness of the child longing to escape the womb for the wide worlds beyond. She lacked something, called for something with a word her parents didn't understand. When one of those incidents happened, it took a long time to comfort her. Acorna had the oddest feeling that just when she and her baby were the closest, the child was lonely.

The baby became a source of contention. Hafiz felt he could offer Acorna the best medical care on MOO. The Council, on the other hand, felt the ideal solution, considering the redistribution of the Linyaari population according to stargoing or planet-hugging proclivities, was for her to give birth on narhii-Vhiliinyar. There, they pointed out, her human and other alien friends could visit and yet she would still be surrounded by Linyaari who could heal any illness or injury, any slight anomaly she might experience during her pregnancy. The problem with that plan was that narhii-Vhiliinyar was not as rehabilitated from the Khleevi attack it had suffered as Vhiliinyar was. By now, thanks to the catseyes and the funds from their sale, Vhiliinyar was almost entirely reterraformed into the world it once had been.

A compromise was struck. Acorna and Aari would remain on MOO throughout the rest of her pregnancy, as long as she stayed healthy. Six weeks before she was due to deliver, she would be transported to their new quarters on Vhiliinyar.

She was very tired of so much attention, even from the people she dearly loved. (I wish you and I could get into Hafiz's wedding gift with our three portable kaf replicators and all and just go away somewhere quiet to do this,) she told Aari. (I am tired of trying to act less irritable than I feel, or to stand up straight when my back aches so. I am tired of being asked every few minutes if I am all right. I am tired of having *others* address my abdomen instead of my face. I wish we could just leave. You could heal me if I got into trouble.)

(Yes, but could you heal me when our mothers learned I had deprived them of the opportunity to help you at this time?)

(And here I have always considered you the bravest of our kind.)

(Khleevi are one thing. Family is another.)

Shortly afterward her labor began. Fifty ships were available to take her to the surface, but Becker didn't consult anyone else. He simply bustled them onto the robolift along with both sets of parents. Neeva and the *Balakiire* crew brought Laarye and Maati.

'I want you in constant touch by com unit!' Hafiz insisted. 'Her fathers and I have a right to know!'

Vaanye smiled, and said, 'Rest assured that I shall personally see to it that you are kept informed, Uncle Hafiz. We fathers must stick together.'

'And bring them back as soon as they can travel!' Karina said. 'We will need to see the baby. There are ritual blessings it must receive.'

Naturally, Acorna gave birth to her daughter halfway between MOO and Vhiliinyar, in the hydroponics garden aboard the *Condor*. Aari, his mother, and Feriila soothed her with horn touches and calming birth songs the women remembered from their own times.

Khoriilya came out of the womb star-clad, as white and silver as her mother and father, once the reddish mess was cleaned off her. Her nub of a golden horn was the delight of everyone. RK hopped up onto Acorna's berth to inspect the newcomer and gave her a lick of approval.

'We may as well turn around and go back to

MOO,' Becker said. 'You'll be as comfortable there as anywhere and you can get fussed over by House Harakamian, Gill, and Calum, as well as everybody else.'

Acorna groaned. Khoriilya gurgled and reached out for RK's tail, which he waved and twitched back and forth in front of her.

'She likes cats,' Becker said when he saw what the baby was doing. 'That's good. Miw-Sher and Nadhari particularly want her to have a kitten from one of the new litters. I think she'll find several that look pretty familiar.' He nodded at RK.

Three weeks after they landed, they saw Gill, Calum, and the Kendoro sisters off and waited to greet Johnny Greene and the star-faring crew of young folk from the *Haven*. Khoriilya toddled around the terminal, determined to deconstruct it, while Aari and Acorna said their good-byes.

Weary as Acorna had become of all the attention, she ached to see them leave.

Maati stepped out of the com room, and said, 'Khornya, Aari, Captain Becker wants you and Khoriilya to come to the *Condor*'s robolift. He says Maak is ready to present his wedding and birthing gift.'

Acorna lifted a protesting Khorii into her arms. The baby could get into entirely too much trouble out in the docking bays.

Becker and RK were on the ground when they reached the *Condor*. The robolift was ascending. 'Mac just went back up to get his present,' he said.

'What is it?' Aari asked. There was no Linyaari

etiquette that considered it impolite to inquire about the nature of a gift.

'You'll see. Picked out her cat yet?'

'No. For the sake of the kitten we thought it best to wait until she's a bit older. They're still quite small.'

'Are you sure about that? Nadhari says temple cats do better if they're bonded young to their people.'

The robolift descended, carrying Mac and another person, a child from the look of him. As the lift lowered even farther, Acorna saw that it was a Linyaari child, a young boy.

'Who is this?' she asked.

'You might say he is my son,' Mac told her. 'Your kinspeople said much about tutors for Khoriilya. But knowing you and Aari, she will not be on the planet long enough to go to tutors or meet other children, if there were many other Linyaari children which I have noticed there are not. So I used some of my spare parts and some other – items – Captain Becker had to create this boy. He is, as you see, a Linyaari android and so can accompany Khoriilya to Vhiliinyar. He can be her playmate and guardian as well as her tutor. His horn acts as a medical scanner. I thought it would be especially good if she heals people because she can always say my son is the one programmed to do it.'

The little boy looked coolly from Mac to Acorna and Aari, but his gaze settled on Khorii, who solemnly returned it.

With Khorii in her arms, Acorna knelt to be at eye level with the child droid. 'Do you have a name?' she asked.

'I researched that quite thoroughly,' Mac said. 'I wanted my son to have a name easy to pronounce by both Linyaari and humans. I wanted it to be a name of noble origin and wide fame. I consulted all of the vids and texts aboard and decided to name him after an Old Terran king. Tell them your name, son.'

'I am Elviiz,' he said.

'Viizzz!' Khoriilya said, and stuck out her arms to him. He gently grasped one of her pudgy baby hands and shook it lightly.

Khorii squirmed to be put down, where she and Elviiz crawled around at first until he stood and encouraged her to do so.

Acorna thought Mac had come up with the perfect solution for her daughter's odd bouts of loneliness. For the first time ever, she leaned over and kissed him on the cheek.

'Does that mean you are pleased, Khornya?'

'Oh, Maak, you've given us your son! How could we not be pleased! You will have to come and visit always.'

Mac seemed a bit puzzled. 'I always visit with you and Aari when you are near, Khornya. Of course I will.'

'Well, let's go look at cats,' Becker said. 'RK is itching to visit some of his offspring, I know. He can't wait till they're weaned. He's hoping the mamas will go back into heat again before they have to return to Makahomia.'

Miw-Sher and Nadhari had already returned to Makahomia, since it could hardly do without leadership for a prolonged period. But they had left the guardian mothers behind with nine acolytes – one per mother per eight-hour watch. Three of these very young Makahomians sat playing with a calamitous confusion of kittens tumbling and bumbling all over them, the mothers, and the room. At least half of them bore brindled stripes and puffed-out facial ruffs similar to RK's. Acorna thought Khorii would certainly choose one of them.

But one little golden-striped kitten with large green eyes headed straight for the child and began grooming her. She giggled and petted it awkwardly.

Viiz joined her on the floor. He didn't touch the kitten but turned his head first one way, then another, and lay down on his back to look up at the kitten's belly. He gently patted the kitten's back, then fingered something shining in the fine but very dense fur around its neck. Then he reached out and touched Khorii's mouth, bringing away a little of her enthusiastic drool and rubbing it against his finger.

'What is it, son?' Mac inquired.

'This kitten is wearing what appears to be Khorii's birth disk, Father. On cursory examination, the DNA code inscribed upon it appears to match hers.'

'But her birth disk isn't ready yet,' Acorna said. 'Mother said it would take the artisans another week or so.'

Becker laughed. 'Nadhari knew how much Aari's meant to you. I'll bet she was going to give it to you, then found out your parents wanted to.'

'Yes, but how did it get on the kitten?' Aari asked, looking askance at the small innocent creature.

'You know kittens. Unintentionally probably. Looks like this is the one the kid wants anyway,' Becker said. 'Now, if I were you, buddy, I'd let him mate a time or two since this planet is a little low on cats. Then if you're going to take him into space with you, and you don't want the whole ship to smell like tomcat' – he lowered his voice as RK looked up – 'get him neutered. But don't do it yourself unless you have some powerful healing horns nearby.'

Becker and Mac returned to the ship after Mac had tweaked Viiz's programming. Aari carried Khorii, and Acorna held Viiz's hand. Solemn and erudite he might be, but he looked like a Linyaari youngling. In the crook of his other arm, Viiz gently held the still-nameless kitten.

Karina and Hafiz walked toward them on the garden path. Fluttering and cooing, Karina turned to her husband. 'Oh, Haffy, aren't they just the sweetest things? The picture of Linyaari domestic bliss – the perfect peaceful little family! I just know they're going to – we all are going to – live happily ever after!'

Acorna and Aari exchanged smiles. (I hope this is one time when Karina's self-proclaimed gift of prophecy is true,) Aari said.

(Yes, wouldn't that be a nice change,) Acorna agreed. (But somehow I rather doubt it.)

Glossary of Terms and Proper Names in the Acorna Universe

aagroni – Linyaari name for a vocation that is a combination of ecologist, agriculturalist, botanist, and biologist.

Aagroni are responsible for terraforming new planets for settlement as well as maintaining the well-being of populated planets.

Aari – a Linyaari of the Nyaarya clan, captured by the Khleevi during the invasion of Vhiliinyar, tortured, and left for dead on the abandoned planet. He's Maati's older brother. Aari survived and was rescued and restored to his people by Jonas Becker and Roadkill. But Aari's differences, the physical and psychological scars left behind by his adventures, make it difficult for him to fit in among the Linyaari.

Aarlii – a Linyaari survey team member, first-born daughter of Captain Yaniriin.

Aarkiiyi – member of the Linyaari survey team on Vhiliinyar.

abaanye – a Linyaari sleeping potion that can be fatal in large doses.

Acorna – a unicorn-like humanoid discovered as an infant by three human miners – Calum, Gill, and Rafik. She has the power to heal and purify with her horn. Her uniqueness has already shaken up the human galaxy, especially the planet Kezdet. She's now fully grown and changing the lives of her own people, as well. Among her own people, she is known as Khornya.

Ali Baba – Aziza's ship.

Ancestors – unicorn-like sentient species, precursor race to the Linyaari. Also known as *ki-lin*.

Ancestral Friends – an ancient shape-changing and space-faring race responsible for saving the unicorns (or Ancestors) from Old Terra, and using them to create the Linyaari race on Vhiliinyar.

Ancestral Hosts – *see* Ancestral Friends.

Andina – owner of the cleaning concession on MOO, and sometimes lady companion to Captain Becker.

Aridimi Desert – a vast, barren desert on the Makahomian planet, site of a hidden Temple and a sacred lake.

Aridimis – people from the Makahomian Aridimi Desert.

Arkansas Traveler – freight hauling spaceship piloted by Scaradine MacDonald.

Attendant – Linyaari who have been selected for the task of caring for the Ancestors.

avvi – Linyaari word for 'daddy.'

Aziza Amunpul – head of a troop of dancers and thieves, who, after being reformed, becomes Hafiz's chief security officer on MOO.

Balakiire – the Linyaari spaceship commanded by Acorna's aunt Neeva.

Basic – shorthand for Standard Galactic, the language used throughout human-settled space.

Becker – *see* Jonas Becker.

Bulaybub Felidar sach Pilau ardo Agorah – a Makahomian Temple priest, better known by his real name – Tagoth. A priest who supports modernizing the Makahomian way of life, he was a favorite of Nadhari Kando, before her departure from the planet. He has a close relationship in his young relative, Miw-Sher.

Calum Baird – one of three miners who discovered Acorna and raised her.

chrysoberyl – a precious catseye gemstone available in large supply and great size on the planet of Makahomia, but also, very rarely and in smaller sizes, throughout the known universe. The stones are considered sacred on Makahomia, and are guarded by the priest class and the Temples. Throughout the rest of the universe, they are used in the mining and terraforming industries across the universe.

Condor – Jonas Becker's salvage ship, heavily modified to incorporate various 'found' items Becker has come across in his space voyages.

Crow – Becker's shuttle, used to go between the *Condor* and places in which the *Condor* is unable to land.

Declan 'Gill' Giloglie – one of three human miners who discovered Acorna and raised her.

Delszaki Li – once the richest man on Kezdet, opposed to child exploitation, made many political enemies. He lived his life paralyzed, floating in an antigravity chair. Clever and devious, he both hijacked and rescued Acorna and gave her a cause – saving the children of Kezdet. He became her adopted father. Li's death was a source of tremendous sadness to all but his enemies.

Dinan – Temple priest and doctor in Hissim.

Domestic Goddess – Andina's spaceship.

Dsu Macostut – Federation officer, Lieutenant Commander of the Federation base on Makahomia.

Edacki Ganoosh – corrupt Kezdet count, uncle of Kisla Manjari.

Egstynkeraht – A planet supporting several forms of sulfur-based sentient life.

Elviiz – Mac's son, a Linyaari childlike android, given as a wedding/birth gift to Acorna and Aari. The android is named for an ancient Terran king, and is often called Viiz for short.

enye-ghanyii – Linyaari time unit, small portion of *ghaanye*.

Fagad – Temple priest in the Aridimi Desert, who spied for Mulzar Edu Kando.

Felihari – one of the Makavitian Rain Forest tribes on Makahomia.

Feriila – Acorna's mother.

Fiicki – Linyaari communications officer on Vhiliinyar expedition.

Fiirki Miilkar – a Linyaari animal specialist.

Fiiryi – a Linyaari.

fraaki – Linyaari word for fish.

Friends – also known as Ancestral Friends. A shape-changing and space-faring race responsible for saving the unicorns from Old Terra and using them to create the Linyaari race on Vhiliinyar.

Gaali – highest peak on Vhiliinyar, never scaled by the Linyaari people. The official marker for Vhiliinyar's date line, anchoring the meridian line that sets the end of the old day and the beginning of the new day across the planet as it rotates Our Star at the center of the solar system. With nearby peaks Zaami and Kaahi, the high mountains are a mystical place for most Linyaari.

***ghaanye* (pl. *ghaanyi*)** – a Linyaari year.

gheraalye malivii – Linyaari for navigation officer.

gheraalye ve-khanyii – Linyaari for senior communications officer.

giirange – office of toastmaster in a Linyaari social organization.

GSS – Gravitation Stabilization System.

haarha liirni – Linyaari term for advanced education, usually pursued during adulthood while on sabbatical from a previous calling.

Hafiz Harakamian – Rafik's uncle, head of the interstellar financial empire of House Harakamian, a passionate collector of rarities from throughout the galaxy, and a devotee of the old-fashioned sport of horseracing. Although basically crooked enough to hide behind a spiral staircase, he is genuinely fond of Rafik and Acorna.

Heloise – Andina's spaceship.

Highmagister HaGurdy – the Ancestral Friend in charge of the Hosts on old Vhiliinyar.

Hissim – the biggest city on Makahomia, home of the largest temple.

Hraaya – an Ancestor.

Hrronye – Melireenya's lifemate.

Hrunvrun – the first Linyaari Ancestral attendant.

Iiiliira – a Linyaari ship.

Iirtyi – chief *aagroni* for narhii-Vhiliinyar.

Ikwaskwan – self-styled leader of the Kilumbembese Red Bracelets. Depending on circumstances and who he is trying to impress, he is known as either 'General Ikwaskwan' or 'Admiral Ikwaskwan,' though both ranks are self-assigned. Entered into devious dealings with Edacki Ganoosh that led to his downfall.

Johnny Greene – an old friend of Calum, Rafik, and Gill; joined the Starfarers when he was fired after Amalgamated Mining's takeover of MME.

Jonas Becker – interplanetary salvage artist; alias space junkman. Captain of the *Condor*. CEO of Becker Interplanetary Recycling and Salvage Enterprises, Ltd. – a one-man, one-cat salvage firm Jonas inherited from his adopted father. Jonas spent his early youth on a labor farm on the planet Kezdet before he was adopted.

Judit Kendoro – assistant to psychiatrist Alton Forelle at Amalgamated Mining, saved Acorna from certain death. Later fell in love with Gill and joined with him to help care for the children employed in Delszaki Li's Maganos mining operation.

Kaahi – a high mountain peak on Vhiliinyar.

Kaalmi Vroniiyi – leader of the Linyaari Council, which made the decision to restore the ruined planet Vhiliinyar, with Hafiz's help and support, to a state that would once again support the Linyaari and all the lifeforms native to the planet.

Kaarlye – the father of Aari, Maati, and Laarye. A member of the Nyaarya clan, and life-bonded to Miiri.

***ka*-Linyaari** – something against all Linyaari beliefs, something not Linyaari.

Karina – a plumply beautiful wanna-be psychic with a small shred of actual talent and a large fondness for profit. Married to Hafiz Harakamian. This is her first marriage, his second.

Kashirian Steppes – Makahomian region that produces the best fighters.

Kashirians – Makahomians from the Kashirian Steppes.

kava – a coffeelike hot drink produced from roasted ground beans.

KEN – a line of general-purpose male androids, some with customized specializations, differentiated among their owners by number, for example – KEN637.

Kezdet – a backwoods planet with a labor system based on child exploitation. Currently in economic turmoil because that system was broken by Delszaki Li and Acorna.

Khaari – senior Linyaari navigator on the *Balakiire*.

Khleevi – name given by Acorna's people to the space-borne enemies who have attacked them without mercy.

Khoriilya – Acorna and Aari's oldest child, a daughter, known as Khorii for short.

kii – a Linyaari time measurement roughly equivalent to an hour of Standard Time.

ki-lin – Oriental term for unicorn, also a name sometimes associated with Acorna.

Kilumbemba Empire – an entire society that raises and exports mercenaries for hire – the Red Bracelets.

Kisla Manjari – anorexic and snobbish young

woman, raised as daughter of Baron Manjari; shattered when through Acorna's efforts to help the children of Kezdet her father is ruined and the truth of her lowly birth is revealed.

Kubiilikaan – the legendary first city on Vhiliinyar, founded by the Ancestral Hosts.

Kubiilikhan – capital city of narhii-Vhiliinyar, named after Kubiilikaan, the legendary first city on Vhiliinyar, founded by the Ancestral Hosts.

LAANYE – sleep learning device invented by the Linyaari that can, from a small sample of any foreign language, teach the wearer the new language overnight.

Laarye – Maati and Aari's brother. He died on Vhiliinyar during the Khleevi invasion. He was trapped in an accident in a cave far distant from the spaceport during the evacuation, and was badly injured. Aari stayed behind to rescue and heal him, but was captured by the Khleevi and tortured before he could accomplish his mission. Laarye died before Aari could escape and return. Time travel has brought him back to life.

Laboue – the planet where Hafiz Harakamian makes his headquarters.

lalli – Linyaari word for 'mother.'

lilaala – a flowering vine native to Vhiliinyar, used by early Linyaari to make paper.

Liriili – former *viizaar* of narhii-Vhiliinyar, member of the clan Riivye.

Linyaari – Acorna's people.
Lukia of the Lights – a protective saint, identified by some children of Kezdet with Acorna.

Ma'aowri 3 – a planet populated by catlike beings.
Maarni – a Linyaari folklorist, mate to Yiitir.
Maati – a young Linyaari girl of the Nyaarya clan who lost most of her family during the Khleevi invasion. Aari's younger sister.
MacKenZ – also known as Mac or Maak, a very useful and adaptable unit of the KEN line of androids, now in the service of Captain Becker. The android was formerly owned by Kisla Manjari, and came into the Captain's service after it tried to kill him on Kisla's orders. Becker's knack for dealing with salvage enabled him to reprogram the android to make the KEN unit both loyal to him and eager to please. The reprogramming had interesting side effects on the android's personality, though, leaving Mac much quirkier than is usually the case for androids.
madigadi – a berry-like fruit whose juice is a popular beverage.
Maganos – one of the three moons of Kezdet, base for Delszaki Li's mining operation and child rehabilitation project.
Makahomia – war-torn home planet of RK and Nadhari Kendo.
Makahomian Temple Cat – cats on the planet

Makahomia, bred from ancient Cat God stock to protect and defend the Cat God's Temples. They are – for cats – large, fiercely loyal, remarkably intelligent, and dangerous when crossed.

Makavitian Rain Forest – a tropical area of the planet Makahomia, populated by various warring jungle tribes.

Manjari – a baron in the Kezdet aristocracy, and a key person in the organization and protection of Kezdet's child-labor racket, in which he was known by the code name 'Piper.' He murdered his wife, then committed suicide when his identity was revealed and his organization destroyed.

Martin Dehoney – famous astro-architect who designed Maganos Moon Base; the coveted Dehoney Prize was named after him.

Melireenya – Linyaari communications specialist on the *Balakiire,* bonded to Hrronye.

Mercy Kendoro – younger sister of Pal and Judit Kendoro, saved from a life of bonded labor by Judit's efforts, she worked as a spy for the Child Liberation League in offices of Kezdet Guardians of the Peace until the child-labor system was destroyed.

Miiri – mother of Aari, Laarye, and Maati. A member of the Nyaarya clan, life-bonded to Kaarlye.

mitanyaakhi – generic Linyaari term meaning a very large number.

Miw-Sher – a Makahomian Keeper of the sacred

Temple cats. Her name means 'Kitten' in Makahomian.

MME – Gill, Calum, and Rafik's original mining company. Swallowed by the ruthless, conscienceless, and bureaucratic Amalgamated Mining.

Mog-Gim Plateau – an arid area on the planet Makahomia near the Federation spaceport.

MOO, or Moon of Opportunity – Hafiz's artificial planet, and home base for the Vhiliinyar terraforming operation.

Mulzar (feminine form: Mulzarah) – the Mog-Gimin title taken by the high priest who is also the warlord of the Plateau.

Mulzar Edu Kando sach Pilau dom Mog-Gim – High Priest of Hissim and the Aridimi Plateau, on the planet Makahomia.

Naadiina – also known as Grandam, one of the oldest Linyaari, host to both Maati and Acorna on narhii-Vhiliinyar, died to give her people the opportunity to save both of their planets.

Naarye – Linyaari techno-artisan in charge of final fit-out of spaceships.

naazhoni – the Linyaari word for someone who is a bit unstable.

Nadhari Kando – formerly Delszaki Li's personal bodyguard, rumored to have been an officer in the Red Bracelets earlier in her career, then a security officer in charge of MOO, then the guard for the leader on her home planet of Makahomia.

narhii-Vhiliinyar – the planet settled by the Linyaari after Vhiliinyar, their original home-world, was destroyed by the Khleevi.

Neeva – Acorna's aunt and Linyaari envoy on the *Balakiire,* bonded to Virii.

Neo-Hadithian – an ultraconservative, fanatical religious sect.

Ngaen Xong Hoa – a Kieaanese scientist who invented a planetary weather control system. He sought asylum on the *Haven* because he feared the warring governments on his planet would misuse his research. A mutineer faction on the *Haven* used the system to reduce the planet Rushima to ruins. The mutineers were tossed into space, and Dr. Hoa has since restored Rushima and now works for Hafiz.

Niciirye – Grandam Naadiina's husband, dead and buried on Vhiliinyar.

Niikaavri – Acorna's grandmother, a member of the clan Geeyiinah, and a spaceship designer by trade. Also, as *Niikaavre,* the name of the spaceship used by Maati and Thariinye.

Nirii – a planetary trading partner of the Linyaari, populated by bovinelike two-horned sentients, known as Niriians, technologically advanced, able to communicate telepathically, and phlegmatic in temperament.

nyiiri – the Linyaari word for unmitigated gall, sheer effrontery, or other forms of misplaced bravado.

Our Star – Linyaari name for the star that centers their solar system.

Paazo River – a major geographical feature on the Linyaari homeworld, Vhiliinyar.

pahaantiyir – a large catlike animal once found on Vhiliinyar.

Pandora – Count Edacki Ganoosh's personal spaceship, used to track and pursue Hafiz's ship *Shahrazad* as it speeds after Acorna on her journey to narhii-Vhiliinyar. Later confiscated and used by Hafiz for his own purposes.

piiro – Linyaari word for a rowboatlike water vessel.

piiyi – a Niriian biotechnology-based information storage and retrieval system. The biological component resembles a very rancid cheese.

Praxos – a swampy planet near Makahomia used by the Federation to train Makahomian recruits.

PU#10 – Human name for the vine planet, with its sentient plant inhabitants, where the Khleevi-killing sap was found.

Rafik Nadezda – one of three miners who discovered Acorna and raised her.

Red Bracelets – Kilumbembese mercenaries; arguably the toughest and nastiest fighting force in known space.

Roadkill – otherwise known as RK. A

Makahomian Temple Cat, the only survivor of a space wreck, rescued and adopted by Jonas Becker, and honorary first mate of the *Condor*.

Roc – Rafik's shuttle ship.

Scaradine MacDonald – captain of the *Arkansas Traveler* spaceship, and galactic freight hauler.

Shahrazad – Hafiz's personal spaceship, a luxury cruiser.

***sii*-Linyaari** – a legendary race of aquatic Linyaari-like beings developed by the Ancestral Friends.

Siiaaryi Maartri – a Linyaari survey ship.

Sinbad – Rafik's spaceship.

Sita Ram – a protective goddess, identified with Acorna by the mining children on Kezdet.

Smythe-Wesson – a former Red Bracelet officer, Win Smythe-Wesson briefly served as Hafiz's head of security on MOO before his larcenous urges overcame him.

Standard Galactic Basic – the language used throughout the human settled galaxy, also known simply as 'Basic.'

stiil – Linyaari word for a pencil-like writing implement.

Taankaril – *visedhaanye ferilii* of the Gamma sector of Linyaari space.

Tagoth – *see* Bulaybub.

Techno-artisan – Linyaari specialist who designs, engineers, or manufactures goods.

Thariinye – a handsome and conceited young

space-faring Linyaari from clan Renyilaaghe.

Theophilus Becker – Jonas Becker's father, a salvage man and astrophysicist with a fondness for exploring uncharted wormholes.

***thiilir* (pl. *thilirii*)** – small arboreal mammals of Linyaari homeworld.

thiilsis – grass species native to Vhiliinyar.

Toruna – a Niriian female who sought help from Acorna and the Linyaari when her home planet was invaded by the Khleevi.

Twi Osiam – planetary site of a major financial and trade center.

twilit – small, pestiferous insect on Linyaari home planet.

Uhuru – one of the various names of the ship owned jointly by Gill, Calum, and Rafik.

Vaanye – Acorna's father.

Vhiliinyar – original home planet of the Linyaari, destroyed by Khleevi.

viizaar – a high political office in the Linyaari system, roughly equivalent to president or prime minister.

Virii – Neeva's spouse.

visedhaanye ferilii – Linyaari term corresponding roughly to 'Envoy Extraordinary.'

Vriiniia Watiir – sacred healing lake on Vhiliinyar, defiled by the Khleevi.

Wahanamoian Blossom of Sleep – poppylike flowers whose pollens, when ground, are a

very powerful sedative.
wii – a Linyaari prefix meaning 'small.'

yaazi – Linyaari term for 'beloved'.
Yukata Batsu – Uncle Hafiz's chief competitor on Laboue.
Yaniriin – a Linyaari Survey Ship captain.
Yiitir – history teacher at the Linyaari academy, and Chief Keeper of the Linyaari Stories. Lifemate to Maarni.

Zaami – a high mountain peak on the Linyaari homeworld.
Zanegar – second-generation Starfarer.

BRIEF NOTES ON THE LINYAARI LANGUAGE
by
Margaret Ball

As Anne McCaffrey's collaborator in transcribing the first two tales of Acorna, I was delighted to find that the second of these books provided an opportunity to sharpen my long-unused skills in linguistic fieldwork. Many years ago, when the government gave out scholarships with gay abandon and the cost of living (and attending graduate school) was virtually nil, I got a Ph.D. in linguistics for no better reason than that: (a) the government was willing to pay; (b) it gave me an excuse to spend a couple of years doing field-work in Africa; and (c) there weren't any real jobs going for eighteen-year-old girls with a B.A. in math and a minor in Germanic languages. (This was back during the Upper Pleistocene era, when the Help Wanted ads were still divided into Male and Female.)

So there were all those years spent doing things like transcribing tonal Oriental languages on staff paper (the Field Methods instructor was Not Amused) and tape-recording Swahili women at weddings, and then I got the degree and wandered off to play with computers and never had any use for the stuff again . . . until Acorna's people appeared on the scene. It required a sharp ear and some facility for linguistic analysis to make sense of the subtle sound changes with which their language signaled syntactic changes; I quite enjoyed the challenge.

The notes appended here represent my first and necessarily tentative analysis of certain patterns in Linyaari phonemics and morphophonemics. If there is any inconsistency between this analysis and the Linyaari speech patterns recorded in the later adventures of Acorna, please remember that I was working from a very limited database and, what is perhaps worse, attempting to analyze a decidedly nonhuman language with the aid of the only paradigms I had, twentieth-century linguistic models developed exclusively from human language. The result is very likely as inaccurate as were the first attempts to describe English syntax by forcing it into the mold of Latin, if not worse. My colleague, Elizabeth Ann Scarborough, has by now added her own notes to the small corpus of Linyaari names and utterances, and it may well be that in the next decade there will be enough data available to publish a truly definitive dictionary and grammar of Linyaari; an undertaking that will surely be of inestimable value, not only to those members of our race who are involved in diplomatic and trade relations with this people, but also to everyone interested in the study of language.

Notes on the Linyaari Language

1. A doubled vowel indicates stress: **aavi, abaanye, khleevi**.

2. Stress is used as an indicator of syntactic function: in nouns stress is on the penultimate syllable, in adjectives on the last syllable, in verbs on the first.

3. Intervocalic n is always palatalized.

4. Noun plurals are formed by adding a final vowel, usually **-i:** one Liinyar, two Linyaari. Note that this causes a change in the stressed syllable (from **LI-nyar** to **Li-NYA-ri**) and hence a change in the pattern of doubled vowels.

For nouns whose singular form ends in a vowel, the plural is formed by dropping the original vowel and adding **-i: ghaanye, ghaanyi**. Here the number of syllables remains the same, therefore no stress/spelling change is required.

5. Adjectives can be formed from nouns by adding a final **-ii** (again, dropping the original final vowel if one exists): **maalive, malivii; Liinyar, Linyarii**. Again, the change in stress means that the doubled vowels in the penultimate syllable of the noun disappear.

6. For nouns denoting a class or species, such as Liinyar, the noun itself can be used as an adjective when the meaning is simply to denote a member of the class, rather than the usual adjective meaning of 'having the qualities of this class' – thus, of the characters in *Acorna,* only Acorna herself could be described as 'a **Liinyar** girl' but Judit, although human, would certainly be described as 'a **linyarii** girl,' or 'a just-as-civilized-as-a-real-member-of-the-People' girl.

7. Verbs can be formed from nouns by adding a prefix constructed by [first consonant of noun] + **ii + nye: faalar** – grief; **fiinyefalar** – to grieve.

8. The participle is formed from the verb by adding a suffix **-an** or **-en**: **thiinyethilel** – to destroy, **thiinyethilelen** – destroyed. No stress change is involved because the participle is perceived as a verb form and therefore stress remains on the first syllable:

enye-ghanyii – time unit, small portion of a year **(ghaanye)**

fiinyefalaran – mourning, mourned

ghaanye – a Linyaari year, equivalent to about one and one-third earth years.

gheraalye malivii – Navigation Officer

gheraalye ve-khanyii – Senior Communications Specialist

Khleevi – originally, a small vicious carrion-feeding animal with a poisonous bite; now used by the Linyaari to denote the invaders who destroyed their homeworld.

khleevi – barbarous, uncivilized, vicious without reason

Liinyar – member of the People

linyaari – civilized; like a Liinyar

mitanyaakhi – large number (slang – like our 'zillions')

narhii – new

thiilir; thiliiri – small arboreal mammals of Linyaari homeworld

thiilel – destruction

visedhaanye ferilii – Envoy Extraordinary

DRAGON'S KIN

By Anne & Todd McCaffrey

Young Kindan has no expectations other than joining his father in the mines of Camp Natalon. However, mining is fraught with danger and a disaster leaves Kindan orphaned. Grieving, Kindan is taken in by the camp's new Harper and finds a measure of solace in a burgeoning musical talent . . . and in a new friendship with the mysterious Nuella. Nuella helps Kindan when he is selected to hatch and train a new watch-wher for the camp, a creature distantly related to dragons and uniquely suited to specialized work in the dark, cold mineshafts.

Meanwhile, long-simmering tensions are dividing the camp. As warring factions threaten to explode, Nuella and Kindan begin to discover hidden talents in the watch-wher – talents that could very well save an entire Hold and which show them that even a seemingly impossible dream is never completely out of reach . . .

For the first time, Anne McCaffrey has invited another writer to join her in the skies of Pern, a writer with an intimate knowledge of Pern and its history: her son, Todd.

0 552 15150 5

CORGI BOOKS

A LIST OF OTHER ANNE McCAFFREY TITLES AVAILABLE FROM CORGI BOOKS

THE PRICES SHOWN BELOW WERE CORRECT AT THE TIME OF GOING TO PRESS. HOWEVER TRANSWORLD PUBLISHERS RESERVE THE RIGHT TO SHOW NEW RETAIL PRICES ON COVERS WHICH MAY DIFFER FROM THOSE PREVIOUSLY ADVERTISED IN THE TEXT OR ELSEWHERE.

08453 0	DRAGONFLIGHT	£6.99
11635 1	DRAGONQUEST	£6.99
10661 5	DRAGONSONG	£6.99
10881 2	DRAGONSINGER: HARPER OF PERN	£5.99
11313 1	THE WHITE DRAGON	£6.99
11804 4	DRAGONDRUMS	£5.99
12499 0	MORETA: DRAGONLADY OF PERN	£6.99
12817 1	NERILKA'S STORY & THE COELURA	£5.99
13098 2	DRAGONSDAWN	£6.99
13099 0	THE RENEGADES OF PERN	£6.99
13729 4	ALL THE WEYRS OF PERN	£6.99
13913 0	THE CHRONICLES OF PERN: FIRST FALL	£6.99
14270 0	THE DOLPHINS OF PERN	£6.99
14272 7	RED STAR RISING: THE SECOND CHRONICLES OF PERN	£6.99
14274 3	THE MASTERHARPER OF PERN	£6.99
14631 5	THE SKIES OF PERN	£6.99
15150 5	DRAGON'S KIN (with Todd McCaffrey)	£6.99
14762 1	THE CRYSTAL SINGER OMNIBUS	£8.99
14180 1	TO RIDE PEGASUS	£6.99
13728 6	PEGASUS IN FLIGHT	£6.99
14630 7	PEGASUS IN SPACE	£6.99
13763 4	THE ROWAN	£5.99
13764 2	DAMIA	£5.99
13912 2	DAMIA'S CHILDREN	£5.99
13914 9	LYON'S PRIDE	£6.99
14629 3	THE TOWER AND THE HIVE	£6.99
09115 4	THE SHIP WHO SANG	£5.99
08661 4	DECISION AT DOONA	£4.99
08344 5	RESTOREE	£5.99
10965 7	GET OFF THE UNICORN	£6.99
14436 3	THE GIRL WHO HEARD DRAGONS	£5.99
14628 5	NIMISHA'S SHIP	£6.99
14271 9	FREEDOM'S LANDING	£6.99
14273 5	FREEDOM'S CHOICE	£6.99
14627 7	FREEDOM'S CHALLENGE	£6.99
14909 8	FREEDOM'S RANSOM	£6.99
14099 6	POWER LINES (with Elizabeth Ann Scarborough)	£6.99
14100 3	POWER PLAY (with Elizabeth Ann Scarborough)	£6.99
14621 8	ACORNA (with Margaret Ball)	£6.99
14748 6	ACORNA'S QUEST (with Margaret Ball)	£6.99
54659 3	ACORNA'S PEOPLE (with Elizabeth Ann Scarborough)	£6.99
14749 [illegible]	ACORNA'S WORLD (with Elizabeth Ann Scarborough)	£6.99
15076 2	ACORNA'S SEARCH (with Elizabeth Ann Scarborough)	£5.99
15135 1	ACORNA'S REBELS (with Elizabeth Ann Scarborough)	£5.99
05151 3	A GIFT OF DRAGONS (Hardback)	£12.99